THE IDENTITY MAN

BOOKS BY ANDREW KLAVAN

THE
IDENTITY
MAN

ANDREW KLAVAN

AN OTTO PENZLER BOOK
MARINER BOOKS
HOUGHTON MIFFLIN HARCOURT
BOSTON   NEW YORK

First Mariner Books edition 2011

Copyright © 2010 by Amalgamated Metaphor, Inc.

ALL RIGHTS RESERVED

For information about permission to reproduce selections from this book,
write to Permissions, Houghton Mifflin Harcourt Publishing Company,
215 Park Avenue South, New York, New York 10003.

www.hmhbooks.com

Library of Congress Cataloging-in-Publication Data
Klavan, Andrew.
The identity man / Andrew Klavan.
p. cm.
ISBN 978-0-547-24328-3
ISBN 978-0-547-59719-5 (pbk.)
I. Title.
PS3561.L334I34 2010
813'.54—dc22   2009047455

Book design by Brian Moore

Printed in the United States of America

DOC 10 9 8 7 6 5 4 3 2 1

This book is for Faith and John Moore.

ACKNOWLEDGMENTS

My sincere thanks to David Heinz for sharing his love and knowledge of wood carving; to Michael "Fish" Fisher for teaching me how to build a house and other cool carpentry tricks; to retired FBI agent Bob Hamer for answering my annoying procedural questions; and to researcher Carolyn Chriss for her always helpful assistance. I also have to mention my debt to the brilliant social and political observer Shelby Steele. My reading of his work informs much of this novel, although of course he's to blame for none of it. I also learned a good deal interviewing and reading the work of the Reverend Jesse Lee Peterson for a feature in *City Journal* (Winter 2010). Reverend Peterson likewise bears no blame for the end result.

My further thanks to my wonderful editor, Otto Penzler, and my likewise wonderful literary agent, Robert Gottlieb, in New York, as well as my movie agent, Frank Wuliger, in Los Angeles.

And thank you, as always, to my wife, Ellen Treacy Klavan, though, as always, no thanks could be enough.

PART I

THE WHITTAKER JOB

A PAGE OF A NEWSPAPER lay sodden on the sidewalk. MINISTER JAILED IN SEX SCANDAL, the headline read. Peter Patterson made out the words before the gusting wind caught the paper up and carried it, wet and heavy as it was, tumbling away through the mist of slashing rain. Patterson watched the paper gray and dim and vanish in the darkness. He kept walking, the wind and water whipping at his face.

The things of the flesh, he thought with an inward sigh. *The things of the spirit. The things of the flesh.*

He was already nervous — already afraid—and now the headline made him melancholy, too. The minister's conviction had been a great disappointment to him, a stomach-twisting glitch in his moral universe. And yet Peter Patterson was grimly determined not to judge. The Reverend Jesse Skyles was a good man, he told himself, a true man of God. He had just fallen to temptation, that's all. Peter Patterson had plenty of experience with temptation, not to mention falling. True, he'd never tapped anything underage, but the object of Skyles's indiscretion had been fourteen. That was no child; they were juicy then . . . In any case, he could say this and that, make this excuse for himself and that one, but the simple truth was he had left his own trail of tears, a trail of misused women and abandoned sons. He was in no position to condemn anyone.

The things of the spirit, the things of the flesh.

3

It was so easy to fall. Easy to choose the life of the moment over the long consequences. A couple of drinks and a woman's perfume began to seem like a thing worth dying for. And to leave her smile sitting there on her face like that, unkissed? Well, it just felt wrong. You'd have to be a corpse or a fool and no kind of man at all . . .

So the next thing you knew it was some ungodly hour of the morning and there you were, standing over the sprawled and sleeping wreckage of her, looking around the floor for your boxers and your self-respect. Because who were you when you were bare-assed, as it turned out? Surprise: you were that guy who'd looked his son in the eye that very afternoon and said, *Do what's right.* Hand on his shoulder, expression stern, finger wagging in his face. *Do what's right, son. Treat the women with respect. Don't be making no babies you can't take care of.* And then that selfsame night after four bourbons and a perfumed smile it was *Aw, fuck it.* Another mother betrayed, another son ushered into the funhouse of his father's hypocrisy, another relationship shot to hell . . .

All part of the journey that had led him to this night.

Man, he thought, suddenly coming back into the moment, back into the full awareness of his corrosive anxiety. *Man, look at this place.*

It was a sight to see, all right, the city in the rain. The night city, empty everywhere, with only the wind moving in it. Without people, without traffic, the avenue was reduced to the shadowy shapes of things. The rectangles of office buildings to the left and right of him, the smaller rectangles of newspaper boxes on the sidewalk, the shepherd's crook of a lamp pole in the light of its lamp . . . Everything seemed two-dimensional like that. Even the depth of the receding street seemed a trick of perspective.

People had taken the evacuation order seriously this time. There was not a body moving anywhere, not a footfall on the street but his. The rain spat and whispered against the macadam as if it were falling in an empty field. At moments, when the wind subsided, you could hear the stoplights changing color. You could see them swaying there above the intersections, one gleaming circle of red after another in the storm-streaked dark. Then there was a double metallic gulp, like a robot swallowing, and all the red circles turned gleaming green. There was something lonesome and almost poetic about it. *The city was practically beautiful,* he thought, *once you got rid of the people.*

Hands in his pockets, shoulders hunched, Peter Patterson trudged the final half block to the corner and ducked under the overhang of the skyscraper there. The moment he stopped walking, he became aware of how wet and miserable he was. His raincoat and his hat had protected him for a while, but now they were both soaked. His socks and cuffs were sodden from wading through the sluicing gutters. The cold was seeping into his core.

It was a hell of a night for a meeting—with the storm going and the river about to blow. A hell of a night to finally do what he had convinced himself to do.

Lieutenant Brick Ramsey saw Patterson reach the meeting point, but he lingered where he was, watching the man through the windshield of his unmarked Charger. Watching the wavering shape of the man anyway. He couldn't see much more of him than that. He didn't want to turn his wipers on. He was afraid the movement might draw attention to him sitting there. Uninterrupted, the rain spilled down over the glass in gusting sheets, then broken streams and droplets. Through the water, the pink glare of the downtown halogen lamps seemed to melt and run in fluid streaks of illumination. The stoplights ran in fluid streaks of red, then green. And beyond the light, in the blur and shadows, there was the wavering shape of Peter Patterson, an average-sized man in a hat and overcoat, hunched and waiting. Ramsey knew he ought to go to him, but he lingered, watched.

Ramsey figured himself for a hard man, but he didn't like thinking about what he was about to do. Peter Patterson was nobody in the big scheme of things. He was nothing in the city hierarchy. Just a bookkeeper. Just a middle-aged drunk who'd come to

Jesus and now fancied himself incorruptible. There should have been a dozen easy ways to shut him up or shut him down. They could've just waited him out probably. The mood would probably have passed.

But they couldn't wait. They couldn't risk it. Peter Patterson had crossed the line. It was one thing to come to Jesus. It was another to go to the feds.

"He wants a meet?" Augie Lancaster had murmured smoothly over the phone. "Arrange a meet. Tell him *you're* the feds and arrange a meet, that's all."

That's all.

It made Ramsey sick inside. But what else could he do? You got into these things step by step, day by day, and then there you were and you didn't really have a choice when you came down to it. There were people who depended on you, expected things from you. Not just Augie Lancaster but the Chief of Ds and the councilmen and all the rest. You couldn't just turn righteous on them, overnight become another man than the one they knew. Anyway, your fate was tied to theirs by this time. If they went down, you went down with them. Even if Ramsey *wanted* to turn righteous, that was way more righteous than he was prepared to be. No, whichever way you turned, the exit was closed and a hundred strings were pulling at you. You had to go on with it, that's all. Just as Augie said: That's all.

The rain drummed hard on the Charger's roof, then crashed on it like thunder, blown by the wind. The calls for backup hissed and whispered from the radio. Looting had started half an hour ago, almost as soon as the city emptied out. *The brothers*, Ramsey thought with a stab of shame and distaste. The brothers were busting up the Northern District, two miles away.

The City of Hope. The City of Equality. The City of Justice.

All those high words. All those fine Augie Lancaster speeches came back to him.

"Where they have taken away your voice, I will speak for you. Where they have robbed you of your dignity, I will make them re-

6

pay you. Where they have built their wealth on your exploitation, I will bring that wealth back from Washington to your neighborhoods and your families."

Ramsey could remember the thrill of hearing him. The thrill of the crowd and the roar of the brothers cheering. Those were the same crowds, the same brothers, who were out there smashing the storefronts of the slant-owned groceries and the chain pharmacies and the Stereo World and the old furniture emporium they had shopped at for ages. Flood sale. Everything must go.

He had the radio turned down low to dim the distraction of it. The soft cries for help seemed like the voices of ghosts in the storm, distant and mournful and lost.

The brothers.

Well, they aren't the only ones to take whatever they can get their hands on, Ramsey told himself. *When it comes to that, all men are brothers.*

He glanced at the clock on the dashboard. He knew it was time. He knew he ought to go and get this over with.

But he lingered, watching.

The things of the spirit, the things of the flesh.

That was Peter Patterson, meanwhile, his restless mind returning to the Reverend Skyles as he stood under the skyscraper's overhang, all shrugged up in his wet overcoat; as the wind-whipped water sluiced down and spattered the shins of his trousers where he stood; as he waited anxiously for the feds to come.

He shivered. He bounced on his toes. He thought: *Where are they already?*

He thought: *How could he do it?* His restless mind returning to Skyles, returning to himself and the things he'd done in his life, the journey that had brought him here, the booze, the women. Because he knew how Skyles could do it. He knew exactly how he could do it, and do it again. You weren't even sorry afterward. Not really. You were ashamed, for sure. When you were sober, when you were satisfied and bare-assed, looking for your shorts, looking for some way to dull the contrast between what you knew full well you ought to be and what in fact you were, you were plenty ashamed then. You hated the consequences, the women screaming at you in their hurt and betrayal, the three sons by two mothers that you never saw, the one boy in jail. But how could you say you were sorry for what you remembered with a dreamy smile? How could you say you regretted what you'd do again in a city minute? Oh yes, you would. If the opportunity arose—and you arose—back you'd be in the Country of King Penis, loyal subject of His Majesty, flying to do his bidding at his least command . . .

Where the hell were they?

He turned his head to the right and the left, searching the rain for his contact. No one. He lifted his gaze to the intersecting street.

That was when he saw the red-white glow above the building tops.

His breath caught. Fire. He knew what it was right away. With the city empty and the high water coming, looters must have swarmed the shops uptown, and now they'd torched the place and had it burning. The glow pulsed into the sky's deep blackness. The slashing rain glimmered silver against it.

And suddenly, for no reason he could put into words, Peter Patterson knew that everything was wrong. This meeting made no sense. This place made no sense. Why here? Why tonight? Why the sudden phone call after all the patient, reassuring overtures back and forth? Why the strange voice, the mysterious instructions . . . ?

He hardly asked himself these questions. He was simply gripped by the urgent conviction that he had to get the hell out of here. Now.

Lieutenant Ramsey was startled to see Patterson break from his shelter. The bookkeeper moved quickly, nearly jogging, with his hands still in his overcoat pockets and his head lowered as if to butt his way through the wind and rain back to his car. Every few steps, he would look over his shoulder and then tumble on even faster as if he'd seen demons chasing him.

Ramsey cursed. In the first moment of surprise, he grabbed the door handle, ready to go after the guy. But then he thought better of it. He had been in situations like this before, plenty of times. Blown meets, blown stakeouts. Things changed, you had to change your plan. You botched things up if you failed to adapt. He decided to follow Patterson and see what was what. He would find the moment. He would bide his time.

One hand left the door and the other went to the keys in the ignition. At the same time, he caught a glimpse of his own eyes in the rearview mirror. He quickly looked away.

Lieutenant Brick Ramsey had—had always had, since his childhood—an appearance of dignity, of restraint, self-control, and moral authority. His mother had instilled these qualities in him. One hand on her hip, the other waggling a finger in his face or sometimes a Bible. *Don't you be like them.* The brothers, she meant. The street-corner gangsters who held up the walls of his neighborhood with their slouching backs. *You gonna do right. You gonna make something of yourself. You gonna be somebody. It don't profit you nothing to gain the whole world if you lose your soul.* Hammering at him with that finger, with that Bible, like a sculptor hammering at marble until she made the shape of him, the dignified set of his broad shoulders, the dignified stillness of his oval face with its pencil moustache over a serious mouth, with its intelligent, watchful, soulful brown eyes. Four years in the marines had added to the pride of his carriage. And five years patrolling the streets had reminded him daily of the degraded neighborhood life he had risen above. But it was his mother's work he saw when he looked in the mirror—and he quickly looked away.

The pounding of the rain on the roof intensified, drowning out the dim calls for assistance from the radio. A fresh sheet of water washed down over the windshield. When it passed, Ramsey saw Patterson reach the line of cars in the parking zone down the street. He saw Patterson reach his own car, a battered blue Chrysler New Yorker, had to be fifteen years old at least. The car's top light went on as Patterson opened the door and lowered himself into the driver's seat. Then he pulled the door shut after him and the car went dark. A moment later, Lieutenant Ramsey saw the New Yorker's headlights, blurry through the water on the windshield. The car pulled out and took off down the street, illuminating the silver streaks of the rain before it.

Ramsey waited a few seconds and then followed in the unmarked Charger, holding back a block, sunk in the darkness, counting on the storm to obscure him.

Up ahead, the New Yorker turned the corner. The Charger reached the intersection a few seconds afterward. It was only then, only when he turned to look down the street, that Ramsey understood what had spooked Patterson.

The throbbing red-white glow gave sudden depth to the strangely flat skyline. The City of Hope. The City of Equality. The City of Justice. It was burning.

The brothers, Ramsey thought, with another gout of disgust and self-disgust.

He brought the Charger around the corner and kept after his man.

Peter Patterson felt strangely safe once he was inside his car. His sudden surge of fear subsided. He felt as if no one could touch him there.

He drove north through the empty city. He drove slowly, careful of the storm. The pavement was slick where it was level and there were troughs and hollows where deep puddles gathered, where the water thundered against the undercarriage and gripped the tires of the old car as they passed through.

As he got away from downtown, the streets grew even darker around him. It took him a while to notice it: the electricity here was out. He looked past the laboring wipers. He saw rain-swept boulevards empty as alleyways, storefronts boarded against the tempest. He was glad to be inside and warm with the heater on. The unreasoning urgency in him—the anxious conviction that he had just been in some kind of danger—was already beginning to recede. Maybe he'd just spooked himself. Maybe he'd just let his nerves get the better of him.

He turned on the radio. Hoping for some news, some voices for company. Nothing came out but static. He pressed the scan button and listened as the tuner automatically ran the band. Still nothing but that hiss, end to end, that hiss with broken fragments of words in it like men sending messages from the belly of a snake.

Look at this. Look at this.

The hollowed brownstones. The vacant businesses. The broken windows like phantoms' eyes. He was in the north now, at the edge of the neighborhoods. He was thinking: *The wages of sin.*

Because it was all the Country of King Penis, wasn't it? The country of misused women and abandoned sons. That was exactly the message Reverend Skyles had been trying to bring to them, that was exactly why his fall was such a disappointment, such a tragedy. He was a good man, a true man of God, the lone voice of truth against the silken temptations of Augie Lancaster. Augie Lancaster telling folks he would give them back their dignity. How do you *give* a man dignity if he doesn't have it for himself? Reverend Skyles told them they had to *be* dignified, had to *do* right . . .

Peter Patterson was lost in such philosophical thoughts he didn't notice the water rising. It was pouring in fast from the east where the river had broken through the levies. It was burbling up out of the sewers with such force that manhole covers were being lifted and rattled aside, one after another, as the deluge crossed town.

Peter Patterson began to feel the grip of the flood on his tires, the steering wheel tugging at his hands, but he was distracted. He figured he was just going through another puddle.

Then his headlights picked out the body of a drowned man.

Oh, it was an eerie sight to see. It was so unreal, he felt a stutter of disbelief between the moment he understood what it was and the moment the terror began to rise in him. Peter Patterson stared through the windshield, open-mouthed. The corpse's ballooning shirt gleamed white in the headlights as he floated face down through the silent intersection up ahead.

"Holy mother of God," Peter Patterson whispered.

An instant later, the tide was on him.

He felt a soft jolt against the side of the old Chrysler. He turned and was startled to find the water outside was suddenly lapping at the bottom of the car's door. The next moment, with one low, electric groan, the New Yorker stalled. It stopped and sat there, dark and dead, a motionless hulk around him.

Peter Patterson reflexively reached for the keys, but the shutdown had such a finality to it that he didn't even bother to try to restart the engine. He just pulled the keys from the ignition. He knew he had to get out, get free, as fast as he could.

He tried to shoulder open the door. It gave a little—just a little. Then the pressure of the water held it. Through the windshield, in the wavering glow of a fire nearby, he could still see the white shirt of the drowned man as he floated, slowly revolving, down the street. A little zap of fresh panic went through him.

You could get caught in here. You could be that guy, he thought.

He shouldered the door again, harder this time, with a little of that I-don't-wanna-die adrenalin pumping through him. It was no good. The weird, living gelatin of the flood pushed back against him. He hit the door again, even harder, even more afraid. At last, it gave way. The water poured in over his feet and ankles, shockingly cold. The door slid open just enough—just enough for Peter Patterson to force himself desperately through the gap.

He stood up in the street. The water reached his knees and was still rising. Shockingly, shockingly cold. Insidious in its swiftness. He could feel the force of it, trying to nudge him away from the car, trying to coax him into the arms of the current. The cold seeped into him like a seductive whisper, trying to weaken his resolve. It was the voice of the storm. The storm wanted to kill him. He could feel it. It wanted him floating and turning down the street like the drowned man. He was already shivering, already growing weak with the cold.

Peter Patterson held on to the car door with one hand, using all the strength that was left in his freezing fingers. He looked around him and behind him, searching for the best way out, praying to God to help him find it. The glow of the fire to the north lit the intersection with an eerie brightness. He could make out the shapes of buildings silhouetted against it. The dark grew thick in the near distance, though, with the electric down. *Hard to find my way, Lord.*

He remembered the keychain gripped in his free hand. There was a small flashlight on it. He lifted it. Had to be careful not to drop it—his hand was getting so stiff—his whole body was shuddering with cold. He pressed the button and shot a thin blue beam in different directions, this way and that. It picked out patches of water, black and boiling on every side of him. He had to pray some more to fight his rising panic. He turned the unsteady beam over the buildings around him. There was a promising one, about a block away. He might be able to break into that. It was blackened brick, about six stories tall. There were boards on the ground-floor windows, but he was sure he could tear them off. There'd be stairs inside. He could climb up to higher ground. *Thank you, Jesus.*

He took a deep breath for courage and reluctantly let go of the car. He began wading through the water toward the intersection. The drowned corpse turned and floated past the corner to his left, like a taunt, like a threat, like an omen. But Peter Patterson tried not to look in that direction. He told himself he was going to make it, he was going to be all right. He kept praying.

The flood was up to the bottom of his thighs now, but he was still stronger than the current. He could still push through. Only the cold worried him. Wicked cold. It ate into him, ate away his strength. It made his arms quiver, as he pressed them tightly against his sides. The rain lashed his face and his sodden overcoat clung to him. Every stride through the thick flood was an effort.

He felt heavy and was getting heavier. He felt like a man made of soft, wet clay trying to reach his goal before the clay dried and hardened so that he became a statue on the city street. His teeth began to chatter. He made shuddering noises, battling to take another slow step and another. *Don't let me die.*

He reached the intersection. The light here was bright and startling, drawing his attention to the west. He turned to look and stopped where he was, stood still, letting out a tremulous breath as the water washed around him.

The flames were bright here, the city on fire. You wouldn't think it could burn like that in all this rain. Only a block away, beyond the revolving corpse in the foreground, jagged lashings of livid orange burst through a broad storefront and scarred the black night. The store's low white roof gleamed red. The taller brownstones on either side of it loomed darkly above the burning. The water flowed and rose on the street out front, reflecting the fire in places or sometimes swallowing its light or sometimes sending up flickering splashes as people kicked through it. The human figures appeared in silhouette, running into the flaming shop and out again, carrying their boxes of plunder. They were busy as insects, but now and then the fire caught the face of a man, his eyes weirdly dead and bright at the same time, dead with the mindless passion of his hunger and bright with the hunger at the same time, dead and bright like the white shirt on the back of the corpse revolving in the current.

Appalled, Peter Patterson stood there for a moment, watching. But only for a moment. The flames were vivid and hot to the eye, but they gave no heat really. The water still had him in the clutches of its cold, numbing him and urging him into its flow. He had to fight it. He had to move. He had to keep moving. *Help me, God.*

He turned to go on—and there was Ramsey towering over him.

Lieutenant Brick Ramsey killed Peter Patterson quickly and efficiently. He grabbed the bookkeeper by the shoulder and thrust the blade of the combat knife deep between his ribs and into his heart, twisting it to sever the artery. The two men were close together. Ramsey could practically read the sequence of Peter Patterson's thoughts in his eyes. Patterson was startled by Ramsey's sudden appearance but then, for a single instant, he tried to make sense of it, maybe figured he was the fed who'd been sent to meet him in the rain. Then Ramsey jammed the knife in and Peter Patterson's eyes went wide in pain and bewilderment. But before he died, the logic of it must have come to him because Ramsey could see that he understood.

Peter Patterson tried to struggle free, but it was only a small instinctive motion. He was already too weak and he knew he was finished, his lips moving in prayer. Ramsey held him against the knife handle easily. As Peter Patterson's knees buckled, Ramsey lowered the bookkeeper into the water and pressed down on the knife to force him beneath the surface. Peter Patterson thrashed once before his final breath came bubbling out of him. Then he sank to the bottom of the roiling flow.

Bent over low, bent close to the water, the cold damp soaking through his sleeves, Lieutenant Ramsey held Peter Patterson down. The firelight penetrated the black depths, and he could make out the bookkeeper's face down there. He was sickened by the sight of the eyes staring up at him, sickened at the gaping mouth, wavery underwater, and the staring eyes full of what looked to him like pity. He had to turn away from them. He lifted his own eyes to the flames: the burning storefront and the dark buildings looming over it on either side. He saw the silhouetted figures of the looters splashing around in the firelight and caught glimpses of their bright, dead faces. He still had one hand on Peter Patterson's shoulder and the other on the knife. With a sickening thrill, he felt—or thought he felt—Peter Patterson's heartbeat pulsing in the knife handle. The pulse weakened and faded away and was gone.

Ramsey wrestled the knife free and straightened, knee-deep in the water. He let the knife slip out of his hand. It plopped into the flood and sank down, gleaming dully and then more dully until it settled, dim silver, on the bottom beside Patterson's body. Strange. For a moment there, Ramsey had felt relief, really wonderful relief. The very moment of the murder had seemed bright and explosive—a bright moment of freedom from the tension leading up to it—a star-toothed, bright, explosive release from the nausea of the self-hatred and shame he had barely been aware of feeling. But as he released his grip on the body, as he dropped the knife and stood, the nova-like blast of freedom shrank back into itself and the blackness at its edges—the blackness of shame, of self-disgust—came sweeping down on him in a torrent ten-fold and it was horrible. Horrible. Before, sitting in the car, it had seemed to him there was no getting out of this. What with Augie and all the people he knew and all the things they expected of him, Ramsey could see no way then to avoid what had to be done. But now, now that it was over, it all looked different. He saw that he *could* have gotten out—he could've said no at any time—of course, he could have. It was *this*—this now—that there was no getting out of. This was done and there was no undoing it. It was like a stain, an acid stain; no washing it away. Ramsey had to force his mind into a kind of deadness so he wouldn't feel the full awareness of it all at once. But it was there nonetheless. The stain, the guilt. The shame, the self-disgust. He had made himself a nightmare with no waking ever.

The clammy water swirled around his legs. The cold of it was beginning to reach into him. The cold made the flames he saw seem strange and unreal, all leaping action and no true heat, like a movie or a memory of fire. Ramsey stood in the flood and shivered and gazed at the burning, drowning city. He felt unbearably alone, unbearably exposed to the eyes of the night, which he knew full well were his mother's eyes and the eyes of his mother's God.

A THOUSAND MILES away, a week or so later, as evening came, Shannon was working with wood. We'll call him Shannon anyway. He'd had a couple of other names in his life and he'll have one more before this story is finished, but he was Shannon now and it'll do. He was running a draw knife over a block of white ash. White ash was a hard wood to shape and it rotted fast, but he liked the color of it. This block in particular had caught his eye in the art supply store. He could see a woman in it, a woman's face. She was not young but not old either. She was very gentle and sweet, feminine and yearning. It was only the face but he could picture all of her. He could see her standing in the doorway of a house at the edge of a field of grain. She was looking into the distance, watching for her man, hoping he would come back to her.

When Shannon had finished shaving the block down to the right size, he would go at it with his gouges and draw out the woman's features. He could do that. He could see the shapes in wood and carve them. It was a knack he had. No one had taught it to him. He'd just found out about it in the shop in the Hall, the first time he was sent away, when he was still a juvenile. He'd gotten six months for misdemeanor breaking and entering, pled down from a felony. He'd gone to the Hall shop to kill time, and he'd somehow discovered this talent of his. When his 8320 counselor found out about it, he arranged for Shannon to get training as a carpenter. That was supposed to give him an honest profession and keep him out of trouble. It hadn't kept him out of trouble. He still was what he was. But in his spare time, he carved wood. He liked doing it. It had a good effect on him. It made him calm inside and still. It was the only thing that did. His mind got into the rhythm of his hands and he got wrapped up in what he was doing. He began to think and wonder about things, things that were different and interesting, questions that had no answers. Now, for instance, as his two hands worked the draw knife back over the tough off-white surface of the block, he was wondering: Where had this woman come from, this woman whose face he saw? Was she really in the wood to begin with or had his imagination just put her there? If she wasn't in the wood, how did he see her? How had she gotten into his imagination? She wasn't like anyone he knew or remembered. Maybe he had met her somewhere or passed her on the street and forgotten. Or maybe they had never met but she existed anyway and had somehow come into his imagination by ESP or something so that he saw her face in the wood as you might see someone in a dream who later turned out to be real. That might also explain how he could have real feelings about her. Because he did. When he thought of her standing there, waiting for her man in the doorway of the house, when he pictured her face brightening with a smile as she first spotted him coming up the road through the field, his heart lifted. He felt glad, genuinely glad, as if he were the man coming home to her. He even smiled—smiled back at her—as he worked the draw knife over the wood. It seemed too bizarre to him that he could feel this way about someone who didn't exist at all.

This was the sort of thing he wondered about when his mind fell into the rhythm of his hands carving wood. It was stupid probably, but it made him calm and still inside and nothing else did.

Shannon wasn't sure how old he was, but he was about thirty-one or -two. His driver's license said thirty-two and he knew it was around there somewhere. He was just over six feet tall, lean, broad-chested, and muscular. He had a long, rugged face with lines down the sides and around the eyes that made him look thoughtful and sad. He was wearing jeans now and no shirt. Sawdust clung to the sweat on his chest and arms.

The warmth of day lingered in the Southern California evening. The air smelled of eucalyptus and the sea. Shannon was standing in the little square of yard behind the three-story apartments, where he lived on the top floor. He was using the workbench he'd set out there among the lawn chairs.

He was about to lay the draw knife aside and open his roll of gouges, but he noticed the long light was finally failing. Another ten minutes and it would be too dark to go on. It wasn't worth beginning the next stage of the sculpture.

Shannon sighed and straightened, taking one hand off the knife and pressing the heel of his palm into his back as he stretched. As quick as that—as soon as he stopped carving—he remembered what he had to do tonight.

On the instant, his good feeling and his calm were gone.

Benny Torrance was coming. They were going to do a job. Shannon knew he shouldn't be doing jobs anymore, but somehow he kept doing them anyway. People called and asked him to come in on something, and he knew he should say no, but he never did. He needed the money, for one thing. The carpentry work had been sporadic lately. But it wasn't just that. Even when he was working full-time, he still did break-ins. He needed the buzz, the thrill of them. It was like he was addicted to it. Day-to-day life got on his nerves after a while. When he was carving wood, he was calm, it was all right, but when he wasn't, he needed something else. Day-to-day life made his skin crawl.

All the same, he had a bad feeling about this job. He'd had a bad feeling about it for days. He couldn't afford any more mistakes, couldn't afford any more convictions. He had two previous knocks for burglaries in inhabited dwellings. Those were serious felonies. One more and the three-strike law kicked in. That meant he'd die behind bars or get out only as a shuffling old man, doughy from prison starch and barely able to tolerate the free light of day. Sometimes the thought of that made him lie awake at night sweating. It made him sick inside with dread. He had to force himself not to think about it.

So there was that. And then there was the Benny Torrance of it all. Benny was bad news any way you looked at it. He was crazy. There were all kinds of stories about him. Ham Underwood, a guy Shannon knew, said he'd once shared a hooker with Benny and Benny went nuts and nearly killed her for no reason. And there were other stories like that, too. But they weren't the worst of it. Just a couple of nights ago, after he'd agreed to do the job, Shannon had been drinking in the Clover and some guys were talking about that home invasion in Carpinteria. The Hernandez killings. Some of the guys said it was a gang thing, but one of them said it was Benny and he sounded like he knew. That's when Shannon started to get his bad feeling, when he heard that. The Hernandez business was some very sick shit. The whole family had been murdered: father, mother, and two kids, a boy and a girl. If Benny was the doer, Shannon didn't want to be anywhere near him. He was a break-in man, not a rapist or a killer. But he had already agreed to go in on the job and now he felt like he couldn't pull out.

Shannon went inside and showered the wood chips off him. He dressed in black jeans and a black T-shirt for the job. He went into the kitchen and cooked himself some eggs and ham. He slid them from the pan to a plate and ate them standing at the sink with a glass of red wine set on the counter. He hoped the wine would take the edge off his bad feeling.

Karen was in the living room. She was watching some TV show about movie stars, which one was screwing which, and so on. Shannon could hear the lady announcer sounding all excited about it, and there were flashes of music like flashes of bright light. When he was done with his eggs, he put the plate in the sink and carried his wine glass to the living room doorway. He leaned against the door frame and looked down at Karen. She was lying on the sofa, drinking a beer and smoking a joint, relaxing after her work day. She had changed out of the clothes she wore at the hotel and was wearing shorts and a pink T-shirt. She had a good body, big breasts, ripe thighs. She had a pretty face, too, when she was made-up nicely. Her dark hair shone in the light from the lamp next to the sofa.

Shannon still liked Karen well enough. He was just tired of her, that's all. He figured they were tired of each other. It was just like anything else: if it went on too long, it made your skin crawl. You needed a buzz. You needed to find something new.

"I gotta go out tonight," he told her.

"Okay," she said. She didn't look up from the television. She knew he did jobs. She knew he did something anyway. She never asked exactly what. Sometimes he wanted to tell her about it, about how he wanted to stop but couldn't, about how he lay awake at night, dreading that he would be sent away for life. But he never did. What could she answer? It wasn't her problem. If he wanted to stop, he ought to stop.

"You mind getting the dishes?" he asked her.

"No, I'll get 'em before I go. I may go out later, too, with Jeanette."

"Okay."

A car horn honked on the street outside, then honked again a long time loudly.

"Why don't you just announce it to the neighborhood?" Shannon muttered. "You dumb fuck."

"Who is that?"

"Benny."

"I hate that guy. He gives me the creeps." Karen took a draw of reefer. She never took her eyes off the television. Shannon couldn't figure what she saw in this stuff. Who cared if one of these movie clowns was doing another one or not?

For some reason, though, watching her watch the show, Shannon felt a surge of affection for her. He walked over to the sofa. He bent down to her, and she lifted her face to him and blew smoke out of the side of her mouth so he could kiss her goodbye.

"I'll see you later," Shannon said. He tasted her lips and the ganja. For some reason, he felt sad to leave her.

"See you, baby," she said.

But they never saw each other again.

As soon as Shannon got a look at Benny Torrance, he knew this was going to be a disaster of a night. Benny was aggie-eyed—his eyes looked like streaked marbles. God knew what he was on, but he was obviously juiced out of his mind. You could practically see his bonzo thoughts whooshing through his brain about a hundred miles a minute, like a wall covered with graffiti seen from a fast train.

"Shannon, my boy!" he rumbled.

He clapped a hand on Shannon's thigh as Shannon slid into the passenger side of the pickup. Then, with a thick guttural laugh, Benny jammed his foot down on the gas. The tires gave a banshee shriek and the black truck fired off into the night with a roar that must have rattled windows. The guy was a cluster-fuck in human form.

Benny was thickset, rippling with muscle. He had long stringy hair. He had a brutal face with three days' stubble. He was dressed in dark jeans and a black windbreaker, zipped all the way up. Blue tats peeked out where his flesh showed—the head of a rattler on his right wrist, a woman's bare leg on his left, curling tentacles coming up around his collar: it looked like he was smuggling a whole fantastic menagerie of dream creatures under his clothing and they were trying to squirm free.

He drove fast and, man, he drove loud, some kind of supercharger jazzing the truck's combustion and boosting the HP. He had to shout at Shannon over the roar.

"Talked to my friend an hour ago. He says the place is loaded. Caveman security. We're gonna be doing the money dance before the night is over."

Yeah, yeah, yeah, thought Shannon. He half hoped some cop pulled them over for speeding or excessive noise before they arrived.

No such luck.

They came onto a stretch of road south of the city center, a dark street parallel to lower Main. Every shop here had its gates down. There was no one on the sidewalks. There were no street lamps. A breeze brought the smell of the ocean from a few blocks away. A couple of palm trees, sunk in shadow, whispered over the low buildings. A car or two went by when the traffic lights changed. Other than that, nothing was moving. The place was dead.

Benny parked the truck in the center of the block.

"Let's do this thing," he growled.

He got out and led the way to a narrow drive between a fabric store and a dry cleaner. Shannon followed him, alert, looking for trouble this way and that. He was wearing a black windbreaker now. He had a canvas roll tucked into the inside pocket.

They went down the drive to where it ended at a quaint house hidden among trees. It was a three-story Victorian clapboard with a porch and a gabled roof and a fanciful turret and blue trim painted around the windows. There was a painted sign at the entrance to the porch steps: THE WHITTAKER CENTER. There were cheerful swirling vine designs around the words.

It was a foundation of some kind. A charity or something. Benny had a friend who worked security there. The guy had given Benny the patrol times and the alarm codes and told him where there was an old combination safe full of cash. Apparently they kept a lot of cash around. People could just drop in and get a handful of dollars if they needed it badly enough.

Shannon took a look around the place as they went up the porch steps. He was reassured by the location, the way the house was set back from the road. No one driving by on the street was likely to notice them and there were no neighbors who might spot them with a glance out a nearby window either.

But one thing did worry him. The front door had a top pane of beveled glass and he could see a yellow glow through it.

"There's a light on in there," he said in a soft voice.

"Just for security," said Benny. They were shoulder to shoulder and Shannon could smell the vomitous scent of old beer on him. "The guard only comes by on the even hours. I told you. They just walk around outside."

Shannon nodded. Benny *had* told him that, but he was not convinced.

Shannon knelt in front of the door. He had a small penlight that sent out a blue beam. He held the penlight in his teeth so that the beam shone on his work. He brought out his canvas roll, laid it on the porch, and spread it open. It was the same kind of roll he used for his gouges when he carved wood. It was lined with pockets for his tools. He drew out a snapper pick for the front door and was through the lock in five seconds. The alarm warning sounded, a steady shrill, but soft, too soft to be heard outside the building. There was a sixty-second delay before the real alarm went off. Benny had told him that, too.

Shannon gathered his roll and strode quickly across the foyer to the keypad. He kept the flashlight clenched in his teeth so that the blue beam played over the keys. He tapped in the code Benny had given him—half expecting it to fail, half expecting the full alarm to blow like the last trumpet. But no, the code worked. The alarm was disabled. The house went silent around them.

Benny had his flashlight out now, too. It was bigger than Shannon's and had a bright white beam. He shone it only long enough to pick out the way to the stairs, then turned it off. He moved to the stairs and went up two at a time. Shannon rolled up his tools and followed him.

Later, Shannon remembered that he noticed something at this point. He noticed there were no lights on anywhere in the house. He had seen that glow through the glass of the door, so there must have been a light on before but now there wasn't. That didn't make sense, but Shannon dismissed the thought before he really considered it. Maybe he didn't want to think about it now that he was in so deep.

On the second floor landing, Benny shone his flashlight beam briefly again and picked out a door across from the stairway. He tilted his head at it. Shannon went to the door and picked the lock with one of his triple-nine bump keys. He went through, into a small cluttered office. Benny stayed by the door, but he shone his flashlight at a wooden cabinet built into the wall behind the desk.

"In there," he whispered.

Shannon went around the desk. He knelt in front of the cabinet and spread out his roll of tools. In another few seconds, he had the cabinet door unlocked and open. There was the safe inside, a combination box, as old-fashioned as Benny had said. Shannon used a stethoscope to listen for the tumblers, but he hardly needed it. He could feel the discs fall into place with his fingers. In another few seconds, he opened the door. His flashlight's blue beam danced over the stacks of money inside. It looked like a lot, thousands of dollars.

Shannon was surprised by the sight of all that cash. From the very start, he'd been expecting everything to go ass up. He'd expected the alarm to go off or the guards to show up at an odd hour or the safe to be empty. But here they were and there was the safe with the money inside. For the first time, Shannon began to hope this was going to come out all right.

And, of course, right then and there—the minute he dared to hope—that was when the disaster struck.

A floorboard creaked on the landing. Shannon tensed, his hand frozen reaching for the cash. He turned to see Benny's dark shape likewise frozen by the door. In their silence, they heard light footsteps running on the hall carpet. All the pieces—all the half-acknowledged thoughts—fell into place in Shannon's mind and he understood: there was someone in the house. There had been someone in the house all along. That's why he'd seen a glow at the door. The someone must have heard them break in. The someone must have turned the light off in order to hide his own presence. Now the someone was trying to get to the stairway and escape.

For another second, Shannon hoped things might still turn

out all right. All they had to do was let the someone go. Then they could grab the money and get out of here before the police showed up. Even with Benny's supercharged engine roaring for all the world to hear, they might still get away without being spotted.

But then Benny moved—and he moved so fast Shannon had no time to stop him or even call out. His shadow flashed through the door like a streak of black lightning. When he flashed back he had the someone in his hands.

It was a woman. Benny was gripping her by the throat. He shoved her up against the wall hard, hard enough to make the room shudder. He shone his flashlight in her face and then down the whole length of her. She was in her twenties, very pretty, with a curvy figure pressing through her blouse and skirt. In the out-glow of the flashlight beam, Shannon could see Benny's bright eyes and the teeth in his fierce smile as he breathed over her. His breath was a low, laughing growl of triumph and desire.

Shannon jumped to his feet. He shone his own flashlight on Benny, the blue beam crossing with the white beam in the dark.

"What the hell're you doing? Let her go," he said in a harsh whisper.

"Shut up. Get the money," Benny said. He shoved his flashlight in his back pocket. He held the girl by the throat with one hand and tore open her blouse with the other. The buttons of the blouse pattered on the carpeting. Benny grabbed hold of the girl's breast. The girl struggled, crying out in anguish and pain.

"I called the police," she managed to say. Then her voice ended in a gasp as Benny squeezed her hard and pressed himself up against her.

"Damn it, there's no time for this shit!" said Shannon.

"Shut up," Benny said. He was crazy. "Get the money."

Shannon hesitated. His blue flashlight beam played over the girl's face. He could see her terror and then her despair as Benny's hand started fumbling under her skirt. Tears streamed down her cheeks. Her eyes went up and her lips moved silently. Shannon could tell she was praying.

His heart went out to her. He was surprised by the force of the feeling. It was just one of those things you didn't know you would feel so much until you were in the situation. Now he was here and he was looking right at her, looking at her tear-streaked face. He could see her praying and choking, helpless in Benny's hands. And he felt awful for her. He knew he ought to forget about it, ignore Benny and just grab the money so they could get out when Benny was done with her. He knew if he started trouble now, they were sure to get caught. That meant prison for Shannon, prison for life.

But look at her, he thought. An image flashed in his mind of the girl getting dressed for work in the morning, turning this way and that in front of her mirror, pleased because her blouse looked pretty on her. And now Benny had torn the blouse and her face was twisted in fear and agony.

Shannon had one more moment of indecision. Then he thought: *Shit.* Then he thought again: *Shit!* Because he realized there was no way he was going to just stand there and let this happen.

Shannon had fought characters like Benny a couple of times in prison, and this is what he knew: there was no talking involved in it. Benny was big and mean and drugged out of his mind. There could be no threats or poses or hard-guy exchanges with him because by the time you got through with that garbage you'd be dead. So he simply bent to his roll and slipped his crowbar out of its pocket. It was small but it was heavy enough. He stepped around the desk and took half another step and he was next to Benny. Benny was choking the girl hard and mashing her hard with his hand under her skirt. Shannon could hear strangled phrases of her prayer: "*Santa Maria . . . Madre de Dios . . .*" That settled it for him somehow. Without another thought, he brought the crowbar whipping around in a low Laredo sidearm and shattered Benny's kneecap.

Benny did a sack of potatoes, dropped right down to the floor, *boom*, clutching his leg and shrieking like a woman in a horror movie. All of which was fine with Shannon, because what a piece of garbage this guy was.

The girl, meanwhile, staggered away from the wall, clutching her throat with one hand and the front of her skirt with the other. She straightened and glanced at Shannon, confused. Then she looked down at Benny. Benny was writhing on the floor. His shriek had sunk away to a series of gibbering sobs. What a piece of garbage.

The girl looked up at Shannon again, hesitating, uncertain. Even in the dark, he could see she was trembling violently.

"My knee!" groaned Benny Torrance.

"Aw, shut up," said Shannon. Then he turned back to the girl. "Go on, sister, get out of here. No one's gonna hurt you now."

He didn't have to tell her twice. She stumbled to the door and out onto the landing. But just as she got there, the long, urgent cry of a siren came to them through the night outside. The police. She really had called them, like she said. By the sound of it, they were turning off the street, coming down the drive to the house. Shannon's heart just about broke when he heard them. He was finished. He was going to grow old in slam. He'd always known this was going to happen if he kept at it and it was his own stupid fault, but that didn't make it any easier now that the time had come.

"You broke my knee!" cried Benny Torrance.

"Shut up, I said," said Shannon sadly.

The girl was still on the landing. She had halted there at the sound of siren. As the siren drew closer, she looked back at Shannon. He could see the whites of her eyes in the shadows. She tilted her head down the hall.

"There's a back way," she told him.

Shannon gaped at her. The sudden rush of hope gave him vertigo. The siren stopped. He could hear the police radio right outside the door.

"Hurry," the girl said.

Dumbfounded, Shannon glanced back at the money in the safe, at his tools on the floor. He glanced down at Benny. Benny writhed and held his leg and went, "Ah God. Ah God."

"Hurry," the girl said again.

Shannon let the crowbar slip from his fingers. He took two long steps and was out on the landing next to her. Instinctively, she recoiled from him, her arm pressed protectively against her breasts. He was close enough to smell her fear and her sex and her perfume and the vomitous smell of Benny on her.

"Thanks, baby," he said.

Still recoiling fearfully, she nodded.

Down the stairs, he saw the flashing red and blue lights of the police cruiser playing over the beveled glass of the door. He saw the shape of a lawman approaching.

"Don't leave me here!" cried Benny Torrance, clutching his knee.

Shannon took off down the hall.

IT WAS A LONG WAY back to his place on foot. Up hills, down empty streets, the night full of sirens. By the time Shannon pushed through the door of his apartment, he was breathless and sweating. He was scared, too. It wasn't hard for him to figure out what was going to happen next.

Benny was done—that was the first point. Benny was diddled, heavily diddled every which way. Once the shock wore off and the girl started talking, she'd get her Mex temper going and give the cops an earful. She was no illegal. You could tell just by looking at her. She had nothing to hide and no reason to hold back. She'd have Benny on agg sex assault and attempted rape and felony B and E, plus God only knew what the law had working on that psycho already. That was it for Benny. Jesus Christ would be back on the street before him.

Which meant Shannon had to hit the wind. He had to grab his bag and go—now, right now. Benny would give him over as soon as he could get the words out of his mouth, before they patched up his knee even. He'd be screaming Shannon's name as they gurneyed him into the ER. Why not, after what Shannon had done to him? It would be sweet revenge and a chance to deal down, all wrapped up in one. It had probably already happened. The cops were probably already on their way. Shannon was just lucky he'd gotten here before they did.

The apartment was empty. Karen must've gone out with her friends like she said she would. Shannon was sorry about that. He would've liked to see her one last time. He would've liked to say goodbye. She was a good girl, easygoing and good-tempered, and always willing to get it on unless she was pissed off about something. They'd had some laughs.

He went to the closet in his bedroom. On his hands and knees, he knocked a panel out of the back wall and pulled his stash from the hole there. He left a couple of fifties for Karen, but he couldn't afford to be too generous. She had her own job and she could sell his car if she needed more cash. He stuffed the money in a gym bag and stuffed some clothes on top of it. He got his traveling kit out of the bathroom and stuffed that in, too.

Before he left, he stood in the center of the living room and looked around, trying to think if he'd forgotten anything. His eyes made natural stops at the wood sculptures decorating the place here and there, sculptures he had made himself: a wall relief of a sailing ship on a stormy sea, a free-standing Indian on the coffee table, a freestanding city skyline on a shelf, a wall clock set in a relief of an eagle gazing at the moon.

He was sorry to go. He was sorry to lose Karen and the life they'd had here. He was sorry he would never see the face of the woman he'd been planning to carve in the block of white ash. He didn't have much hope for the future. He didn't think he had much chance of escaping in the long run. A traffic stop, a D-and-D —anything—and he'd be behind bars until he died. He was sorry about all of it.

As he stepped out of the apartment door, he heard a siren approaching on the street below. He halted in the doorway, his stomach turning sour. But the siren passed by.

Calm down, he told himself. *Don't go paranoid on me.* It was only a break-in, after all. He didn't even get away with the money. It wasn't like the cops were going to send the dogs and choppers after him.

That's what he thought anyway. He had no idea how bad things really were. But he was going to find out soon enough.

About half an hour later, not four blocks from where he'd done the job, he was outside the Greyhound station. He stood across the street, watching the place. A late wind had risen, a warm wind smelling of dust. The tangled fibers of eucalyptus bark rolled down the pavement like tumbleweed.

The bus station had storefront windows on two sides and was brightly lit so he could see the interior clearly. There were a couple of travelers on the benches in there and a couple of scurvy characters who might be ticket-holders or might not. No cops for now, but Shannon knew they'd be around in the normal course of things. They would drop by to chase the bums and scout out whatever types were hanging around or passing through.

Shannon figured this was as good a time to go in as any. He put on a self-assured demeanor. He crossed the street with swift, businesslike steps and pushed into the station, out of the hot, dark night and into the cold, stinging brightness of the interior. He crossed to the Plexiglas window of the ticket booth without looking to the left or right. He was aware of the voice of a newswoman speaking from the TV hung on the wall behind him.

The woman in the ticket booth was old and bent and shapeless. She moved to him slowly and stiffly, as if her bones hurt her. He asked her for a ticket to Vegas. He'd checked the schedules and it was the next bus out of state. It left in an hour. He figured Vegas was a city he could get lost in, find work in. He'd make some contacts there, score himself a new name and driver's license. Maybe eventually head farther east.

The woman pushed his ticket to him under the slot in the window. It was the first time she'd looked up at him. He thought she hesitated when her eyes reached his face, as if she recognized him and knew he was a fugitive. But that really *was* paranoid. It was only a break-in. Why would she know?

Just the same, he took the ticket and left the station quickly, feeling her eyes on his back all the way to the door. There was a bar across the street, the Cocktail Hour. He figured he'd wait for the bus in there. That way, if the police patrols came by the station, he'd be able to see them through the bar's big window.

The Cocktail Hour was small and dark. There was room for a bar and two tables and a video game and that was pretty much it. There was a fat guy playing the video game and two other fat guys sitting together at the bar, talking. There was rock music playing.

Shannon sat on the side of the bar where he could look out the window and keep an eye on the bus station. The bartender came over to him there. She was a woman in her forties. She was pleasantly slender in her black skirt and white blouse. Her face was showing some wear on it, but it was a friendly face. Shannon asked her for a Miller draft.

There was a TV behind the bar. It was hung up high, a rectangle of colored light and motion against the wall's dark wood paneling. The TV's sound was off because of the rock music, but the captions were turned on so you could read what people were saying.

That's how Shannon found out what had happened.

The bartender set his beer in front of him and turned away. Wiping her hands on a towel, she looked up at the TV, her profile to him. Shannon drank. He watched the TV, too. The local news was just coming on. Shannon had his glass at his lips when his own face appeared on the screen.

He nearly choked on his beer. The picture was a mug shot from five years ago, but it was a good enough likeness. Shannon's eyes shifted quickly. He saw the bartender draw a deep breath. He saw her body stiffen. She was careful not to look at him, but he could tell she had recognized him from the picture.

But that wasn't the worst of it, not by half. The words spelling themselves out under his mug shot told what the newswoman was saying: *Local and state police have launched a massive manhunt for John Shannon, a suspect in the Hernandez killings.*

Shannon stared, his lips parted. *The Hernandez killings? What the fuck?*

A detective was speaking on the screen now. His words spelled themselves out beneath him. *Benjamin Torrance was arrested earlier this evening during a robbery of the Whittaker Charitable Foundation,* he said. *Under questioning, Torrance confessed to the home invasion two months ago in which a family of four were brutally slaughtered. Torrance implicated Shannon as his accomplice in that crime.*

Shannon felt the room telescope to nothing around him. He felt suddenly spotlit, white bright, as if everyone must notice him, must see that he was a wanted man. The Hernandez killings. The cops had Benny on the Hernandez killings and in a fury, for revenge, Benny had told them Shannon was in on them. He'd given Shannon up for slaughtering an entire family.

Shannon's wide, suffering eyes returned to the bartender. She was still trying not to look at him, but he knew she would. How could she help herself? He waited for it and when, in fact, she stole a glance his way, he shook his head at her back and forth: *I didn't do it.* Terrified, the bartender quickly looked away at the TV again.

At that moment—as if his luck was collapsing stone after quickening stone, gathering into an avalanche of bad news coming down on top of him—at that moment, a red light caught his eye, and he turned to see two police cruisers pulling up at the curb in front of the Greyhound station.

The rock music in the bar went on playing. The fat guy went on playing the video game, the screen flashing with make-believe explosions. The two other fat guys went on talking, eating peanuts from a bowl and ignoring the TV.

Two cops got out of one of the cruisers across the street. They went into the bus station. Two other cops got out of the other cruiser and just stood there, scanning the area, their eyes passing right over the place where Shannon was sitting.

Shannon turned back to the bartender. She was still staring up at the TV, trying to pretend she hadn't recognized him. Shannon, nauseous, dying inside, followed her gaze.

There on the screen now was the girl, the girl from the job, the one that Benny had molested. Shannon read what she was saying as the words spelled themselves out under her.

It doesn't make sense to me. He could have let this man rape me. He could have taken the money, but he helped me instead. I don't think he could be a killer. It just doesn't make sense. The police must've made a mistake.

When she read that, the bartender couldn't help but glance at him again.

Shannon poured his thoughts into his suffering eyes: *Please, sister, believe her. I didn't do it. I'm not that guy.*

This time, the bartender did not pretend to look away. She looked over her shoulder at the window. Shannon looked, too. The two cops in the Greyhound station were talking to the ticket lady. She was lifting an unsteady hand to point at the bar across the street—at him. She must've seen him come in here.

Shannon and the bartender looked at one another. He poured his thoughts into his eyes, begging her to help him. He didn't dare speak out loud. He knew if one of the men in the bar realized what was happening, he would be done for. The men would turn him in. They would figure he was probably guilty anyway and if he wasn't, then let the law work it out. But a woman—a woman might go with her instincts. A woman might feel some sisterhood with the girl on TV. She might feel the romance of reaching out to him in his most desperate hour. A man would do the smart thing, the right thing, but a woman might help him. He begged her to help him with his eyes.

Outside, the two cops were pushing back into the night through the door of the bus station. One of them was talking into his shoulder mike, calling for backup. They joined the other two cops standing by the cruiser. Then all four cops began to cross the street toward the bar—although they had to wait a moment as a truck rumbled past.

Shannon turned to the bartender once again and now she was standing right in front of him. She put her small fist on the bar between them and when she withdrew it, there was a keychain lying there with about twenty keys on it. Shannon put his own hand over the keys, then lifted his eyes to her. She made the slightest gesture with her head. He followed it and saw there was a door in the wall behind her.

It was the second time that night a woman had helped him get away from the cops. He felt a passion of gratitude to her and to her entire sex, fools that they were for a man in trouble, fools that they had been for him all his life, he didn't know why. This, too, he expressed through his eyes when he looked up at her for the last time.

But now, the four cops were coming fast across the street, their expressions alert, their hands on their holsters. Shannon closed his fingers around the bartender's keychain. He stood off his barstool and, as he did, the bartender lifted the flap in the bar to let him pass through. With a final glance over his shoulder, he saw the four oncoming cops reach the sidewalk just outside the Cocktail Hour. Then he pushed through the door behind the bar.

He came into a narrow, crowded pantry. A long table filled the center of it. Shelves and boxes lined the walls. Shannon had to squeeze between the table and the boxes to get to the heavy metal door at the far end. The door was locked with a deadbolt. Shannon started flipping through the keys on the bartender's keychain, searching for the right one. He could hear the rock music playing in the bar, but he couldn't hear whether the police had come in yet. He thought they must have. And he thought the fat guys at the bar must've noticed him leaving. There wasn't a lot of time before the cops pushed into the pantry behind him. He fumbled hurriedly through the keys.

There it was: the key he wanted. Quickly, he had the heavy door unlocked. He left the keys dangling there and pulled the door open.

He stepped out into a parking lot. It was a dark expanse with only a single car parked in it. All over, in the cool night air, there were sirens—sirens coming from every direction, growing louder from every direction. Shannon's throat closed with desperation.

He understood the truth now: they were all—all of them—coming for him.

The metal door swung closed. Just before it shut with a clank, he heard the rock music grow louder as the pantry door burst open inside. The cops were right behind him.

A moment later, he was running as fast as he could into the darkness.

FOR THREE DAYS he lived in a graveyard. It was on a cliff top overlooking the sea. There were acres and acres of gently rolling lawn. There were paved walkways winding through the grass. There were stones and steles, crosses, and the occasional statue rising white on the green hills amid shrubs and eucalyptus and palm trees. Shannon knew one of the groundskeepers here, a sad-eyed, egg-shaped dude named Hector Medeiros. They had done a few jobs together. Hector helped him hide out.

During the daylight hours, Shannon kept out of sight in a mausoleum near the edge of the cliff. It was a small classical temple of white marble. Inside there was a stone bench against one wall. On the opposite wall there were square stone panels with brass plates on them. The plates had the names of the people whose corpses were behind the panels. There was a small window on another wall. It was stained glass, yellow with a dark yellow cross in the middle. You couldn't see much through it, only shapes moving when someone went by.

Being in the mausoleum made Shannon jumpy and claustrophobic. The place was the size of a prison cell, only a few paces wide and long. He couldn't go out during the day because there were groundskeepers out there and visitors sometimes. He couldn't see through the window so he was constantly paranoid about someone approaching, someone coming in on him, even though Hector told him no one would. He gathered some sticks and whittled them with his pocketknife to calm his nerves. Even so, after the first day, he began to feel he was buried in here, the same as the dead people. Once, when he fell asleep on the stone bench, he had a dream the dead people had come out of the wall and were standing over him—just standing there, looking down at him. He woke up with a start, sweating.

It was better in the evenings. When the groundskeepers went home, he would carefully emerge from the mausoleum. Hector would let him into the groundskeepers' building, a one-story house with offices and storerooms and a kitchen. Shannon gave Hector money and Hector brought him food and a newspaper. Then, once dark fell, he could go outside and get some air among the graves—as long as he kept an eye out for the security guards who came through on patrol all night long.

Staying at the cemetery, he had time to take stock of his situation. The more he thought about it, the worse it seemed. Benny had screwed him but good. Setting him up for the Hernandez killings—well, it paid Shannon back in full for the kneecap, that's for sure. It was an excellent vengeance. It really got to him, got on his nerves, got into his imagination, especially in that first rush of panic and anxiety after he heard about it in the bar. He had no alibi for the killings. They had gone down two months ago in the small hours. He'd probably been in bed at the time. He couldn't even remember. He could imagine himself getting convicted for the crime. He could picture himself on death row. The strap-down. The needle. The images ate at him.

Later, when he'd had a chance to calm down a little, Shannon told himself the rap would never stick. The police weren't stupid. They had fingerprints and DNA and all that stuff. They weren't going to pump him full of poison on the say-so of a little psycho like Benny. Were they?

But that was the thing: it didn't matter. That was the beauty of it, speaking from Benny's point of view, that was the excellence of his revenge. It didn't matter if the rap stuck or not. By setting him up for the Hernandez killings, what Benny had done was make sure that the cops would hunt him down. They'd put it all on him: feds, choppers, dogs, the TV news. There was already a quarter-of-a-million-dollar reward on his head. So they'd bust him for sure eventually, and even if they cleared him for the Hernandez job—he'd skip the needle; great—but he was a three-time loser. He'd still go down for life.

So nice work, Benny.

But then, on the third night he was at the cemetery, something happened, something flat-out bizarre. This is really where the whole story about Shannon gets started.

It was evening but still light. The grounds crew had gone home and Hector had let Shannon into the building. He had brought him some food. A chicken wrap and a Coke and some potato chips and another sandwich for later.

Shannon was famished after sleeping and pacing in the mausoleum all day. He plunked down at the table in the kitchen and tore into the wrap. While he ate, he read the newspaper Hector had brought him. That was when he saw the news about the price on his head, the quarter of a million reward. Just as he saw it, he felt Hector's eyes on him. He looked up. Sure enough, Hector was standing just behind him, gazing at him. His expression was full of sorrow and greed, like a poor but honest man gazing at the loaf of bread he was about to steal.

"What're you looking at, you squirrelly wetback?" Shannon asked him.

Hector looked away quickly. "Nothing, man, nothing."

"You saw about this reward, didn't you? Gonna sell me out, Hector? Gonna get you your quarter of a mil in blood money? Huh?"

"No, no, my friend, of course not, never."

Yeah, he was. Shannon could tell. Maybe tonight. Or maybe he'd wrestle with his conscience tonight, but then he'd do it tomorrow for sure. He'd go home and talk to Carmen and she'd point to their forty-seven kids or however many it was and say,

"A quarter of a million dollars, Hector," and then you could butter Shannon's ass because it was basically toast.

So Shannon knew his time was running out. When the sun was going down, he went outside. He went to the edge of the cliff and sat on the grass under a palm tree. His hands whittled a stick, but his eyes were on the ocean, watching the orange light of the sinking sun moving on the waves. He watched the water go slate gray as the sun went down.

He had to get out of here. There was no point waiting for things to cool off. They would never cool off. There was no point heading for another city either, Vegas or anyplace else in the U.S. With the Hernandez killings hanging over him, they'd be after him everywhere. He'd have to try for Mexico, maybe even South America. He hated the idea. It was no picnic down there for a foreigner on the run. Hard to get work, dangerous to steal. Anyone with a sharp eye could turn you in or own you. And with the hellhole jails down there and the dirty cops and the gangs and the feds up here still after him, he could just imagine what he would turn into over time, scurvy and low four seasons of the year, lower with every season, a perennial bottom-feeder creeping feverishly from job to job.

But what choice did he have?

He sat on the edge of the cliff as night fell over the field of headstones. The wind rose and the surf below him whispered and plashed.

Finally, when it was fully dark, he took his cell phone out of his pocket. It was turned off. He kept it that way because he knew the police could track a cell phone even if you didn't make a call from it. He probably should have ditched the thing, but somehow he couldn't. It was his only link to his old life, the only antidote for his crushing feelings of loneliness and regret. Once a day, he took the phone out and turned it on—just for a minute—too short a time for the law to track it—or at least he hoped so. He wanted to check his messages, hear some familiar voices, hear Karen's voice maybe. Anything.

The first night, when the news broke, Karen called him. "Oh my God, Shannon. Are you all right? Call me back." He didn't dare call her back, but at least he could listen to her voice. It made him feel better.

The second night, though—that was not so good. There had been a message from a cop, some smart-ass detective.

"Hey, Shannon," the cop said. "This is the police. You're surrounded. Come out with your hands up and no one gets hurt." Then he muttered, "You murdering piece of shit" and hung up. Shannon blanched and turned the phone off quickly.

Tonight, the third night, Shannon didn't know what to expect. He hoped Karen had called again. He missed her painfully. It had been easy to get tired of her when she was around every day, but now that he might never see her again, he remembered the good times they'd had together. He remembered the pleasure of lying next to her in the dark.

He turned on the phone. He waited nervously. He imagined the cops pinging him with their devices and zeroing in on his location. He kept an eye on his watch to make sure he didn't keep the phone on longer than a minute. The seconds passed and there didn't seem to be any new messages. Karen hadn't called. He was sorry about that. He figured she realized it was all over for good.

He was about to turn the phone off, when a light started blinking on the screen. There was no phone message, but there was a text message. Maybe that was from Karen. He pressed the button to bring the message onto the readout.

The message said: *Shannon. You've made a friend. I can help you. The Pacific Mall at midnight. Eyes.*

Shannon went through torments of uncertainty before he decided what to do. He argued it back and forth and back and forth in his mind. He was sure the message was a setup. Probably the cops. Luring him out to the mall where a dozen cruisers waited for him in the shadows. Their lights would suddenly flash red on every side of him. Their sirens would howl as they closed in on him like wolves. Or maybe it was something else, some killer cousin of Benny's, waiting to stick a knife in his heart: "This is for what you did to my boy." He would lie on his back in the parking lot and bleed to death, staring into the starless sky.

What else could it be? What kind of "friend" could he have? What kind of friend could help him? It didn't make sense. It had to be the cops or some killer from Benny. It had to be.

But with his situation as desperate as it was, he wanted to believe there were other possibilities. It *could* be real, couldn't it? It could be, say, the girl from Whittaker, the girl he'd helped out when Benny went for her. Maybe she had a brother or sister who wanted to show their gratitude and would bring him down to Mexico and hide him among their happy family. He worked up a daydream about that, about the children playing in the sun and *Mamacita* bringing him bowls of rice as he waited out the long, hot Mexican days. Then he worked up another fantasy, more elaborate, about this guy Whittaker who ran the foundation. Maybe Whittaker had seen the girl on TV and seen how Shannon had helped her and how he hadn't taken the money from his foundation after all. Someone who had a foundation—he must be at least a billionaire, right? Maybe he was sitting in his red leather wingchair, smoking a pipe in his bathrobe, and he saw the girl on TV and said to his butler, "By gadfrey, Jeeves, I think I'm going to help that young fellow."

Shannon had to choose. Time was running out. Hector was going to turn him in. He could tell. He either had to leave for Mexico tonight or meet this mysterious friend of his at the mall and hope for the best.

Eyes—that's what finally tipped the balance. He knew the mall well—he'd cased it for a job once—and he knew Eyes. Eyes was an eyeglasses store. It had a unique location, set on a sort of island in the middle of the mall's enormous parking lot, away from the other stores. If you were a cop—or even a killer—it wasn't the place you would choose for a meeting. It was too easy to scope out. Shannon could approach it from any direction, get a good

43

look at the surrounding area, and make a run for it if there was any trouble. Plus, he could come and go anonymously because, while there were security cameras all over the rest of the mall, the only camera near Eyes was inside the store. It was hard to think of a place in town that would give Shannon more advantages in any kind of ambush. That had to be why this "friend" of his chose it. It had to be some kind of gesture to gain his trust.

Finally, desperate as he was, he decided to go to the mall.

The mall at midnight was vast and empty. The quick, steady traffic hissed and flashed past on upper Main and Pacific, the streets that bordered the place on two sides. But in the mall itself, there was nothing moving. The parking lot seemed to go on forever, an immense expanse. On one side, the Pacific side, was the supermarket, the Vons. Way over on the other was the huge white block of a Macy's department store and the long, low white gallery of shops and restaurants that ran from the Macy's to the huge white block of a Sears, for all your home and garden needs. In the middle was the gray pavement of the lot, going on and on. There were no cars there at this hour, which made it seem even larger, oceanic, a shadowy gray sea with the white parking stripes like whitecaps on it. Street lamps made an archipelago of bright pink patches across its brooding, solitary distances.

Shannon entered the lot from Pacific on foot, skirting the Vons to avoid its security cameras. He was dressed in black again and carrying his gym bag, ready to leave town. His eyes were moving as he crossed the lot, but it was plain to see there was no one in the whole great expanse of it. He headed toward the center, toward the isolated island, toward the small glass box of the eyeglass store, Eyes.

He moved fast, his black sneakers quiet on the asphalt. He avoided the outglow of the street lamps and stuck to the dark. Now that he was here, his first doubts had resurfaced. He was sure he was walking into trouble like an idiot. It had to be a setup. Had to be.

He neared the store. He still saw no one, but he had an intense sensation of being watched. Maybe it was just the effect of the glasses in the store window, row after row of eyeglasses peering out at him. Or maybe it was the store sign, the two enormous eyes in spectacles that rose above the line of the roof.

He made his final approach to the place in a large looping circle, getting a look at it from every side. There was no one near. Shannon paused in the shadows a few yards away. He watched the store. The glasses in the window watched him back. The bespectacled eyes above the roof stared down at him.

Gradually—and then with a sudden, sickening start—he became aware of a figure in the darkness, a figure standing in the empty parking lot a few yards from the store, just standing there and staring at him like the dead people who had stared down at him in his dream. Shannon's breath caught. How had the figure snuck up on him like that? It was almost as if he'd appeared from nowhere.

Shannon turned sharply to face him. At once, the figure started walking toward him. Shannon waited, poised to run. The figure came close enough for Shannon to see him in the gray light. It was a man, in his sixties or even seventies maybe, small, heavyset, with rough features. No cop, if Shannon was any judge. He was dressed in a shabby tweed jacket and a button-down shirt and jeans that looked too tight on him, as jeans often do on older men. He had a lot of hair, silver and red, slicked back in an old-fashioned way, the kind of style you would've gotten in a candy-pole barber shop for five bucks fifty years ago. He had bushy eyebrows that seemed to sprout sloppily in various directions. Shannon thought there was something low-life and foreign about him.

The man stopped where he was, and Shannon's heart leapt as he held something up in his hand. But it was only a cell phone.

"I call for car, yes?" the man said. Shannon was right: he was a foreigner. He had a thick accent of some kind.

Shannon shook his head. "You call for car, brother, I'm outta here. What the hell is this? Who are you?"

"You make friend, like message said. Rich friend, powerful friend. He sends me to help you."

"Who? I don't have any friends like that. Who?"

The heavyset man shrugged. He shrugged like a foreigner, too. "You are smart man. You can know."

Whittaker, Shannon thought. It had to be. Who else? It might be a foreign name. Hard to tell.

"What does this friend want to do?"

"He send me to help you. To save you." He held up the phone again. "I call for car."

This was nuts, Shannon thought. *Nuts.* It had to be a setup. He was a stone idiot for coming. He had to go. Right now. He had to.

But he didn't go. He just didn't. The next second and the next, he was still there, still standing there with the rows of eyeglasses in the window watching him and the bespectacled eyes above the roof staring down. He was thinking about Mexico or South America or wherever he would have to run to. It felt to him almost as if that alien country, whatever it was, surrounded the mall, as if it lay just beyond the mall's perimeter. It felt to him almost as if he would suddenly be there if he left the mall. He would be there hunted, alone, lost forever to his motherland, a stranger and an outlaw and prey to anyone.

"How can you help me?" he said, stalling for time so he could make his mind up.

But the foreigner with the bushy eyebrows only flipped his phone open. "Send car," he said into it.

Instantly, Shannon saw the headlights turn in off Main. They bounced toward him across the lot, going in and out of the gray dark and the pink light. It was a blue Cadillac, Shannon could see as it drew near. He could see the shape of the driver behind the wheel, but he couldn't make out his face. The Caddy pulled up close beside the foreigner. The foreigner pulled the rear door open.

"We should not stay," he said. Then he got into the car's back seat, leaving the door open for Shannon.

Well, he was right about that anyway. They shouldn't stay, not with the light of the car drawing attention, and all those eyeglasses staring.

Shannon took a deep breath. Almost before he decided to do it, he was walking to the car. He tossed his gym bag to the floor and lowered himself onto the back seat. As he was pulling the door shut, the car started moving.

He sat back, dazed. What the hell had he just done? He stared blankly at the pane of dark Plexiglas that shielded the front seat. He couldn't see the driver on the other side. He only saw his own reflection.

After a moment, he collected himself enough to turn to the foreigner. There were lights burning low on the doors and he could see him clearly. "Where are we going?"

The foreigner didn't answer. He seemed to be studying Shannon, peering at his face as if it were a statue in a museum. He was twisted around toward him on the seat with his arm up resting on the seatback. He was tilting his head this way and that as if considering his options.

"What're you looking at?" Shannon asked him.

The man reached out with his thick, liver-spotted hand. He tried to take hold of Shannon's chin. Shannon slapped the hand away.

"Get off me. What're you doing?" The foreigner just went on studying him. It gave him the creeps. "Who are you anyway?"

"I am identity man," the foreigner murmured as he studied him. Only he said *mang* instead of *man*. "I am identity mang." Now, finally, he turned away. He reached for something on the other side of him. Shannon craned his neck and peered hard to make out what it was in the dark. It was a medical bag. The foreigner opened it, rooted through it with his thick fingers, glancing at Shannon over his shoulder. "Yes? You know this? Identity?"

Shannon shook his head. "What—you mean, like, you get people fake ID?"

"Oh! Please! Not fake ID." The foreigner went on looking at

Shannon but went on rooting in his medical bag at the same time. *"Real* ID. New. I give you new everything. I give you new face. I give you new name, new papers, new work, new place to live. Yes? Is good, huh? I save you. I give you new life entirely."

Then, with unbelievable swiftness, animal swiftness that outraced the mind, he whipped his hand around and plunged a syringe into Shannon's neck.

Shannon began to lift his hand in self-defense, but his hand fell back as he sank into unconsciousness.

PART II

THE WHITE ROOM

THE GANGSTER WAS fifteen years old. He called himself Super-Pred—he actually called himself that. He had his own following among the scattered crews warring over the city's Northern District, or what was left of the Northern District after the looting and the fire and the flood. He had a rep for the unimaginably sudden and grotesque: frothing fits of rage that left his enemies de-boweled or otherwise damaged irrevocably. There was, for instance, one thirteen-year-old in his posse nicknamed Eyeball because Super-Pred had torn one of his eyeballs out in a property dispute over some twelve-year-old cooch—who, by the way, had been missing ever since.

Thus Lieutenant Brick Ramsey watched dispassionately as Detective Gutterson beat the little cancer down.

They were in a steel shed, what had been a storage shed out back of an auto parts shop years back. The shop itself was long gone but the shed stood even after the flooding. Corrugated steel walls and a dirt floor. That's where the boy was—on the floor, hands over his head to protect it. The blood from his nose had made a round stain about the size of a silver dollar in the packed earth.

Well, these things had to be. The Northern District was lawless now. Murders every hellish day. Gunfire all the time—so much gunfire that citizens had stopped calling it in—it was just rattling background noise to them like cicadas in the trees. Super-Pred's squad—and other squads like them—prowled the ruined streets in dark and daylight. Slink-backed coyotes, drooling for Vics. With rap-star T-shirts and golden dollar signs on golden chains and baggy pants like their convict heroes wore. One night, a pack of them broke into a woman's emergency trailer—one of those trailers the feds gave to people who'd lost their homes in the storm. They broke in and raped her to death right there in her own bed, her four-year-old daughter crouching in the corner.

That was bad enough. But last night, someone *really* crossed the line. Someone popped a cruiser. A cop car establishing a presence on Northern Boulevard. A couple of patrolmen doing a slow pass, giving the evil eye to the whores and dealers there. Some joker hunkered like Baghdad behind a Dumpster in an alley opened up with a Kalishnikov and peppered the car's passenger door, could've hurt the rookie riding shotgun. Shooter was gone before they could chase him down. That crossed the line. That couldn't be allowed to stand. When the police passed by, you faded, motherfucker, you vanished like the Cheshire Cat till there was nothing left of you but your shit-eating grin. That was the law of the streets.

"I'm going to leave here with your scrotum in my pocket or the name of the fool with the AK," Lieutenant Ramsey said quietly.

Detective Gutterson kicked the boy in the stomach by way of punctuation, making the punk let go of his head and clutch his belly now, all curled up and writhing on the shed's dirt floor.

Gutterson smiled down at his work. And what a likely thug *he* was, Ramsey thought. Two hundred and fifty pounds of pure contempt disguised as a human being. A six-foot-four frame of deteriorating muscle. A smirking, resentful expression plastered on that crewcut potato of a head, an age-old mask of hatred that spoke trouble to a brother's very DNA. Back in his dreamed-of yesteryears, Ramsey figured, Gutterson probably would have been an overseer on a southern slave plantation, all whip and hard-on. Now he was a bullying cop in whatever was left of this bled-dry city, and it was one of Ramsey's few remaining sources of job satisfaction that he could tell a dog like this to fetch and it would go fetch, despising his colored master only a little more than he despised himself for having to obey.

Gutterson was loving this, just loving it. It was probably the highlight of his week. And the junior g, Mr. Super-Pred down there—he knew it, too. He knew that his only pathway out of this mini-perdition was through the sympathies of Lieutenant Ramsey.

"You let that peckerwood do a brother like this?" he whined, clutching his gut, squinting up at Ramsey through his swollen mug.

Ramsey squatted on the shed floor so he could peer directly in through the purpling lumps of the gang-banger's cheeks to the dim gleam of the swimming child-eyes buried in them. The lieutenant smiled. A quiet, distant smile to let the boy know that the road of racial solidarity ended at the brick wall of his heart. Then he faked a friendly glance up at Gutterson.

"Used to be a preacher in my neighborhood when I was a boy. Reverend Mack. He could do a Sunday morning, all right. Full of the spirit. One day, I got up to some mischief or other. My mama hauled me into his office so he could put the fear of God in me. Her holding me half up in the air by my elbow and him standing behind his desk, looming over me like Mount Sinai, sending up smoke and fire and the word of God. And all I could think about was this picture hung up on the wall behind his desk. He must've found it in a book somewhere. Tore it out and framed it. It was a picture of Jesus stomping out sin. Couldn't take my eyes off it. Sin was this—this kind of a twisting, hissing, black serpent all writhing under Jesus' foot, with this half-man, half-dragon face, something out of a horror movie. Just writhing there, helpless, spitting hatred up at the Lord." Above him, Gutterson chuckled heavily. Ramsey choked back his hatred of the man. Looked away from him, looked down at the boy. "That's what you remind me of, son. Twisting there, writhing there on the ground. You remind me of that picture."

Super-P panted through his pain. "I'm just a brother trying to get by on the mean streets, daddy."

"That right?"

"Just a brother trying to get by, same as you."

Lieutenant Ramsey smiled down at the boy patiently but the smile was a fake, and it felt to him even at that moment like the fake it was. His whole demeanor of self-restrained dignity—his lifelong demeanor—felt to him at this point like a hollow construction, a shell he lived in like a hermit crab. The man he seemed was the shell of the man he had once set out to be, his mother's son. But inside, he was not that man. He knew he was not that man.

And because he knew, Super-P's you-and-me-brother strategy was getting to him more than he let on. In fact, his own mental image of that bygone picture on the preacher's wall was getting to him, too. Crouching over the banger in the shed, he could almost feel that snake of sin writhing and twisting and spitting sourly in his belly. And because it really did remind him of Super-P, it was almost as if it was Super-P himself writhing inside him. Not that Ramsey's sin was this gangster's beatdown. That was nothing. That was street business. That just had to be. No. His sin was Peter Patterson, killing Peter Patterson. Even now, weeks after the storm, the memory of the bookkeeper's pitying eyes stared up at him from the memory of the flame-streaked black water, the dead man's face liquid and wavering.

"You loose this cracker on me?" Super-Pred whined. "You think he your beast, but he own you same as slavery. You and me both."

Lieutenant Ramsey gave a single silent laugh but the laugh was a fake, too. This punk didn't know how close he was, how close to getting Ramsey's goat, setting him off. The lieutenant went on smiling but he wanted to shut this punk up with a bullet. Shut him up with a bullet and then do Gutterson, too—do him slow—kneecap, then belly, and finally no-longer-smirking-but-pleading-sweating-cowardly face. Kill them both as if they were the snake inside him.

"You're gonna tell me the shooter's name, little man," he said. "That's a fact." He spoke with his lifelong tone of quiet self-control and moral dignity, his fake tone now that he had Peter Patterson's pitying stare and his own writhing shame inside him. "Detective Gutterson has all day to deal with this. But me, I've got better things to do."

He stood up, making as if to leave.

That did the trick. Panic went flaring through the beaten boy. A day alone with Detective Gutterson would be a day without sunshine for damn sure.

"No, wait! Now hold on! Hold on, daddy."

Ramsey waited. Looked down with his demeanor of lofty dignity at the punk on the floor.

Super-P's body sagged there, the twisting, snakelike tension dying in him. He was finished. He just needed a moment to swallow his shame now, swallow his self-disgust at breaking down, at showing his ass and giving over. There was always that moment at the end before they gave over.

He gave over. "Fatboy," he said.

Ramsey sighed. Fatboy. Figured. Sixteen-year-old lardbutt bully-bait trying to make his bones by unloading on the police. He could be tried as an adult for this, do twenty years, two decades grabbing his ankles, asshole spiked on jail yard meat. It was a world without justice.

"Don't feel so bad," he told Super-P. "You're ashamed 'cause we see your ass? You're ashamed 'cause it turns out you're no tough guy like the rapper on your shirt or your big brother in prison? Turns out you're just another scared, fatherless punk doesn't know how to be a man and you're ashamed? Well, guess what. Rapper on your shirt? Your big brother in prison? They're scared, fatherless punks, too. Show their ass for a dollar and a kick in the shin. It's just who you all are, boy. You just gotta swallow it. Swallow it like a whore swallows cum." He spat in the bloodstained dirt. He sighed again. Fatboy. Then, to the ape Gutterson he said, "Come on."

He gestured the big thug toward the shed door and began to head that way himself. Gutterson paused to snort his disdain over the broken child in the dirt. Then he followed.

But Super-Pred wasn't done. Or that is, he was done, but he needed to pretend there was still some man in him.

"You think you're better than me?" he called up from the floor, called at their backs. "You no better than me, daddy. You just the same."

Ramsey felt Gutterson glance at him as they walked away together. Ramsey only just bothered to roll his eyes to show how little he cared. But he did care, the snake writhing in him.

"What are you but a g with a badge?" ragged Super-Pred from the floor, trying to salvage some self-respect. "Why shouldn't Fatboy fight his turf? You just another crew out here, my man. You think we don't know? What about Peter Patterson? Whole street knows about him."

Ramsey stopped in his tracks. Gutterson didn't catch it. The big thug kept going, reached the shed door, had his hand on it. Only then did he look behind to see Ramsey frozen.

Ramsey turned slowly back toward Super-P. "What do you think you know?" he said quietly. Demeanor of lofty moral dignity. His mother's son.

The boy gangster knew he'd gone too far, tried to backtrack. "I don't know nothing." Ramsey took a single step toward him. That was all it needed. Mr. Super-Pred started babbling, "I'm just rapping. Just a tag, man. Give a brother some slack. Trying to get your goat, that's all. Just a tag I saw."

"A tag? Where?" said Ramsey in the same quiet tone. "You saw it where?"

"A house. Old house we hang in sometimes."

Ramsey nodded slowly. With that lifelong demeanor. With the

snake writhing in his belly. Peter Patterson's pitying stare through the wavering water.

"Tell me the address," he said.

There was a magazine between the two front seats of the unmarked Charger. Standing in the hollow armrest between where Gutterson sat behind the wheel and where Ramsey sat on the passenger side. It was a national newsweekly. A leading national newsweekly with a picture of Augie Lancaster on the cover. Lancaster was striking a heroic pose. Fists on his hips, eyes on the horizon. They'd photographed him from below so he looked like a moral giant.

Fighting to Save His City.

That was the headline. That was actually the headline.

If stupidity were a communicable disease, Ramsey thought, journalists would have to be herded into a pit and shot like infected cattle.

He looked out his window. It was late afternoon on a dull gray day. No beam of sun—no shock of blue or any color—appeared to mitigate the bleakness of the scene. There was devastation on every side and an inhuman stillness, a heavy hollowness in the atmosphere—or maybe that was Ramsey himself, an emanation of his own interior state. In any case, brownstones stood gutted, their black windows like skull-eyes gazing back at him. Houses lay crippled and broken, sunk in mud that used to be lawns. Shops—he could see through the shattered storefronts—had been scoured of all their goods and were empty and abandoned, the walls stained brown up to the waterlines near their ceilings. There were words scrawled and painted on doorways and walls, words that had been scrawled and painted there to alert rescuers at the height of the flood. They came to Ramsey like disembodied voices, whispering out of the wreckage: *Help us. Four trapped inside. One dead here. Save us. Help us.*

The whole area stank. Stagnant water and sewage. It made you flinch at first, but then it made you sad. It was such a mortal sort of odor, the stench of an abandoned corpse. It made you sad and then, after a while, you got used to it and just couldn't smell it at all anymore.

Fighting to Save His City.

Ramsey's eyes went over the scene, flicking instinctively to whatever was alive. A woman wearing a gym suit and carrying a shopping bag, young but bent over as if the earth itself were on her back. Two old men sitting in chairs against a wall, staring at the wrecked world like a movie. An angry mother yanking at her toddler's arm. And here and there, again and again, the slouching, shift-eyed, yellow-eyed young coyote-men prowling the afternoon, casing locations, casing prey, meeting on corners to clasp each other's hands in an expert and near-invisible exchange of cash and contraband.

Fighting to Save His City.

Had it ever been true? Ramsey wondered bitterly. Even at the beginning when Ramsey had first followed him, even loved him, even then had Augie Lancaster ever fought to save this city? Had he ever even meant to? Well . . . in daydreams maybe. Daydreams like we all have of ceaseless cheering, of an endless parade, of himself, Augie, slowly passing in his top-down limousine, the hands of the poor upraised in gratitude at the spangly gold showering from his beneficent fingertips. Maybe he really hadn't known—maybe he really hadn't understood that even the dream of doing good can be the hunger for power in disguise. Maybe he hadn't recognized the strangely red-visaged angel who had whispered to him he could be king of saints only to slowly tutor him to be king of kings—king of the city kings with his vacation homes and his cars and his boat, and the vacation homes and cars and boats of his cronies . . .

Fighting to Save His City.

All those times he had called these people his brothers. All those times he had told them that the white man was their enemy, that only he could save them as he saved them—look!—in his dreams. All those beautiful speeches—*City of Hope, City of Justice*—spurring them on to this protest or that, to boycott a Jew store owner who had shot a neighborhood thief, or to picket a radio station where some DJ had made some racial crack, or to protest a white jury's verdict that had sent some black mad-dog to prison. All those times he had inspired them to bare their chests and display the scars of injustice, mobilizing them as an army of victims to blackmail another dollar out of the citadels of white guilt and fear. It was all good—all good for the king of the city kings, but for the brothers? Useless, meaningless diversions while their fatherless children prowled the streets in drooling coyote crews and their fatherless mothers smoked bone for crack cocaine which their fatherless fathers sold to them in the broken buildings that all the spangly gold from his fingertips somehow never did rebuild.

Fighting to Save His City.

Sure. Because the journalists had their daydreams, too, the guilty white journalists made gullible by their desperate yearning for virtue. The same strangely red-visaged angel whispered in their ears, too: *Well done, thou good and faithful servants, here are your Pulitzer Prizes and your I-Love-a-Nigger Decoder Rings for, lo, you have lifted a dusky-colored saint into the slowly passing top-down limousine of his parade where the spangly gold may fall upon the brown-skinned masses, transforming their infirmities and all your sins into an ever-to-be-remembered goodness.*

Herded into a pit and shot like infected cattle, Ramsey thought. *The stupidest pack of fools on earth.*

Except maybe for him. Except maybe for Lieutenant Brick Ramsey himself, who had also followed Augie, who had even loved him and also believed.

Gutterson swung the wheel and turned the Charger off the boulevard.

They came onto a short lane. The houses here stood ghostly, lopsided and broken. You could see through the staring windows that they were empty, their interiors ravaged. You could see overturned furniture in there and piles of debris and brown stains rising to the high waterlines on the wall.

The lane dead-ended at an empty lot, a dirt-brown expanse where plastic bags and papers tumbled over concrete shards and discarded mattresses and discarded refrigerators and ovens and scrap. It made a mournful backdrop.

"This is the one," Gutterson said.

It was the fourth house down on the left, about halfway to the dead end. It was made of large wooden shingles painted pale green. Ramsey could already feel its haunted emptiness as the Charger pulled to the curb in front of it.

"This is where they hang?" said Gutterson. "Look at it. Bunch of animals."

Ramsey choked down his hatred for the man and with it any answer he might've made.

The two of them got out of the car. They started across the front yard—the ruin of the front yard. The lawn was dead and littered with rubbish: cans and bags and pieces of lumber and rebar. They stepped through it gingerly, the debris crunching and clanging and crackling under their shoes. Gutterson's hand hovered over his nine, in case anyone was in the house and up to mischief. Ramsey's hands were at his sides. He was certain there was no one in there.

They reached the front door and stood one on either side of it. A breeze off the river brought a fresh stink to them. Ramsey's nostrils stung with it and with the first hint of the smell within. Gutterson glanced at Ramsey. Ramsey nodded. Gutterson reached out and banged on the door with his fist.

"Police!" he started to say. But with a soft, damp sound, the flood-rotten wood of the doorframe splintered. The door swung in and the word died half spoken.

Another glance at Ramsey. Another nod. Gutterson drew his gun and charged the place. Ramsey more or less strolled in after him.

"Oh . . . !" Gutterson strangled on a curse. The stench inside was hellish. He clapped a hand over his nose and mouth. "Fucking animals," he said through his fingers. "It's like living nose-deep in shit."

He went off to search the place, moving tensely behind his gun.

Ramsey, meanwhile, put his hands in his pants pockets and ambled into the living room. The smell was even worse in here. He tried breathing through his mouth but the air tasted bad, too. It was an awful brew: sewage, garbage, rotten food, maybe some dead things, drowned rats in the walls or a cat somewhere, and just the all-around putrescence of water damage. The whole place must've been under the flood at some point. The sofa had been soaked to a hulking mush. It looked as if it had melted and then resolidified. Chairs and tables were all overturned, broken and only half recognizable, what was left of them flung randomly about like body parts in a minefield. The walls were crumbling, broken through in places to the beams and insulation. The ceiling was mildewed and sagging as if it were about to come crashing down.

"Clear!" Gutterson announced, coming in behind him.

Ramsey had already found what he was looking for, was already standing in front of one moldy wall. Gutterson moved up beside him and the two cops stood shoulder to shoulder, looking at it.

The wall was spray-painted and chalked from top to bottom, covered in tags, scrawled all over with ornate and sweeping gang handles and gang signs. Black skulls, green waves, gray thorns, red fire. Nicknames formed by tortuous swirls of color. Ramsey's eyes went over them. He knew the merciless thugs who made these marks and he despised them. He had always known them, always despised them. They were what his mother had hammered at him not to be. What the marines had sweated out of him. He had thought he'd lost his last sentimental traces of pity for them during his patrolmen years, seeing the creatures they were, cleaning their victims' entrails off the macadam. But it was strange. Looking at these marks today, he felt some distant stirring of . . . compassion . . . something. The flamelike rise of their embroidery seemed to him like supplicating hands raised to the sky, the masculine energy of their creation sounded in his mind like the

61

soul-cries of fatherless young men, a great inarticulate bubble of boy-prayer desperately bursting under an empty heaven and then desperately gone.

"Like pissing on a tree," said Gutterson. "Animals."

Ramsey, with his air of quiet moral dignity and the writhing sourness inside him, didn't answer. Reluctantly, already knowing what he'd find, he shifted his gaze to the wall's low corner on his right hand, to the words stroked there in dripping blood-red letters.

"What the fuck?" Gutterson muttered.

The dripping blood-red letters said,

Ramsey murdered Peter Patterson!

SHANNON KNEW TIME was passing but he didn't know how much. Days? Weeks? He had no way of telling. He would float upward toward the surface of consciousness but never quite break through. He would see the world above as if through water, a liquid blur of life just beyond him.

The foreigner was up there sometimes. The crazy old bastard who'd injected him. Shannon remembered. The mall parking lot. The watching eyeglasses. The back seat of the car . . .

The foreigner would give him drinks through a straw. He would talk sometimes, though the words also came to Shannon as if through water and he could never recall from time to time what the foreigner said. He would try to answer. He would struggle to break through the surface, to come awake fully. But the drugs—it must've been drugs—would suck him back under. Light narrowing to a pinpoint, depths closing over him. He would hear the foreigner's voice like a fading echo: "Sleep."

And he would sleep.

Now he awoke. It was different this time. He felt it right away. His mind was clearer. He was aware of the room around him, of the bed underneath him. He had a new sense of his own material presence.

He was in pain—he was aware of that now, too. His face was stiff, aching, throbbing. The pain pulsed from the center of his head to radiate through his entire body. His left arm stung like hornets had been at it.

He began to lift a hand to his face.

"Don't touch yet," the foreigner said.

Shannon stared at the hand groggily. He let it sink down again to the sheets. Slowly, he turned toward the voice.

The foreigner was standing beside his bed. He was wearing a doctor's get-up, a white coat, a stethoscope around his neck. He was adjusting a blinking machine that stood on the top shelf of a green cart. Shannon noticed now that his bed had a rail like a hospital bed and that the mattress was partly raised like a hospital mattress so he could sit up. The machines the foreigner was tinkering with looked like hospital-style machines, too. There was an IV bag with its tube stuck in Shannon's arm. Another tube ran out from under the blankets—a catheter. It was all hospital stuff.

But Shannon sensed that this was no hospital. A dim fire of panic sprang up in him, a dim fire of fear he understood was there but could hardly feel. He looked around the room. No windows. No pictures. Nothing. Just blank, white walls. No furniture but the bed and one chair. Where the hell was he?

At that point, Shannon's eyes started to sink shut. He started to slump on the upraised mattress.

"Sit. Sit up, stay up," the foreigner said briskly, coming to the bedside, pushing at his shoulder. "You have to keep elevated for swelling."

Shannon shook his head, stretched his eyes, trying to stay awake. "Where am I? What'd you do to me?"

"I cut off your legs and replace them with grinning doll heads."

"What?"

"Ta, ta, ta. Don't be fool. I joke with you. I give you new face, like I tell you. So the police, they won't know you. Is good, yes?"

"My face? You changed my face?" Shannon started to lift his hand to it again.

"Don't touch. Here. Drink."

The foreigner held up a water bottle made of blue plastic, a sports bottle with a built-in straw.

"No more drugs," said Shannon thickly.

"Drink. Is apple juice. I drug you here," said the foreigner, pointing to the IV tube.

Shannon realized he was very thirsty. He let the foreigner hold the bottle under his lips. He sucked at the straw. The apple juice tasted good—cold and sweet. Shannon took another sip, then sat back against his pillow.

His mind was getting clearer. He rolled his head so he could focus on the foreigner. He could see the man better in here than he could before, out in the parking lot, in the night. There really was something seedy about the guy. The doctor outfit couldn't change that. The whole look of him was shady and suspicious. The red-and-silver hair slicked back in its own oil and the eyebrows sprouting all over the place. The liver spots on his unsteady hands. The fluffy white hair that looked like dead dandelions growing out of his ears. And something else: that sinister laughter in his eyes, that unwholesome sparkle of chaotic wit. You got that with foreign guys sometimes. Shannon had seen it before. They acted like they'd been around forever and knew everything, like they knew the whole world was just one big joke and you were a naive American fool if you took it seriously.

"You just went and changed my face?" Shannon made himself sound pissed off about it but really he wasn't sure how he felt. It was *his* face, on the one hand, and no one had asked him. On the other hand, the whole business was coming back to him—the Whittaker job and Benny Torrance and the Hernandez killings. He could see where the foreigner might have done him a favor.

"Is good, yes?" the foreigner repeated with his sinister eyes sparkling. "So police won't know you."

"You could've asked me first."

The foreigner shrugged. "I also could've made you look like monkey's asshole." He diddled some more with the machine.

"No more drugs," said Shannon.

"A little for the pain."

Shannon was clear enough in his head to start thinking now, to start remembering and putting things together.

"How long've I been here?"

"Two days."

"And this was all because of Whittaker, the foundation guy? Is he the one who wanted to help me out?"

"Your friend, you mean. Your friend wishes to remain anonymous."

"What do you mean, anonymous? What the hell is this?" Shannon felt like he ought to make trouble, for form's sake, but he was beginning to suspect he had stepped into a good thing.

"Ta, ta, ta," the foreigner said again. He finished with the machine. He drew the chair up to the bed and sat down on it, murmuring, "Now we see." He leaned forward, studying Shannon's face, peering at him from underneath his untamed eyebrows. He reached out and when Shannon made to slap him off, he said, "Et-et-et" and pushed past him. He held Shannon's cheek and chin gently with his fingertips, turning his face this way and that.

"You are very ugly now, like monster," he murmured. "But soon you will be Handsome Dan, like in movies." *Handsome Dang.*

Now Shannon did push the foreigner's hands away. "You ought to ask before you cut up someone's face."

"Yes, yes." The foreigner seemed unrepentant, even amused. He went on studying Shannon a while in silence. Then, in a low voice, as if meditating out loud, he said, "Let me tell you how will be, how always is. I give you new face, name, papers, work to do. I even change your fingerprints and DNA."

"What? I thought you couldn't do that."

"In body, no. In computers, yes—which amounts to same thing."

"What do you mean? You mean you can get into the computers? The records? All of them? The feds, the cops, the prisons? You can change all the records of my fingerprints and DNA? You can do that?"

"I am identity mang. I tell you."

Shannon's face grew blank and distant as the implications occurred to him.

"You see?" said the foreigner, nodding. "This is what you want, yes? This is beyond wildest dreams. You will escape police now, live new life now, yes?"

"Yeah," said Shannon, thinking it through. "Yeah . . ."

"Yeah." The foreigner mimicked him, mocked him. "Maybe for month. Maybe for year, maybe two years, maybe sometimes three, who knows? Then you begin to make mistakes, do little things same as like you used to. You are thinking, 'It does not matter now. I am new man now.'" *New mang.* "'I escape police.' Then one day you don't escape. You steal, you fight, you run traffic light, you drink in street, police arrest you. Maybe you get away one time — because fingerprints are changed, face is new, you have papers. But soon you are back. You steal, you fight. You go to jail. You go to prison. Three strikes. Or you kill someone. It is all again. All my work, what's the use, what's the purpose, yes? A month, a year, two years, maybe sometimes three. Then it is all again. All the same like before."

Shannon gestured for the apple juice. The foreigner held it to him and he sucked at the straw. As he leaned back, tired with the effort, he shook his head. "No," he said. "Not me. I get what you're saying. But not me. I'm done with that life. You give me a fresh start and I'm gone, baby, gone, so help me."

"Yes, yes, yes, 'so help me.'" The foreigner waved his spotty hand. "You all think this. Fresh start. Like magic, you think. Because you are American. Because you are dumb. You think: 'This is big, wide country. I come to new place, no one knows me, I change. I have therapy, I read book, I take medicine, I have operation, I am new mang.'" He shook his head, those sinister, laughing eyes glistening. "You are never new mang. I am identity man who tells you this. You have identity like stain in flesh, it never leave you. You have history, like stain in mind. Look at arm. Hmm? Look."

Shannon looked at his stinging left arm. There was a bandage wrapped around it, but he could see red, raw flesh peeking out from beneath the edges. "What's that . . . ?"

"They are gone now. The little scars. I take them away from you. Soon the flesh will heal. There will be nothing."

Shannon stared—at the bandaged arm, then at the foreigner, then at the bandaged arm again. His reaction to this new piece of information surprised him. He had always hated those little round scars on his arms. He had never noticed them without a pang of rage. There were nights when he lost sleep over them, angry at his crappy luck, generally furious and forlorn. And yet now—now that they were gone, he sorrowed for the loss of them. He felt violated, wronged, an intimate piece of him stripped away while he slept.

"What'd you have to do that for?" he murmured, half to himself. He already knew the answer.

"Because they are identifying marks, no? I take them off records, but maybe someone remembers. They make for questions. So I take them." He watched, amused, as Shannon mourned over his lost scars. "So what? So I take scars—so what? Is history gone? Did mother not burn you with cigarette now? Do you not lie awake at night in anger and pain because you have no love in life, no love in heart until you die? You know this. Shannon—is not even real name. You change already. You are new mang? No. Identity like stain. You have nature, you have history. These I cannot take away. So," concluded the foreigner breezily, throwing his hands in the air and letting them plop back down into his lap, "you are fucked." He stood up. "You are not changed. You cannot change. You will do again same like before and like before, same things will happen to you. But . . . for now you have new face. So that is something, yes? I do what I can do."

Shannon glanced at his bandaged arm again. He couldn't shake that weird sense of loss.

"So what do I look like?" he asked. "My face, I mean."

"I show you later," said the foreigner, "when you are Handsome Dang."

"Just give me a mirror. What do I look like?"

But already the older man was toying with the machine at the bedside. "Sleep," he said.

And Shannon sank away into sleep.

The next time he woke up, he was alone, although he had the sense that a door had just closed, that someone had just left him. His mind cleared faster this time. He cranked his eyes wide. He worked himself into an upright position on the bed. Looked around him.

The IV bag and its silver pole were pushed against the wall. The tube was wrapped up on a hook on the pole. He looked down at his right arm. Nothing there now but a square of gauze taped in the crook of his elbow where the needle had run in. The catheter was gone, too. So were the bandages on his left arm. He could see the red, naked patch where the burn scars had been. He was still in pain, a lot of pain, more throbbing pain in his head than before, in fact. But that was all right, he could take it. He was glad to be free of the tubes and off the drugs.

He moved his feet over the edge of the bed and sat up. He had to wait there until his stomach stopped roller coasting. While he waited, he noticed a couple of painkillers, Vicodin, on the bedside table next to the juice bottle. That was reassuring. He'd go without them as long as he could, but he was probably going to need them soon.

He was wearing a hospital gown, one of those papery smocks that opens in back so your ass hangs out. He looked around the room for his clothes. No sign of them. That annoyed him. He wanted to get dressed. He wanted to get out of here. He wanted to get some air and be his own man again.

He wanted to see his face, too, see what the foreigner had done to him, get a look at this "new mang" he was supposed to be. There was a bathroom just past the end of the bed, the door open. That got him moving. He managed to stand up. Hanging onto the bedrail, he edged his way unsteadily across the floor.

He went into the bathroom. What the hell? No mirror. Everything else was there—a sink, a toilet, a shower—but no mirror. This foreigner was a real comedian, wasn't he? If he wasn't careful, Shannon might give *him* a new face, see how he liked it.

Without thinking, he reached up and gingerly touched the stubble on his cheek. He flinched. The skin underneath was still swollen and stiff and raw. Well, maybe he was better off without a mirror. He wasn't going to be able to shave for a while anyway.

He made his way out of the bathroom, to the door of the bedroom. He was still fighting off nausea, but it was getting better. He grasped the knob and hesitated for a moment. The spooky idea came to him that he might be locked in here. He would hate that. But no. The knob turned, the door opened. He padded out.

Here was another room, another white room with no windows or pictures or anything, just white walls. It was bigger than the bedroom, much bigger. There was some furniture here, too. A table, a couple of chairs, a low white dresser against one white wall—plus a white refrigerator. There was also another door. Maybe a door to the outside. Shannon decided to ignore it for now. He wasn't feeling steady enough to go out. Not to mention the fact that his butt was waving in the breeze.

He went to the refrigerator instead. Opened it. Found a sandwich inside and a carton of milk and a whole chicken wrapped in plastic. There was also a bowl with some oranges and apples. He tried a bite of one of the apples, but he could barely swallow it. He was too sick. He tossed what was left back in the bowl. It was nice to know it was there anyway. It would come in handy when his stomach stopped feeling like Adventureland.

He went to the dresser. Pulled open a drawer. Clothes! Now this was good. This was a big find. It lifted his heart. He opened the drawers one by one. Black jeans and blue jeans, underwear, socks, sweatshirts, T-shirts, even a couple of pairs of sneakers, all in his size. He lost no time about it. He got himself dressed right then and there, ignoring the throbbing pain in his head when he pulled the sweatshirt down over it, wincing through the burn on his arm when he worked it into the sleeve. No, this was really good. Getting dressed. It made him feel much better, much more human.

Now he was ready to try the other door. He went to it and again he hesitated. It was painted white like the rest of the place, but it was wooden, heavy. He tried the knob. Locked. He had known it would be. It was a police lock, too. He could tell by the plate. There would be a big iron bar jammed in a slot in the floor on the other side. No way through that, not without some heavy machinery.

He turned away. He took an unsteady breath. He was trapped in here—trapped. Had to keep calm. Had to keep smart. He told himself it was all right. He was still better off than he was back in the mausoleum, much better. Then, the cops were after him. The Hernandez killings—three strikes—either way, he was looking at prison for life. Now, if the foreigner was telling the truth, he had a new face, new records, a second chance at everything. It was a good deal. He was better off. Much.

Still he was claustrophobic. Angry, agitated. He couldn't help it. He was frustrated at being trapped in here, trapped in the white room.

He didn't like it. He didn't like it at all.

Hours went by. It was tough. Tough. A white room. Nothing to do, nothing to look at, not even a TV or a magazine. It was like prison, the stretches he'd done in prison where time became a kind of distance, time became like a long road you had to walk and walk and you couldn't speed up or slow down or stop but only walk at the same pace—that was the punishment—the monotony of the pace—a purgatory of walking down the road of time. At least in prison there was something to see and hear. There were noises and voices and other people, something to break up the tedium. Here, what was there? When he felt stronger, he ate the chicken. He took the Vicodin. He did some pushups, some crunches, as much as he could tolerate through the pain. Then that was it. There was pretty much nothing else to do. A couple more hours went by and he felt like he'd been here for years. He felt like he was going crazy. He felt like his skin was made of spiders, like his skin was crawling all over him. This was the way he felt when he hadn't done a job for a long time. When he was just working and coming home and there was nothing happening. The boredom of everyday life made him crazy just like this, just like prison did with its purgatory road.

Crazy thoughts started to come into his mind. He couldn't stop them. All his worries raced around inside his head like mice on speed. The police and the Hernandez killings and Benny Torrance. Racing around and around in his head. Karen and his old life—gone like that, like the snap of a finger. Gone forever. He thought of her, wriggling out of her skirt, smirking at him in her bra and panties, putting perfume on for him. It was enough to drive him insane with longing. What had he done? Why had he gone on another job? He knew his luck was running out. He knew it. He'd never had a big supply of luck to begin with. He looked at his arm where those little round scars used to be and he felt the old hollow rage that came to him in his sleepless hours and he felt this hollow sadness that the scars were gone and he thought: *A new mang. A new mang.*

Then he was back to remembering how good his old life had been. Okay, sure, he'd gotten crazy from the boredom sometimes, but there were other times when life was really good. Like right at the tail end there, out in the backyard with the daylight the way it got toward evening, golden before it went gray, and with the draw knife in his two hands working over the block of white ash that had the woman's face hidden in it, the woman he would have carved into being, sweet and feminine with long hair playing around her cheeks as she stood on her doorstep at the edge of a field of grain, searching the distance for him, eager to see him coming home on that endless, endless road. He thought of her and he would not have believed he could have felt such longing, longing so bad it seemed it might kill him where he stood.

72

But it was like that, here in the white room. It made him nuts, with nothing to do hour after hour, with the same thoughts running through his mind like mice: *Why did I do that last job? And with that psycho Benny?* Looking at his red, raw arm and thinking: *I knew I never had any luck.* Looking at the ceiling of the white room and thinking: *You never gave me any luck, you son of a bitch.*

There was no clock here, so he didn't know how long this went on. Probably only hours, though it began to feel like days. He began to feel as if his head would explode, as if the foreigner would come back and find him standing there in the middle of the room with just his neck on, the flesh of it ragged, blood splattering the walls—and the thought-mice, freed from the cage of his mind, juiced and hare-brained and running all around the floor of the white room.

Then he heard the police lock slide over with a *thunk*. Finally! He was at the door in a flash.

"Get the hell out of my way," he said, and shoved roughly past the foreigner. The older, smaller man turned aside without resistance. Shannon charged out of the room—and then stopped cold.

He was in a hallway. White—of course, what else? Blank walls—what else? A blank white hallway about twenty paces long with another door at the end, only this door was outlined in daylight, daylight coming in through the top and bottom and along the sides so that the door was kind of a glowing rectangular shadow in the middle of it. Shannon saw he could get out that way, all the way out. That's what stopped him.

"I have key," the foreigner said, picking up his thoughts. He dangled a keychain from his thick fingers, bounced it, made the keys clink and jingle, mockingly. "Take. Go. With monster face. Go. So people say: 'Look, I see mang with face like monster. I remember. Police ask me, I tell them.'"

"I'm going crazy in here, you skeevy foreign bastard."

"In here, you go crazy two weeks, and then you are new mang. Out there, you go crazy in prison—and then you are *old* mang, yes? Unless they give needle for murder, then you are dead mang." He jingled the keys. "But take. Go. My work is for nothing. That is life sometimes."

Shannon wrestled with his anger and his craziness and his pride, but in the end, really, what could he do?

"Skeevy foreign bastard," he muttered—and he shouldered his way belligerently back into the white room.

"Healing is good," the foreigner said. Shannon sat on the edge of the bed. The foreigner stood over him in his doctor get-up. He held Shannon's head with his fingertips, turning it gently this way and that. "Soon you are Handsome Dang."

"Yeah, great," said Shannon. "Get me a TV or something in here, would you? I can't even tell if it's night or day or what day it is . . ."

The foreigner ignored him. "You are carpenter, yes?"

"Yeah? So?"

"We put you in place where there is many buildings, much work. We give you name of contractor, union card . . ."

"Won't they have the word out in places like that? Won't they be looking for me?"

The foreigner's eyes twinkled with that contemptuous foreign wit of his. He turned Shannon's head this way and that, admiring his own handiwork. "It will not matter. They will not know when they see you. I am good identity mang." He let Shannon go. "You will have good life. Plenty work, plenty money. Until you ruin everything and go to jail again. Identity like stain."

"Yeah, just get me a TV. Even a radio. Something. It doesn't do me much good to be *new mang* if I'm babbling-out-of-my-mind crazy. I can't just stare at the walls here."

That made the foreigner smile. "Yes, yes."

"And you could get me some booze, too, or at least some reefer."

"No," said the foreigner. "No booze. No reefer. But I get you something."

He brought a TV set. Left it in the white room while Shannon was sleeping. Shannon stumbled out of the bedroom in the morning—or whatever time it was when he woke up—stumbled yawning out of a Vicodin haze and saw the set on the table. It was like Christmas morning. Like the first time he saw a girl take her shirt off.

"Hallelujah," he said.

He hurried to it. Turned it on. It wasn't anything fancy—no fifty-inch plasma HD or anything—just a squat little box with a twenty-two-inch screen and a DVD player built into the bottom of it—something your grandmother might have. But Shannon actually stroked the side of it as if it were a pet puppy as he waited for the picture to show up.

But it didn't show up. There was nothing. A blank screen. He changed the channel. Nothing.

"No, no, no, no, no," said Shannon. He had started talking to himself in here.

He bitch-slapped the side of the TV, but it still wouldn't give him anything. His hopes and dreams of a better day fizzled within him. Then he noticed the carton in the corner of the floor.

It was the kind of carton you might find stacked in a supermarket storeroom. It used to have tomato cans in it, according to the picture on the side. But now . . . ah, now, it was full of DVDs.

His eyes to heaven, Shannon let out a sigh of relief and a prayer of gratitude. Okay, it wasn't a TV. It was a DVD player. Not as good, but it was something. It would have to do.

He spent the rest of that day—and the next day—watching the DVDs, one after another, three in a row sometimes. Sometimes he did pushups and crunches in front of the box, keeping his eyes trained on the screen as his body moved up and down. Sometimes he ate while he watched. Other times, he just watched.

The DVDs were all movies, old-school stuff—really old. They

weren't even in color. They were black and white. Shannon had never seen a black-and-white movie before, not from beginning to end. He wasn't much of a moviegoer in general anyway. He watched mostly sports on TV. When he went to the theater or rented a film, it was usually an action picture with a lot of slow-motion kung-fu and explosions or maybe a horror flick where all the girls showed their tits and then got killed off one by one. Occasionally, he might watch a comedy with Karen. He liked the goofball stuff where guys drank beer and peeked through knot-holes at coeds in the shower and so on. He also liked sports comedies where some retard tried to play football or basketball or whatever way out of his league. Karen liked those comedies, too. Some of those actors could make her laugh so hard the beer came up through her nose. Then, once or twice, she sweet-talked him into watching one of those chick flicks she liked, where some poor excuse for an asshole got all tangled up in lies with his girlfriend and finally had to apologize to her so everyone could live happily ever after. Guys were always apologizing in chick flicks, that was basically the whole plot. Shannon hated them. Watching them made him feel like someone was drilling a hole in the side of his head. Sometimes, Karen got mad because she said he ruined the picture for her with all his groaning and complaining . . .

But anyway, these were the kinds of things he usually watched when he watched movies. That's what was around.

But this black-and-white stuff—this was different. Just the look of the movies was strange to him at first. The look of the cars and the look of the guys in hats and ties and the women in their old-style dresses. And everyone was white—white with short hair and clean-shaven—with only the occasional shuffle-footed "darkie" coming in as a servant or musician from time to time. Oh, and the talking! There was a lot—a lot!—of talking in these pictures. Some of them were really slow and really corny.

But then some of them—some of them were good, genuinely good, once you got used to them, once you just forgot all the old-fashioned stuff and focused on the stories. There was this one

Western he really liked, for instance, about a bunch of people stuck riding together in a stagecoach. They were all trying to escape from something or get somewhere and each one had a secret or a tale to tell. He liked the hero, who was taciturn and watchful and cool—and who'd been framed for a murder, just like Shannon himself. He even liked the love story part where the hero fell for the girl even though she used to be a hooker. He liked when the hero killed the guys who'd framed him. And then there was a good chase with the Indians coming after the coach. The hero risked his life to help beat the Indians so, in return, the marshal helped him escape to Mexico with the girl, which was a pretty good ending.

There was another movie he liked where the hero ran a casino during the war with the Nazis. The hero didn't want to get involved in the war but his old girlfriend showed up and now she was married to some top secret agent. The hero wanted her back and it looked like she was willing, but in the end he sent her away to help her husband beat the Nazis and he became a secret agent himself to help fight the war, too. That was a good story. Shannon thought about it a lot afterward. He sort of daydreamed about being in it. It'd be tough to give up a girl like that, he thought. The girls in these old movies never showed enough skin—the movies always faded away during the sex scenes so you never got to see anything. But the girl in this movie was smoking hot even with her clothes on. Just the way she looked up at the hero—like he was everything to her and her fate was in his hands no matter what: that was the thing—that's what would make her so hard to let go of. Shannon wasn't sure he'd be able to do it in real life, but he daydreamed he would.

There was another movie about war that he liked with the same hero who was in the Western, the same actor. In this one, he played a tough drill sergeant who had to teach young recruits how to be good marines. In the end, he got killed by a Jap sniper, but his recruits remembered him and went on to fight the war on their own. Shannon actually teared up at that last part, especially when they played the song about the halls of Montezuma. He'd always sort of thought about being a soldier or a marine and was sorry sometimes that he'd never been one.

"There was even a chick flick in there that was pretty good," Shannon told the foreigner when he came a few days later. Who else was he going to talk to? He sat on the edge of the bed while the foreigner turned his head this way and that in order to look his face over. "Karen—my old girlfriend—she would've liked this picture. But it was good!"

"Yes?" the foreigner murmured. "I never see."

"There were these two rich guys fighting over this girl. Or one of the guys was rich. He was the one who used to be her husband. They all lived in this big mansion."

Shannon was full of the story and had to tell it to someone. It was the last picture he'd seen before the foreigner came. The girl in it had been kind of an ice maiden, too good for anyone. She needed a slap upside the head, basically, which was probably what Shannon would've given her. But the rich guy handled her pretty well. He only slugged her once, in the beginning. The rest of the time he was cool and funny with her, and it finally brought her around. The girl in this movie wasn't as hot as the girl in the casino picture, but in the end she looked at the rich guy the same way, with that same look, and Shannon could see how you could go for her and how it had been worth the rich guy's trouble to straighten her out.

"At least he didn't have to apologize to her in the end," Shannon told the foreigner. "Those apology guys make me sick."

The foreigner let go of him. "Very good," he said. "Almost you are ready. I bring you mirror next time. You see."

"Hey. No kidding. Great," Shannon said. That was what he wanted to hear. Movies or no, he couldn't wait to get out of this place. And the curiosity and anxiety about his new face were killing him. He had tried, between one film and another, to make out his reflection in the dark TV screen. It came back to him dim and distorted. It was a disturbing experience. He had spent hours looking at all those handsome movie stars and pretty girls on the screen, and then suddenly he was there himself with his distorted "monster face," as the foreigner would say. After a while, he stopped trying to see it.

"So we're getting to the end of this, huh," he said now. He was excited but he was worried, too. He was worried about his face and about . . . about everything. "I can get out of here soon."

"Very soon," said the foreigner. "Very soon."

The last movie Shannon watched in the white room—the last DVD in the tomato can carton—was kind of stupid but kind of good, too. If anyone had been around while he was watching it, he would've said it was kind of stupid. But since it was just him sitting there, he had to admit, secretly he thought it was pretty good. It was a story about a guy who wanted to kill himself because his life sucked. He lived in this small town in the middle of nowhere. He was one of these guys who was always sacrificing himself for other people. Every time he tried to get out of this town and get a better job or get some excitement, someone would need something, and he'd have to stay and help them. Finally, time passed, and there he was, just this nobody in the middle of nowhere. That was his whole life. On top of that, his crazy uncle lost some money and the hero got framed for stealing it. So now the police were after him, too. Shannon knew what that was like. He felt for the guy. Finally, the poor bastard decided to throw himself off a bridge. But before he did, he said a prayer for help. The angels heard him in heaven and one of them came down to lend a hand. It was that kind of story. This angel showed the hero what the world would be like if the hero had never been born. It was a pretty bad place because the hero had helped a lot of people who now never would have been helped because he wasn't born. Anyway, this made the hero realize what a good guy he was and so he was happy after that, even though his life pretty much still sucked.

When the movie was over, Shannon looked inside the tomato

can carton just to make sure and, yeah, there were no more DVDs. That was the last of them. The white room was silent around him, the way it had been before. He knew he could watch one of the movies over if he wanted to, and he figured he probably would if he didn't get out of here soon. But for now, he just sat in his chair, thinking about the last one.

It was sort of depressing to think about it. Because if an angel ever came down to show Shannon what the world would be like if *he'd* never been born, the world would be more or less the same as it was now, maybe even better, because there were some bad things Shannon had done that wouldn't have been done. Well—he argued in his own defense—probably somebody else would've done them if he hadn't. And what about that girl at the Whittaker Center? Benny would've left her in absolute pieces if Shannon hadn't been around to help her out. But then, if there'd been no Shannon, maybe Benny wouldn't even have been there in the first place. So that was sort of a wash. In any case, the point was, if he'd never been born, it wouldn't really matter much at all. Which was a depressing thought. He had to tell himself, hey, that guy in the movie, he could afford to be a good guy, he had a lot of advantages. He had a father for one thing. And a mother who was really nice to him. And that small town was boring maybe, but it looked like a nice place to live and not like the places Shannon had grown up in. Plus, later on in the movie, the guy had this dynamite wife, the kind of wife who really did things for him, made his house nice and kept the kids out of the way so when he came home from his crap job he could at least relax a little. Because, let's face it, Shannon could miss Karen all he wanted, but she was nothing like that. First of all, she was half in the bag most of the time. She had a reefer lit and a beer popped almost the second she walked through the door. The wife in the movie was always working on the house or making dinner, where if you asked Karen to get off her ass and get you a drink, it was a two-day negotiation, you never heard the end of it. The guy in the movie just had advantages, that's all Shannon was getting at. It was easier for him to be nice to people and always doing things for them. He had a reason to be that way.

Shannon slouched in the chair with his legs splayed out in front of him, absent-mindedly rubbing the place on his arm where those little round scars used to be. He felt nostalgic. He missed the past, the old days. But it wasn't *his* old days he missed, it was the old days of the guy in the movie. He missed the house in the small town and the mother and the father who loved each other and were nice to him. It was strange—because how could he miss something that had never actually happened to him? It was kind of like when he saw things in the pieces of wood he was carving, things he had never seen in real life, the face of the woman waiting at the door or whatever. It was as if the things in his head were as real as real things. It had always been like that for him. Even when he was little, he had missed this movie life he'd never lived. Even before he had known there *was* such a life, he had somehow known it, and had known his own life was wrong. How had he known such things? Maybe before his real life, he had had another life in which everything was the way it was supposed to be and he missed that. Or something.

He sat in the chair, wondering about it. He wondered: If he *had* lived that movie life, would he have been a better person? Would he have been like the guy in the movie, always doing things for people?

Anyway, that was the last DVD. The box was empty. And then —hallelujah—the foreigner came to bring him his new identity.

"Look, look," the foreigner commanded impatiently. "Look. Go on."

But for another long moment, Shannon hesitated, his heart hammering. He was afraid. Afraid to lift the round shaving mirror from where it lay on his thighs, afraid to peer into the glass at his new face. What if he really was a monster now? Or just so different from what he'd been that he couldn't recognize himself, had become a stranger to his own countenance? Bad enough to be imprisoned in the white room, but to be locked inside a body that wasn't his own . . .

"Go, go," said the foreigner. "Is not so bad. Look."

Shannon took a deep breath and lifted the mirror.

His first sensation at what he saw in the glass was terror, a quick, lancing jag of nauseating fear. Where had he gone? Who was that there? Who was he? But the moment passed. He was still himself. The features were changed, reshaped, but they were still his features somehow. He could still make himself out in the eyes and in remaining traces of the face he'd known. And he was still himself inside.

His terror abated. He was relieved. It was not so bad. It was good, in fact. No one else, not even people who knew him well, would ever recognize him. But he felt the same. He was who he was.

"You are Henry Conor now," the foreigner said.

"Henry Conor," Shannon murmured, gazing at his reflection. He let the name play in his mind. He didn't like it much. It sounded to him like the name of some pencil-head in a suit, a lawyer or something like that. "Why can't I pick my own name?"

"Because I make papers," the foreigner said. "This is name I put."

Shannon shrugged. A name was a name.

He went on looking. He felt better and better about the face looking back at him. Whatever else it was, it was no way the distorted monster face he'd seen reflected in the TV. The beard made him look like kind of a wild man, but he could shave that off soon enough. Underneath, it was all right.

"You do good work," he said.

The foreigner straightened from the briefcase he had opened on the bedroom chair. He handed Shannon a couple of manila folders. "Here are papers. License, passport, Social Security. Also tax returns for five years. Work history, references boss can call so he knows you are good worker." He handed him the folders.

"Nice. This is a whole big operation."

"You will have tools to work with and number to call where you can get job."

Shannon opened a folder. Saw the driver's license in there. Saw the address under the photograph.

"That's a long way away."

"This is good, yes? Far from where you were."

"Yeah, I guess that is good. I never been out there. Where'd you get the picture of me?"

"Computer morph. It's what I work from when I do face. You will shave to look like picture."

"Right. I'll look good without the beard. Should be able to get laid now and then anyway."

"That's why I leave same testicles," the foreigner said.

Shannon tossed the folders aside onto the bed. He searched the foreigner's droll and disdainful expression. "So all this is 'cause I saved that girl? I mean, this whole setup—this is all Whittaker paying me back for my good deed?"

The foreigner didn't answer. He just stood looking at him—looking at him, Shannon thought, as if he were a monkey in a cage or a child being observed on one of those hidden nursery cameras, a child playing dress-up alone in his room who didn't know the camera was there. The foreigner stood and watched him, in other words, as if he were some kind of lesser creature who didn't know he was being watched and whose antics amused him.

"What?" Shannon said. "What're you looking at?"

The foreigner merely went on watching him in that way another few seconds. Then finally he said, "Shave face. Get ready."

Shannon got ready. He shaved. He studied his new look in the mirror until it grew familiar. Then the foreigner came back for the last time.

"Here," he said. He put out one of his knobbly hands. He was holding a couple of capsules.

"No, I'm good," Shannon said. "I don't need them anymore."

"Take. Or I put needle in neck again." Shannon scraped the pills

83

up off the foreigner's palm. "They will make you sleep. When you wake up, you have new life, like princess in fairy tale." He handed Shannon the juice bottle with the straw.

Shannon swallowed the pills, sitting on the edge of the bed. "Where'll you be?" he asked. It wasn't that he'd miss the foreigner exactly, but he was curious. He'd gotten used to the old guy, the only person he'd seen in . . . well, he didn't know how long.

"Lie down or you will fall on new face."

Shannon lay back on the bed, looking up at the foreigner, at his disreputable old-world countenance with the hair sprouting in all the wrong places.

"You just go off to another job or what?" he asked him.

"I disappear like smoke," the foreigner said. "Close eyes."

"Identity mang has no identity, huh," said Shannon sleepily. He was already going under, starting to blink heavily. He fought it for another second or two. Now that the time had finally come, he was nervous about all this, his new life and so on. It'd been boring in here, in the white room, but it had felt safe anyway. Without newspapers or the TV news, the cops and Benny Torrance and the Hernandez killings had all seemed very far away. He'd forgotten what it was like to be out there in the world, on the run with the law after you.

Anxious or not, he couldn't keep his eyes open any longer. He let them fall shut slowly. He lay still, countering his nervousness with images of the house from that last movie, the house in the small town with the lights on in the windows and Mom and Dad inside . . .

He gave a long nostalgic sigh. He missed those old days.

PART III

THE WOODEN ANGEL

RAMSEY DREAMED he was standing on the flooded street again with the city burning all around him. The water had risen to his thighs and Peter Patterson's body was sunk in it, staring up at him through the rain-rattled surface. Then the water began to thicken and grow opaque. The bookkeeper's corpse grew dimmer. Only his stare remained bright. Ramsey heard a voice. He turned and saw his mother, long dead, walking toward him from a block or two away. She was dressed in her print dress for Sunday meeting, holding a black umbrella over her head. She was pushing steadily between the flaming buildings, through the driving rain.

"A man who is full of sin is full of shame!" she cried out, shaking her Bible at him.

He looked down again and Peter Patterson's corpse was no longer visible because, Ramsey suddenly realized, the water had turned to blood.

The dream haunted Ramsey as he tied his tie that morning standing before the bedroom mirror. He had woken from the nightmare with his heart racing and the image of his long-dead mother walking toward him through the storm made his heart race again as it came back to him.

A man who is full of sin is full of shame!

Where had he heard that phrase before? Somewhere. He tucked the tip of the port-red tie down into the Windsor. It looked good against the dark blue shirt. It would add to his air of authority and dignity. That would help at his meeting this morning with Augie Lancaster. He had always suspected that Augie was a little intimidated by him, overawed by his aura of street wisdom and self-control.

As he pulled the knot tight, he remembered: Skyles. That's where the phrase in his dream had come from. The Reverend Jesse Skyles. *What brought him to mind?* he wondered.

The Reverend Jesse Skyles was the most dangerous man in the city. That's what Augie Lancaster had called him anyway, though in Ramsey's opinion, Augie's hatred for the reverend had sometimes shaded over into personal obsession. Every time word got out that Skyles was setting up another of his makeshift churches, Augie would have Ramsey assign precious police resources to find it. He would send building inspectors and fire inspectors to shut it down, or bangers—and off-duty cops pretending to be bangers—to bust it up. At one point, he was threatening to raid the next place right during the service. He had some fantasy about SWAT storming in, rousting suspicious characters, dragging the minister himself away in handcuffs on some trumped-up charge. Ramsey had had a job of it making him see reason. *These are good folks gathering,* Ramsey said, *your folks, home folks who love them some God.* You couldn't go in there like it was Baghdad. It would only turn people against you, and give Skyles credibility, too. It might even alert some news media—the national news media, who weren't in Augie's pocket back then. *Let me go over there,* Ramsey said. *Let me go over and have a look.* Augie liked that idea. He got the picture of it. Ramsey's very presence during the service—the presence of a respected lawman who had risen up from these very streets—would send a chill of suspicion and danger through the congregation. They would ask themselves: *What's the lieutenant doing here? Is the reverend up to something wrong? What's the lieutenant going to think if he sees me here? Maybe I should stay home next time, stay away from this, I don't need the trouble.* It might even intimidate Skyles himself.

That Sunday, the reverend held his service in a storefront in the Five Corners. He and his deacons must've thrown the place together Saturday night. Nothing but metal folding chairs for pews and a card table for an altar. No light in the cramped room but the morning sun through the big window and a couple of desk lamps set on top of stools, their extension cords running to the outlets next door. They'd put out the come-to-meeting at the last possible minute, with phone calls and runners to keep it within the congregation. It was the only way they could outsmart Augie's inspectors and the bangers and the off-duty cops.

But Ramsey found them. Of course. Ramsey pushed gigantically through the door just as the sermon was beginning. He stood in the back of the room large as life and watched with his grim, threatening dignity hanging over the church like a vulture. The worshippers felt him there from the outset. They shifted uncomfortably in their folding chairs. They cast sidelong glances at him.

But not Skyles. Skyles had the spirit in him that morning. It was as if he had swallowed a Roman candle: he was jumping around and there were sparks flying out of him every which way. No lawman—and no man's law—were going to hold him back.

"The white man in America is full of sin and a man who is full of sin is full of shame. He's full of the shame of racism, the shame of slavery and Jim Crow. And he'll do anything to make that shame go away. He'll give you money—welfare money for doing nothing. He'll give you government jobs you didn't earn and don't deserve. He'll say: 'You wanna take drugs? You wanna get your girlfriend pregnant? You want to live without morality? Why, that's okay, little black man, you go right on ahead. I give you abortions to kill those babies. I give the mother money so you don't have to marry her. I give you some *pro-grams* for those drugs. *Pro-grams*, that'll set you right up. Just don't be calling me racist. I'll give you anything you want, just set me free of my shame.'"

In appearance, Skyles was a prim little man. Old—Lieutenant Ramsey noticed with some bitterness—old enough to remember segregation and the rest. Wore a three-piece suit. Had a receding hairline and wire-rimmed glasses. When he was standing still, he had the punctilious, slightly sour aspect of a man who sold ladies' underwear and found it rather distasteful—though in fact he ran a Donut Land franchise over on Pearl Street. But when the spirit was in him like this, he never did stand still. He jumped and strutted like a chicken on fire. Back and forth behind the folding table with the flames and sparks shooting out of him and the words bubbling out of his mouth in a high frantic rasp.

"You say to me, 'No, no, no—no, no, no, Reverend Skyles, we don't take nothing from the white man. We got the black man in power now. We got Augie Lancaster in power. *He* give us that money. *He* give us them abortions. He give us some *pro-grams!* We do love us some *pro-grams,* Reverend Skyles, they set us right up.' But I tell you truly. I tell you: Augie Lancaster *is* the white man. Augie Lancaster has made himself the tool of the white man's shame. He understands the agony of their sin. He goes right to Washington, he says, 'If you don't want me to call you racist, you better give me some of that money you take from people who *earn* their livings. You don't want that shame, you gotta give me some more jobs, some more *pro-grams.*' That's how he buys his homes and his boats and his mistresses. That's how he buys his friends—by giving them those jobs. And that's how he buys you, too. That's right. He buys you, too, just like the rest. And yes, I see his police thug standing in the back there—" he shouted suddenly. He didn't even deign to glance at the imposing Ramsey. He just shouted: "You don't need to be stealing looks back there at him, you keep your eyes on the truth! You keep your eyes on the Word!"

That got some *amens* going for a moment, little eruptions of them here and there. Annoyed, Lieutenant Ramsey let his eyes move sternly over the heads of the parishioners. *I'm seeing you,* he was telling them. *I'm seeing your faces.* The people cast their sidelong glances at him. Fear and anxiety tightened their lips. The *amens* petered out and died.

But Jesse Skyles went on, unstoppable. He had the spirit in him.

"Now the white man has enslaved you again, but it's worse this time, because this time you're his accomplice. Augie Lancaster is an accomplice, and you're an accomplice in your own slavery. You looking to massa to help you instead of helping yourself. You're taking his money and giving up your self-reliance. You take his abortions and give up your responsibilities. You take his *pro-grams* and give up your morality. You getting fat on the milk of his sin, on the honey of his shame. You get all that sweetness by blaming the white man, so you don't need to take no responsibility for yourself."

Ramsey continued to stand there, lithic and imposing, his hands folded in front of him, his roving stare picking off *amens* like they were ducks at a shooting gallery. He was aware of the anger burbling volcanically in the core of that tightly controlled self of his. He was beginning to see Augie's point about this loudmouth. What did he have to be saying *this* kind of thing for? Didn't these people have troubles enough? They needed those jobs and programs Augie got for them. What else did they have? And who else would give them? So why make them feel bad about it? Why make them look bad to themselves—or to the white man if he was listening? And why make Augie look bad? Ramsey was beginning to understand why Augie was so intent on bringing Skyles down.

"Let me ask you a question." Skyles shot the words at his congregation, undeterred by their intimidated silence, hopping back and forth, back and forth behind the folding table. "Who is it who does you like this? Who gives you money but takes your self-reliance? Who gives you jobs but robs you of your desire for excellence? Who takes care of your babies for you but steals your morality and your dignity? Let me ask you this question so you understand: Who gives you the things of the body and lures you away from the things of the spirit?"

"The devil!" an older woman shouted from the folding chairs—the spirit had caught her and she couldn't help herself. Half a dozen worried sidelong glances went toward Lieutenant Ramsey. The woman realized what she'd done and half glanced at him, too. But then she must've figured it was too late. She settled back into her folding chair with a defiant sniff and an I-don't-care wiggle of her bottom.

And Jesse Skyles's spirit fed off hers. "The devil!" he answered back, riding a fine, high wave of indignation. "It's the devil who gives you the things of the world and lures you away from the soul things, the real things. It's guilty white folks trying to buy their way out of history. It's Augie Lancaster making his money and his power off their shame. And it's the devil himself. And if you ask me, they all three's the same!"

Lieutenant Ramsey shrugged into his blue blazer now and examined himself one last moment in the mirror. He had the effect he wanted: distinguished and commanding. He looked into his own eyes.

The nightmare was still in his mind and the memory of Skyles was in his mind, too, and out of the interplay between them, a truth came to him.

Down deep, way down deep, he had agreed with Reverend Skyles that day. He understood that now, only now. He had been angry at Skyles for defying him and for saying what he said, but down deep he had agreed. How could it have been otherwise? What Skyles was telling the people was no different from what Ramsey's mother had told him, what his mother had pounded into him as she sculpted his heart with that hammering Bible. Self-reliance, morality, dignity, self-control. Don't be looking to anyone else to take care of you. Pull yourself up and walk like a man.

That day at that makeshift church—that day marked the first inkling Ramsey had in his heart that the logic of his life had been skewed and twisted, even corrupted and spoiled by Augie—by Augie and his promises and his high rhetoric and his flash. It was the first time he was forced to brush away the suspicion that there was no excuse for this man, that his ends did *not* justify his means, that he was in fact empty and disreputable in every particular, and had led Ramsey astray step by self-justifying step. That's why Ramsey had come to feel that Augie was right about Skyles, that Skyles was dangerous. Because down deep he realized that Skyles could overturn everything, the whole city. Because down deep, he realized that Skyles was speaking the unholy truth of his own mistakes.

That's why he had agreed to help Augie destroy him.

He turned from the mirror and left the bedroom. He went into the living room and stood beside the small round dining table near the kitchenette. He lifted his coffee mug from the table and brought it to his lips for a last sip, even though he knew the coffee had grown cold and bitter. He looked over the mug's rim at the apartment. Hard to believe he'd been living here almost a year now. Hard to believe it was a year since his wife had asked him to go. The apartment was small and drab, furnished as impersonally as a hotel room. Even looking straight at it, he barely saw it anymore.

A man who is full of sin is full of shame.

So it was, no question. His mama never lied.

He paused before he took another sip of the coffee. All his life, he reflected, he had kept control over his emotions. It was no different now. His shame was just one more emotion he had to control, bad dreams and all.

He set the mug down and left for his meeting with Augie.

He was asked to wait in the Media Room. The Media Room, they called it now. That was new. It was the Conference Room last time he was here. But today it was, "Of course, Lieutenant, go right in and have a seat in the Media Room," from the white boy at the front desk. The white boy was new also, one of the volunteers who'd come in from the coast after the flood.

The flood had changed a lot of things around here.

The Media Room was a long chamber paneled in dark wood with one wall of windows overlooking the city park. The glass table was still here from its more modest Conference Room days. And there were still those fancy overpriced chairs around it, the ones with the aerated backs: your tax dollars at work. Now, though, your tax dollars were working overtime, because there were also three, count them three, flat-screen TVs on the wall opposite the windows. TV on the left showed local channel eight; TV on the right showed local channel five; and TV in the middle showed CNN in a little square surrounded by a lot of other little squares showing other news channels. And what do you know? Right this minute, as if it were planned, as if it were timed for Ramsey's edification, all three stations, eight, five, and CNN, were featuring none other than the increasingly famous Augie Lancaster. Augie had made a speech last night before the Council on Justice. It had been touted in the media as his debut on the national political scene. So there he was at the lectern, gazing like a visionary into the distance or at least into the TelePrompTer. The audio on the TVs was off, thank God, but the TV on channel eight was running captions, the white words on the black background appearing under Augie's image, line by line: "We can't have faith until we have hope and we can't have hope until we learn to dream again as a nation . . ."

Nigger, what you on about? Ramsey thought, and the hint of a shadow of a whisper of a smile played at the corner of his lips.

Shaking his head, he turned his back on the TVs and faced the window. He gazed out at the park three stories below. From here, the city looked whole and brilliant. This little corner of the city anyway, the square of government buildings surrounding the sculpted lawn. Men and women walked busily to and fro on gracefully curving asphalt paths. They wore colorful spring shirts and blouses, solid reds and oranges and yellows. The tulips were red and orange and yellow in their beds. Above it all, the dome of city hall presided stately and golden against the blue sky. *City of Hope. City of Justice.* From here, the little square looked like Augie Lancaster's rhetoric made real.

Watching the people below, it occurred to Ramsey that it was a beautiful, warm spring day out there. It occurred to him that he had taken no joy in it, that he'd barely noticed it as he walked from his car to the building. It occurred to him that all his joy in life, in fact, was gone.

Just then, the door opened behind him.

Ramsey turned and saw a young woman come in. It was a terrible and wholly unexpected moment. As soon as he saw her, he felt a kind of spiritual vertigo, as if a trapdoor had opened inside him, the Inner Man falling through. Nothing in his expression changed, of course. His aura of authority and dignity glowed as brightly around him as ever—brighter because of the extra effort required to keep it there, a hollow persona willed into place around a now empty core. But just that one look at the woman and he understood everything that was about to happen.

He'd never seen her before, but he knew her all right. Graduate from some hall of intellectual mirrors. Bard, Sarah Lawrence, Earlham, one of those. Just out of grad school or law school or still in or about to go. Studying something about the environment probably. Advanced Self-Righteous Hysteria 101. With her porcelain skin and the golden blond hair and that body they seem to issue these women along with their degrees nowadays: the taut, slender body with just enough Girl in it to get them what they wanted but not enough so they could be blamed. She had been in her dorm room when she'd first seen Augie on TV. Or maybe in her bedroom at her parents' house or in the apartment they'd bought her. After hours of wallowing in teary-eyed indignation, staring at images of helpless brown victims, listening to grim-faced newscasters calling it "the worst flood since Noah," hearing wise men, movie stars, and pop singers tell her that the gibbering black punks who'd set their own city on fire were nothing but symptoms of the white man's uncaring: she was primed for Augie, and then along he came.

We can't have dreams until we have faith and we can't have faith until we learn to hope again as a nation.

Wasn't it just so true?

So here she was, wearing her white sin like a mink, proud of her shame and searching for her virtue, hoping to receive her virtue like the holy host from Augie's victim-colored hands. Ramsey wondered if Augie had fucked her yet. Maybe not. But he would, he assured himself angrily, and in every possible sense of the word.

"Lieutenant Ramsey?" she said—warm, respectful, solicitous, arrogant, superior, agonizingly self-aware, and wholly self-ignorant at the same time. "I'm Charlotte Mortimer-Rimsky." Of course she was. She extended her slender porcelain hand, a startling flash out of the take-me-seriously black sleeve of her sexless suit.

Ramsey stood dizzy with humiliation. This—this uncooked slice of poon, this blond creation of her own dreamy delusions—*this* was what Augie sent to him? To *him*? It took all his discipline not to leave her hand hanging there, not to cry out "Where's Augie? I had an appointment with Augie!" like a cheated child.

But he did it. He fought down every coarse insult that leapt into his head and shook her hand politely.

"Nice to meet you," he said, just as his mother had taught him.

"Augie sends his apologies. He's been called to a meeting with Senator Lundquist and he just couldn't get out of it. But I'm his new law enforcement liaison, so he thought this might be a good opportunity for us to get to know one another."

"Law Enforcement Liaison." The words dripped like venom from Ramsey's lips. "Well, Miss . . ."

"Mortimer-Rimsky."

"Miss Mortimer-Rimsky . . ."

"Charlotte, please."

"I'd love to get to know you at some point, but I'm afraid this isn't the time. My business with Augie is urgent and requires his immediate personal attention." It was the best he could do. And what good was it really? Everyone involved in this transaction—he and this woman and Augie as well—they all knew that he was being stripped right here and now of every vestige of prestige and even masculinity. There was no pretending it was otherwise. And yet pretense was the only fig leaf he had to cover the place where his balls used to be.

The woman, for her part, did her best to look pained and sincere. Ramsey thought she must've taught herself that expression before breaking up with her high school boyfriend. A pretty little kiss-off.

"I don't know what to tell you. It's just not going to be possible today. I did manage to get you this, though."

She had a blue file folder in her left hand. She gave it to him and then stepped aside toward the windows. She gazed down discreetly at the park below, giving him a moment to open the blue folder.

There was a single photograph inside. Printed out from a computer onto ordinary paper. Dark, blurry. An enlargement of a picture taken with somebody's cell phone, Ramsey guessed. He recognized the house in the background. It was the house on the dead-end lane, the green shingled house where he and Gutterson had found the graffito.

Ramsey murdered Peter Patterson!

"Where did you get this?" he said.

"Some of my city contacts. They're telling me this is the man who wrote that graffito. He's been spreading similar rumors on the street."

He looked at her, at her tailored back, as she faced the window. He let the silence of his doubt play over her, weigh on her. They both knew she didn't have any goddamned city contacts. Only Augie himself could've thrown his net wide enough to haul in something as random as this. She was protecting Augie. She'd been in town for ten minutes and she had the gall to stand between him—between *him*—and Augie Lancaster.

She kept her eyes on the window, on the scene outside, but he could see by her uncomfortable posture that she felt his accusation. She felt compelled to explain. "The thing is, Augie is at a transitional moment," she said finally, with a defensive glance back at him. "I don't have to tell you that. It's a key moment, maybe *the* key moment in his trajectory."

"His trajectory," Lieutenant Ramsey said with an aspect of stone.

She faced him. He wanted to rip that porcelain mask of earnestness right off her. "Yes. I mean . . . look . . . It's a transformational moment in the whole country. We all know that. It's a time of real hope and . . . and change."

So he *had* fucked her. Well, good for him. That was fast work. He must've explained all this to her in the afterglow. *We can't have hope until we have dreams and we can't have dreams until you suck my black dick . . .*

"Augie has a real chance to become one of the new transformational figures. Isn't that what we've all been working for? To get beyond race? To bring some of the same progressive policies to the federal level that Augie's implemented here at the municipal level?"

Even in his rage and shame, Ramsey nearly laughed out loud. Had Miss Dreams ever gone ten steps beyond this pristine government complex? Had she ever set her baby blues on exactly what Augie's progressive policies had accomplished at the municipal level? *The city is in fucking ruins, you dumb bitch!*

"Look, we all know," this girl—who was too young to know much of anything—went on desperately. "We all know that in the rough and tumble of city politics . . . associations are made . . . things get done by the people around you . . . Augie would never turn his back on his friends, believe me. It's just that . . . with this degree of scrutiny on the national level, he has to take appearances into account in a new way. For a period of time, I mean."

He stared at her. He couldn't help himself. For a moment, he was simply dazed, astonished at the wonderful perfection and complexity of Augie's treachery, as if it were some kind of magnificent crystal suddenly revealing its infinite network of facets to the light. Then, as his astonishment receded, anger rushed back into its place with a new force. Ramsey had seen this kind of fury in the faces of men twisted up like pretzels on cell floors, the froth of seizure on their lips, words of such filth and savage desire spewing from them it was enough to make you believe in hell and the devil. He had seen it, but he had never felt that sort of titanic rage himself until this minute. He wanted to shove this girl, this created suburban thing, against the wall, wanted to seize a handful of her throat and a fistful of her breast and ram himself up inside her like he was planting a flag on the moon. He wanted to cram his face a whisker's breadth from her terrified eyes and tell her everything, everything that was going to happen to her next. *Come a day*, he wanted to spit into her porcelain face through his gritted teeth, *come a day, you will stand before judgment, so help me, before a judge, in fact, or a Senate committee or God his own fat, happy self, and Augie will do as much to you as he has done to me here now. "I never knew her," he'll say. "I never knew what she was up to. We had a fling. She took it too seriously. She was overzealous on my behalf. That wasn't what I meant at all." Then oh then, so help me, so help me, you will strip off that sexless suit of yours, you will ditch your degree in environmental horseshit and scurry to put on some tears and lace blouses and any other waiflike wile of femininity that might just charm your sweet white ass out of prison or your sorry soul out of the flames of hell. And even if you do escape, that's your life ever after, cooz. That's the definition of your future life: a bewildered slag announcing your redemption-through-rehab to some bored reporter from www.excelebrityfelons.com, a ragged exile from your daydreamed self, a half-damned half-spirit in a perdition of philosophical somersaults and rationalizations and glasses of wine — anything — any trick you know to stave off the hour when you make a priest of your mirror and confess to yourself what you did here today.*

He wanted to tell her that, throttling her, clutching her, pumping into her until he finished to the pounding rhythm of the final syllables and ejaculated acid in her, burning right through her womb to poison her bleeding heart . . .

But instead, expressionless, he nodded once, the image of dignity, of authority and calm. He looked away from her studied earnestness, down again at the blue folder open in his hands, at the picture in the folder. His eyes went from the green-shingled house to the line of cars parked at the curb outside. His eyes went to the figure behind the wheel of one of those cars, a man in shadow with his features obscured by the glare of the streetlight on the windshield, the same streetlight that illuminated the right half of the car's license plate. Just enough of the license plate so that Ramsey would be able to track the man down.

This was all Augie would give him, the last thing he would give him—and he would never admit that he had given him even this. This picture. This figure. This man who had written the graffito in the green-shingled house—or who had made the remark to the gang-bangers there that caused the graffito to be written—who somehow—somehow—knew:

Ramsey murdered Peter Patterson!

The image of dignity, of authority and calm, Ramsey lifted his eyes. He looked away from the doomed white girl, done with her. He gazed thoughtfully instead at the televisions on the wall. Augie on all three screens. Standing behind the lectern, before the new post-racial world. Gazing visionary into the TelePrompTer.

We can't have Me until we have Me and we can't have Me until we learn to have Me-Me-Me as a nation.

Augie sailing off into the new age—and here was Ramsey left behind in the Media Room with this picture, this picture some-how magically in his hands. That was the way of these things, wasn't it? Someone had to stay behind. Someone had to clean up the mess. Someone had to find the man in the picture, had to find out what he knew and how he knew it.

And someone, in the end, was going to have to kill him.

SHANNON OPENED HIS EYES. At first, he was startled to find himself somewhere new, somewhere other than the white room. He lay still on the strange bed, wary. Then he remembered. He sat up, dragging his hand down his cheek, trying to swipe away the tranquilizer haze.

Stretching, craning his neck, he took in his surroundings. A small studio apartment. Gray walls with a couple of pictures hung on them. Nice wooden floors with a braid rug by the bed. A dresser, a desk, a chair, a mirror on the back of the closet door. He could see himself in the mirror, sitting there with his jockey shorts and his brand-new face on. Look at that: a brand-new face. This time, the sight of it struck him as wonderful. He broke out in a big silly grin. It was just like the foreigner said. He was new mang.

Excited, he got up to explore. He looked out the windows first. There were only two of them, both on the same wall. Not much of a view. Two brownstones across the street. The entrance to a wide alley next to a small grocery. Just the same, after all that time locked up in the white room, he was eager to get out there. Was he ever! Out in the open air again! He couldn't wait.

He checked the front door. Yup, it opened. He was free. A new mang and a free mang, too.

Humming to himself, he wandered around the apartment some more. The fridge in the kitchenette was stocked with food. The dresser was stocked with clothes. The foreigner's folders were on the desk, the ones with all his new identity papers in them—Henry Conor's papers. There was a computer there, too. When he pressed the keyboard, the machine whirred and the monitor lit up, showing classified ads. Carpenters wanted all over the place. Next to the computer: a receipt for the first two months' rent on the apartment. Plus car keys with a Honda logo. Plus a wallet with three hundred-dollar bills in it. Nice.

Maybe the best thing, though, was what he found in the closet. A big red bag with hammers and wrenches in the outside pouches. He unzipped it. He cursed under his breath with wonder.

Tools. A beautiful set of brand-spanking-new Milwaukees, bright silver and red. A framing nailer, a roofing nailer, a Skilsaw, a chop saw, cordless hammers, screwdrivers—must've been three thousand bucks' worth of stuff. It made his heart beat harder. He loved good tools.

Crouched over the bag, he looked around him, nodding to himself. He thought of the foreigner. He felt gratitude to the old dude. Even some affection for him.

New mang. New life. Like princess in fairy tale.

He stepped out of the brownstone. He stood at the top of the stoop. It felt like the times he'd gotten out of prison—that same dizzying sense of open space. Your soul shrank when you were inside for too long. It shriveled to the size of the cell you were stuck in. When you finally came out, there was all that wide world whirling around without you in it. It was unnerving. You were afraid that if you let yourself go, if you let your soul expand again, there might not be enough of you to fill all that emptiness. You might drift away like some kind of mist and finally evaporate and be gone forever. Some guys never did dare to do it. They lived the rest of their lives all shrunken up inside as if the cell walls were still around them. Shannon had seen it happen. If they put you in prison long enough, you were in prison forever, even after they let you go.

But that was the whole point here, wasn't it? He wasn't going back to prison. Not at all, not ever. He had a new face, a new identity. New mang, free mang.

He went down the stairs like a top-hatted dancer. Down the street like the mayor. Taking in the sights. Excited. Growing bigger inside with every breath. He passed a woman pushing a baby in a stroller. He passed two men and a woman flirting on a brownstone stoop. He passed two older women in skirt suits. They smiled at him as they went by. They had Bibles in their hands. They were coming home from church. He could hear the bells ringing. It was Sunday morning. Nice day, blue sky, temperature spring-cool with an undercurrent of the coming summer heat.

He went on down the block of brownstones. Past cars parked under green sycamores. That reminded him . . . He reached into his pocket. He pressed the button on the key to his Honda. A horn honked nearby. Sure enough, there it was: a blue Civic, his own car. About a year old, clean. In pretty good shape, it looked like. He'd have to give it a spin later. But not now. Now he was walking, like a top-hatted dancer, right out in the open, like anyone, like the mayor.

Then he reached the corner and turned and stopped short.

Suddenly, he was staring at a scene of devastation. It stretched into the distance, as far as he could see. In the foreground: brownstones gutted by fire, their windows broken, their brick charred. Beyond those, there were stucco apartment buildings, stricken and slumped like stroke victims. Beyond those, there were piles of churned mud and litter where lawns had been in front of piles of debris that had been houses. In the distance, he could see emergency trailers standing by empty lots, the garbage in the lots making a weird, rocky landscape of appliances and rubble, metal and stone. And all this led at last to the skyline, broken and jagged against the horizon. Light shining through the scorched framework of ruined towers. The city's signature spire snapped off as by a giant's hand. Shannon was never one to watch the news or read the papers much or to fiddle around much online. He'd heard about the floods here and the riots and the fire—you couldn't help but hear. He just hadn't thought about it much. He hadn't thought it could be this bad.

Standing there, staring, stunned, at the extent of the destruction, he tried to maintain his exuberant mood. He tried to tell himself it wasn't so bad. Hell, he could always leave if he wanted to. He was a free man, that was the whole point, that was the really important thing.

But it was no good. He'd had such high hopes there for a minute, but now his heart was sinking. He felt sick with disappointment, with bitterness even, even with anger.

All the places the identity man could've left him, and he left him here, in the ruin of the world.

He spent the next few days exploring the city, sometimes on foot, sometimes in his car. He drove slowly past toppled trees that blocked the sidewalks, past mountains of stinking garbage, past houses washed right off their foundations and abandoned in house-shaped jumbles by the curb. The sights depressed him. He cursed the identity man. He wished he had enough money to start over somewhere else.

He walked through neighborhoods overrun with gangsters, prowling young thugs with their eyes all over everything, their hands itching to strike out and make some kind of grab, probably any kind. Watching them, he could feel their antsy energy inside himself, that old agitation. He caught himself following their glances, casing their lawless neighborhoods for jobs. If only he had enough money . . .

Identity like stain, he thought. He shook off the antsy feeling. No, no, no, no. Not here, not this time. New life. New mang.

The gangsters stared at him balefully and he stared back. They knew a hard guy when they saw one—new face or no new face—and they left him alone.

He walked on, hands in his pockets, shoulders hunched, depressed.

• • •

One day, he parked across the street from a hobbled brownstone. He watched from his car as three ambulance guys rolled a body out of the ground floor on a stretcher. The corpse was enormous, impossibly bloated. It must've been lost in the flooded basement all this time.

A clutch of onlookers shook their heads and covered their noses. A bunch of homeless guys laughed about it, drunk on their bagged bottles. Even where he was sitting, Shannon caught the stench of the waterlogged dead.

Man, what a town. What a town this was.

Patrolmen were standing guard over the scene, their eyes shifting and their hands on their holstered guns. They were the first cops Shannon had seen since he'd gotten here. Their nearness startled him.

One cop's roving gaze came toward him. Shannon seized up inside, afraid of being spotted and caught. He almost hit the gas and sped away. Then he realized: he didn't have to. He didn't have to worry anymore. He had his brand-new face on. He sat there boldly. The cop's gaze never hesitated. It just passed over him and moved on.

Shannon smiled to himself as he watched the bloated corpse shoved into the back of the ambulance. He felt again the power of his anonymity, the possibility of a fresh start.

As he drove away, he thought to himself: *New mang. Don't blow it.*

The next day, he was still thinking along the same lines. He was walking on a narrow street. Ruined brick apartment buildings slanted and loured on either side of him. He felt a tingle on the back of his neck. He looked over his shoulder. He saw this guy stepping out of a pale green Ford, a Crown Victoria with a white scrape on the side. He was a small guy, hungry-thin or maybe drug-thin. He was dressed in a cheap black suit, white shirt, narrow tie. He had a shaved head. He had smart, searching, dangerous eyes. They looked in Shannon's direction—then quickly looked away.

About half an hour later, Shannon caught a glimpse of him again, the same guy, on a corner several blocks to the north. It made him nervous. Was this fucktard following him?

He ducked into a restaurant to see what would happen. He watched through the front window as the guy wandered off.

Then, since he was here, he decided to get something to eat. It was a nice place, a family place with lopsided wooden floors and wooden plank walls painted cheerful red. It was called Betsy's. Betsy served the food. She was a warm, friendly lady in her sixties with a small face, sad-eyed but also cheerful. When she brought him his waffles and chicken, he realized how hungry he was and tore into them. Betsy stood over him, nodding with approval. "There's a man who can eat," she announced to the other people in the restaurant. The other people nodded, too. Some of the little children covered their mouths and giggled.

Betsy and her restaurant and the friendly people here made him feel better about things, less depressed. As he ate his waffles, he started to think that maybe this wasn't such a bad town to be in after all. He thought of the bag of tools in his closet and he remembered what the foreigner had said to him: *We put you in place where there is many buildings, much work.* There'd be many buildings and much work here, all right. He could make good money if he put his mind to it.

He started to see the logic of the thing. Maybe the old foreign buzzard wasn't such an idiot after all.

Later that afternoon, he sought out a neighborhood where there was some construction going on. Crews were clearing away the wreckage of several houses. Other crews nearby were laying fresh foundations. There was even a wooden frame or two beginning to rise against the sky. He began to imagine himself working here. He would be part of a big project: building the city back up again. He could go to Betsy's for lunch on Sundays and eat waffles and chicken and tell her about his week. Tomorrow, he decided, he'd start calling the numbers in the help-wanted ads on the computer.

Evening was coming as he made his way back to his brownstone. He didn't know the streets and got a little lost. Just as the sun was going down and the color draining out of the sky, he came upon a sight he would never forget.

There was a house on a street called H Street. A beautiful old clapboard house, all white, two stories plus an attic under a pitched roof. Behind its security bars, it had mullioned windows flanked by black shutters, white drapes visible on the inside. There was a white picket fence enclosing the front yard.

All around the house, there were empty lots, expanses of rubble and wreckage, overgrown with weeds. It was as if the flood and fire had destroyed everything near the white house, and yet passed over the house itself, leaving it unharmed.

It was a striking contrast: the house untouched in the midst of the ruins. Shannon stopped to look. That's when he noticed the woman in one of the upstairs windows. The light was on up there. The window was a rectangle of yellow glowing against the dusk. It was too high to reach from the ground so there were no security bars blocking the view. He could see the woman clearly. She was standing just by the drapes, gazing out through the glass into the distance. She was crying—crying terribly. He could see her whole body shaking with the force of her grief. Now and then, she pressed her hand to her mouth as if she didn't want anyone to hear her sobs.

The crying woman was in her twenties. She was pretty and slender. Shannon stood gazing at her, entranced by the depth of her suffering and by the secret intimacy of watching her unawares.

After a while, he realized he'd been staring at her for long seconds. He became afraid she would look down and see him spying on her sorrow. He forced himself to turn away.

As he did, he caught a glimpse of movement. He had a sense that something—someone—had just darted off into the shadows. He scanned the empty lots on every side of him. At first, he saw nothing, no one.

Then a flash of red caught his attention. He turned and saw the red brake lights of a car. The car was just turning the corner, heading off down a side street. It had its headlights off and its body was sunk in twilight. But as it drove away, it passed under a streetlamp. Shannon saw the car was green. Maybe a Ford. Maybe—he wasn't sure—a Crown Victoria . . .

He remembered the man he had seen earlier in the day: the small, drug-thin man with the shaved head and the cheap suit and the smart, searching, dangerous eyes.

NOW IT WAS a few weeks later. Shannon was working as a carpenter. He'd been taken on by a contractor named Harry Hand. "Handsome Harry" everyone called him, which was a joke because he was a little fat guy with a puckered face. He looked like a munchkin gorilla.

Handsome Harry had some kind of city connections. That was probably how he landed his job, overseeing a rebuilding development in the northeastern section. He was always slipping envelopes to guys in suits. Cops and inspectors, Shannon figured. That was the way the city worked. Shannon himself had to pay a "threeper"—a 3 percent kickback to stay on the job. But he was pulling down thirty-three an hour and the good working weather was holding day after day, so he had no complaints on the money front.

In fact, for a while, he had no complaints at all. There he'd be of a fine spring morning, up astride the second-floor joists in the cool and faintly liquid breezes, lost in the rhythm of air-nailing fire blocks between the vertical studs, lost in a sweet dream. He'd look up, look around, and what would he see? The other frames of other houses nearby him, the fresh brown of new wood rising from the colorless rubble and mud. It was as if he was part of something big, a big project to rebuild the broken city. It gave him a good feeling. It was just as he'd imagined it would be.

• • •

Sometimes little boys liked to come and watch the construction. They probably should've been in school, but they hung around the site watching the work. There was this one cute little guy who would hang around Shannon in particular. When Shannon was perched on a cinderblock eating his lunch, the boy would stand over him, asking all kinds of questions about his tools and about how you build things. Some of the other boys would hang around behind this one boy too sometimes, listening in.

"My Daddy, he build things, too," the boy said to Shannon once.

"Oh yeah?" said Shannon, chewing his sandwich.

"Yeah, he build all kinds of things. He come home, he gonna build us a house like this one."

Shannon figured the boy was making it up. He figured the boy's father was really in prison. It made him feel sorry for the little guy. The next weekend, he went out and bought some carving equipment, chisels and gouges and turning tools and so on. When he came back to work, he went to the lead man on the site, Joe Whaley, and asked if he could use some of the blocks sawed off from the studs. Joe said sure, because they just got thrown away anyway. Shannon cut the blocks and carved them and made a dump truck, with a bed that lifted and a gate that opened and wheels that turned and everything. He gave it to the little boy as a present. The little boy got all big-eyed and open-mouthed, like the truck was worth a million dollars. It made Shannon feel good. He made a couple of other trucks for some of the other kids and he carved a few soldiers and whistles for some of the others.

One day, Handsome Harry was checking out the site and he noticed this going on.

"Hey, Conor, look at that, that's all right," said Handsome, admiring one of Shannon's trucks, holding it and turning it this way and that in front of his scrunched-up gorilla face. "Where'd you learn to do that?"

Shannon shrugged. "I can just do it. I always could."

Handsome nodded with appreciation. "Look at that," he said. "That's all right."

So it went. One fine spring day after another. Out at the site, up on the joists, wind in his hair, song in his heart basically. Sometimes he'd get worried, nervous. He'd scope the newspapers or watch some true crime show on television to see if anyone mentioned him. Once or twice, someone did. The police were still "searching nationwide for murder suspect John Shannon," as one TV newswoman put it.

But day after fine spring day, no one came looking for him. No cops cruised slowly past, eyeing him from the patrol car window. No curious civilian tilted his head, and thought, *Where have I seen that face before?*

And so, slowly, day after day, it became real to him: he was free. The foreigner had done it, done just what he'd promised: new face, new papers, new life entirely, like princess in fairy tale. No more three strikes. No more Whittaker job. No more Hernandez killings. No more John Shannon at all. John Shannon was gone. He was Henry Conor now.

Ironically, that's when he started to get crawly. As soon as he started to feel safe, as soon as his new life started to fit him comfortably and he started to get used to it, he began to get that itchy feeling he got sometimes where his skin felt like it was made of spiders. He couldn't sleep at night. He stayed awake, pacing, rubbing his arm where the scars used to be. He got angry. He thought: *What am I supposed to do, just hammer nails every day for the rest of my life? Well, fuck you.* It took half a bottle of bourbon sometimes just to put his lights out.

He needed a woman, that's what. He went out and prowled some bars. He picked up a girl who said she worked in a hair salon. She took him back to her room. Sat him naked in a chair and climbed aboard. For two days, she rode him as if he would take her to the coast nonstop. It was pretty wild. He thought maybe they'd have a thing together. But that was it for her. One weekend and she was done with him. She liked to go with different guys, she said. She didn't want to stick with anybody. A few days later, Shannon was just as crawly as he'd been before.

Now this guy Joe Whaley, the lead guy on the site: he was a watchful character. He was the kind of guy who could just look at a person and tell you a lot about him. He had all kinds of insights about the workers on the site, and the bosses who came by, and the inspectors who came by for payoffs. He must have noticed what was going on with Shannon, how crawly Shannon was, because one day he said to him, "Hey, Conor. Let's have a beer after work."

Whaley was about forty. He was big: broad shoulders, a gut on him. He had a smart, sly face that looked like it had been places. He sat across from Shannon in a booth in a tavern. They each had a mug of beer. It was a quiet place, with no music.

"Where you from, Conor?" Whaley asked.

"Utah, originally," Shannon said. He got that from the movie he'd watched in the white room, the Western about the people on the stagecoach. It had been filmed in Monument Valley, Utah—it said so in the credits. The freedom of its desert distances and the mystery of its stark rock formations had appealed to Shannon. He dreamed of what it would have been like to grow up in the clean wilderness air. But he'd never actually been to Utah and didn't know anything about it, so he added, "But we moved around a lot."

Whaley didn't care. He hadn't brought Shannon here to talk about Utah. He hunched forward over the table. He spoke in a low murmur out of the corner of his mouth.

"There's a lot of money to be made in this town, you know."

"Yeah," said Shannon. "A lot of work."

"There is. And other stuff, too."

"What do you mean?" Shannon already knew what Whaley

meant. He wondered how he could just pick him out like that. *Identity like stain,* he thought.

"Look around, man. Fucking place is lawless. All the gangbangers everywhere. Minute the sun goes down, there's AK's and nine-a's firing all over the place. You can hear them as we're sitting here."

Shannon nodded. He heard them. *Bang, bang. Rat-tat-tat.*

"Police have their hands full," Whaley went on. "They can't be everywhere, right? Lot of nice houses on the west side, nobody patrolling them. And the phone lines are still wonky, too. I know people at the alarm companies. Alarms don't always work, know what I'm saying? No one to blame, just wonky wires."

Shannon nodded.

"Know what I'm saying?" Whaley asked again.

"Yeah," said Shannon. He was thinking: *No. Don't do this. You're free. Don't blow this.* But he felt crawly and crazy, too, and he was feeling, *Well, if identity like stain then it's like stain, right? What can you do?*

"I might have something for you Saturday."

"Saturday," Shannon repeated.

"A job. You interested?"

Shannon nodded, sort of as if he was thinking about it, and sort of as if he was saying yes. "Saturday."

A couple of days later, with the weather still so fine, Shannon decided to walk to work. When he was a couple of blocks away from the site, he passed by a green Crown Victoria parked at the curb. He remembered the guy with the shaved head and looked around to see if he was anywhere nearby. He wasn't, of course. Shannon couldn't even be sure this was the same car although — look at that — it did have a scrape on the side just like the one he'd seen before.

He approached it. He looked in the window. There was nothing special in there. Just some stuff lying on the passenger seat: a packet of Kleenex, some cheap sunglasses, some kind of gum or candy wrapper, and a receipt. Shannon read the receipt. It was from a restaurant called the World Café.

He looked around again. There was still no sign of the guy with the shaved head. He thought, *You don't even know it's the same car. Not for sure. You're being totally paranoid.*

And he went on to work.

But all day long, he had the feeling he was being watched. He kept looking around to see if there was anyone there.

Late in the afternoon, he was skinning the second story, laying in some plywood, when he got that feeling and glanced over his shoulder. There, beyond another frame rising in an empty lot, there was a brick apartment building, about five stories tall. At that time of day, the building cast a long shadow on the sidewalk. Shannon thought he saw someone in that shadow, someone just standing there suspiciously. Shannon was too far away to be sure, but he thought it could've been that guy, the Crown Victoria guy with the shaved head again. He stared harder, trying to make the man out, but just then . . .

"Hey, Conor!"

Shannon was so startled he nearly toppled off the joist. He looked down, his heart pounding. It was only fat little Handsome Harry, standing on the ground right below him, tilting his gorilla face up at him, shielding his eyes from the sun.

"Hey, Conor. Come down here a second."

Shannon glanced back at the shadow of the apartment building. If there had been anyone there before, he was gone now. *Paranoid.* Shannon edged around the plywood and climbed down the metal ladder to the ground.

He stood with Handsome at the base of the frame. The construction went on, and they had to talk loudly over the banging hammers and the buzzing saws and the spitting nail guns.

"I got a guy who wants to talk to you," Handsome said.

Nervous as he already was, Shannon now tasted a coppery spurt of fear on his tongue. "What guy?"

"Just a guy, looking for someone."

"Looking . . ."

"To do some work."

"Oh, looking for a carpenter, you mean?"

"Yeah, only he wants, like, a sculptor guy, a carver. A guy who can carve things—like you were doing for the kids. That's what made me think of you. Those trucks you were making for the kids."

"Oh. Oh, yeah." Shannon felt himself relax. *Don't be so jumpy all the time,* he told himself. *Don't be so paranoid. You're a new mang.*

"You can pick up some extra money on the weekends," said Handsome Harry.

"Is it legal?"

"What're you, the pope? Yeah, it's fine. It's nothing. I get a hundred off the top, finder's fee. Then you're on your own."

Shannon thought about it. There was no harm in talking to the guy. "Where is he?"

"Right over there."

Shannon looked where Handsome pointed. There was a battered blue station wagon that must have been a hundred years old standing by the curb. Standing by the station wagon was an older guy. He was a dignified college professor sort. Short, kind of tubby. Wearing a brown cardigan over a button-down shirt and khaki slacks. He had clipped salt-and-pepper hair and elegant features except for the squashed Negro nose. His eyes were mild but searching and intelligent.

Shannon walked over to him and offered his hand. "I'm Henry Conor," he said.

"Frederick Applebee," said the professor type. "Are you the sculptor?"

"Yeah, I guess so. Why?"

"I wasn't sure where to look for one. They're a lot harder to find than you'd think, especially around here. Someone suggested I try a carpenter." The man had a gentle, pleasant voice, soothing to the ear. "Take a look at these for me, would you?"

He handed Shannon some snapshots. They were pictures of a

115

carving of some kind. A wooden screen with a lot of background tracery on it, then up in front, two angels with trumpets, one on each side, facing each other. In the middle, between them, there was a third angel, lifting his hand as if he was making an announcement. In one or two of the photos, the sculpture was intact and the angel in the middle was whole. In most of the pictures, though, the thing had been scraped up and damaged and the center angel had been broken. The angel's head and one of his wings were gone.

Shannon looked through the snapshots briefly. Some were close-ups of the figures. Some were taken from far enough back that you could see the whole thing.

"What is it?"

"It's a reredos," said Frederick Applebee. "An altarpiece from a church."

"Oak, it looks like."

"That's right. Made in England about one hundred fifty years ago but in the fifteenth-century style. It was damaged in the flood. The angel's head and wing are gone. I've looked everywhere for the pieces, but they must've been carried off in the water."

"Too bad. You a preacher or something?"

"No. No, not at all. It just came with my house when I bought it. It's not even very valuable, really. I've just always been fond of it."

Shannon handed the pictures back to him. "What do you want me to do?"

"Well, I've asked around. The carving is obviously very fine, and I understand oak is a difficult wood to work with. It'd be more than I can afford to get someone who could actually repair the archangel, the one in the middle. I was wondering if maybe you could just remove him and somehow take out the center of the piece, match the tracery of the two halves together, and make the whole thing smaller with just the two heralds on it, if you see what I mean. That's the only solution I can come up with. I hate to lose the central piece but . . ." He gave a self-deprecating chuckle. "I find the idea of a headless archangel a bit disturbing."

Shannon smiled at that. He liked this old guy. "Let me see those again." Shannon took the photos back. Studied them more closely. Shrugged. "Y'know, I could probably just fix this middle one for you. Probably be easier. Smooth down the breaks, drill a couple holes, slap some dowels in there. Put a piece on for the wing, a piece on for the head, carve them right into the shape of it. I could hide the breaks in the wing feathers and in that part—the folds there—of his clothes. You wouldn't even be able to see where I fixed it unless you looked really close."

Frederick Applebee narrowed his eyes at him, doubtful. "You'd have to make a new head, a new wing. You'd have to carve them."

"Well, yeah. That's what I'm talking about."

"The original carving was . . . very fine."

"Yeah, it's good. I can see that." Shannon handed the pictures back to him. "I'm pretty sure I could copy it, though, working from the pictures." He *was* pretty sure he could, in fact. The wing would be easy and he was already beginning to see the head in his mind's eye. It was just a question of finding the right piece of wood for it. It'd be fun. He could do some sculpting and get paid for it into the bargain. Hell, he would've done it for free.

Still, this Applebee character went on giving him that doubtful look, narrow-eyed. He smiled, embarrassed. Gently, he repeated, "I'm told this sort of wood is quite difficult to work with."

"Yeah. Well . . . listen," Shannon said. "If it's no good, I can always cut the angel out, right? Do like you said. But why don't you let me try to fix it? Then, you don't like it, I'll just take it out and make the whole thing smaller."

"I haven't got a lot of money . . ."

"You don't like what you get, you don't have to pay me. I gotta kick a hundred back for the moonlight. Take care of that and, one way or another, you'll get something you can use, and you can pay me what you think it's worth."

Frederick Applebee was shorter than Shannon by a good few inches. He had to look up at Shannon to search his face. That's what he did, standing there for a long moment in silence. It made Shannon kind of uncomfortable: those mild, intelligent eyes going over him, judging the make of him. He had to tell himself again not to be so paranoid. The guy just wanted to make sure he wasn't going to mess up his altarpiece, that's all.

Applebee came to his decision. "All right," he said in his mild voice. "Give it a try. Do you want me to bring it to you somewhere?"

"I haven't got anywhere to bring it. I don't have anyplace to carve."

"Well, we have a small yard out back you can work in. Here, let me give you the address. You can come by on Saturday."

"Saturday," Shannon repeated slowly. That was the day Joe Whaley wanted him to do the job.

When the old man was gone, Shannon stood for a few moments, rubbing his arm, thinking. He was thinking about the job Joe Whaley wanted him to do. He thought he could probably do the sculpting work during the day and do the break-in for Joe Whaley at night. But something else bothered him, something on the edge of his understanding. He couldn't even put it into words at first. Then it came clear to him. His crawly feeling was gone. The minute he found out he'd be doing some sculpting work, the crawly feeling had receded. He knew from experience it would go away completely once the work was underway. He didn't have to do the job for Joe Whaley now. Not if he didn't want to.

He found Joe Whaley in his trailer. He stood around and waited for Joe to get off the phone. Joe hung up and tilted back in his swivel chair behind the mess of papers on his gray metal desk. He put his hands behind his head and lifted his chin as if to ask what was up.

"Listen," said Shannon. "That thing Saturday."

Whaley looked around as if he thought someone might overhear them, even though there was no one else in the trailer.

"Listen, thanks a lot, Joe, but I don't think I want to do that," Shannon told him.

"What do you mean?" said Joe Whaley.

"I mean . . . I don't want to do that. I don't think I'll do that."

"We talked about it," said Joe Whaley. "You said you were interested."

"Well, I thought about it. I don't want to do it."

"Man, that's not right. I was counting on you. You said you were interested."

"I didn't say I'd do it," said Shannon, though he knew he'd said as much.

"Well, man, that's not right. That's not the way it works. I mean, when you say something, you gotta walk the talk."

Shannon didn't answer. He felt a powerful impulse to just give in, just go along. It would be so much easier than starting trouble. But he didn't want to.

After the silence went on a few seconds, Joe Whaley said, "You know, this is a big development here. There's a lot of work around and for a long time. Handsome Harry listens to me about who to hire."

So that was the way it was. If he didn't do the job for Whaley, Whaley would screw up his work life. *It was always something like this,* Shannon thought, pissed off. People were always tangling you up in things. He didn't have enough money to leave town and he knew he could get blackballed pretty easily in a city like this. He hesitated. But still, something inside was telling him, *Don't do this job. Once you do this job you'll be tangled up forever. Identity like stain.*

"You gonna get me fired, Joe?" he said. He gave Joe Whaley a hard look. If Joe was going to do this to him, let him say it to his face. "I don't do this job, you gonna blackball me?"

Joe looked back. Then, after a moment, he backed down. He averted his eyes. "Ah. You're a good carpenter," he muttered. Then, more forcefully, he said, "But don't come crawling back to me when you need extra money. Know what I'm saying? I gotta be able to count on people. You're out now, you're out for good."

"I got you. I won't come back. Sorry, Joe." He felt the need to make an excuse. "It's a personal thing," he said. "I got—personal things going on."

Joe Whaley waved him off, disgusted. Shannon left the trailer sheepishly. Part of him was sorry to let Joe down, but was he ever relieved to be out of that situation! He hadn't realized how tied up in knots he was about it until now.

On Saturday, he drove to the address Frederick Applebee had given him and he couldn't believe what he saw. Amazed, he sat in his car, parked at the curb, looking out at the place through the window. He thought: *What are the chances of that?*

It was the white house—the white clapboard house with black shutters on H Street—the same house where he'd seen the woman crying in the window.

FREDERICK APPLEBEE MET HIM at the door, holding the barred door of the security cage open. As Shannon stepped inside and followed the old man through the house, he looked around him. Since he knew this was where the crying woman lived, he was looking for signs of her and for clues about what she was like.

The house, he found, was kind of old-fashioned. Shabby and musty but very . . . *respectable* was the word that came to his mind. *Respectable* and *homey*. It made him think back to the hero's house in the black-and-white movie about the angel. The furniture was worn, but very proper-looking: straight-backed chairs and a tidy little sofa—and one big old armchair next to a table stacked with books. There were white napkins on the lamp stands in the living room, and a fireplace with framed snapshots on the mantel. As he tromped behind Applebee in his jeans and sweatshirt, the whole place seemed to watch him with disapproval like some old gray-haired lady looking over the tops of her spectacles.

It was the old man's house, Shannon concluded, not the young woman's. It had been decorated by the old man's wife a long time ago. For some reason, he got the feeling the wife was dead now. He found she had no presence in the place except for lingering traces from the past. At one point, he spotted some ladies' magazines in a basket in the corner, but they were the sort of magazines a younger woman would read—the crying woman maybe, not the old man's wife.

"We were lucky in the flood," Applebee told him as they walked through. "This area was hit hard, but we're on slightly higher ground."

"How come your angels got broken then?"

"The reredos? It was in the cellar. When my wife was alive, she always said it made the house look too much like a church, so she put it down there. I'd completely forgotten about it until I came back after the evacuation and went downstairs to check the damage."

Applebee led him to the broken altarpiece. It was on a mantel in the dining room now. Shannon ran his tape measure over it so he could get the wood he needed. Applebee watched him, standing nearby with his hands in his pockets. After a while, a little boy wandered in and stood next to him. Applebee put his hand on the boy's shoulder.

"Mr. Conor, this is my grandson, Michael."

"Hey, how you doing, little man?" Shannon said over his shoulder. The kid was a solemn little fellow for—what?—a six- or seven-year-old. He was skinny and small with short hair and big sad eyes. Shannon worked it out in his mind: if this was Applebee's grandson, then that meant the woman crying in the window was probably his daughter, not his chippy girlfriend or second wife or whatever. What about the boy's father then? That was the question that came into Shannon's mind. Was the boy's father still around?

Shannon went on measuring the broken places on the altarpiece, but he asked the boy over his shoulder, "You live here?" Trying to find out what was what.

The boy was too shy to answer, but Applebee said, "Michael and his mom are staying with me for a while."

Michael and his mom—so the father was out of the picture for now anyway.

Then the boy suddenly spoke up. "My daddy died in the war."

Well, that answered that. "Oh, hey, that's sad," Shannon said. "I'm sorry, little man."

"In Iraq. He was a very brave soldier," said Frederick Applebee —speaking for the boy's sake, Shannon guessed. "He died saving the lives of two other people. Didn't he, son?"

The boy nodded solemnly. Shannon felt a pang of jealousy. He didn't know why. What was it to him if the woman in the window had a hero husband? The guy was dead for one thing, so he was no competition. And what difference did it make if he was competition? Shannon didn't even know this woman.

He thought about it later after he left the house. He thought about her, about the woman he'd seen crying in the window. It wasn't that he'd fallen in love with her at first sight or anything. She'd just made an impression on him, that's all. He didn't know what it was about her exactly. The image of her standing there crying just stuck in his mind.

He had to drive a long way to find a specialty wood store. The nearest one was set up in an old barn about fifty miles outside of town. After a couple of minutes looking around the place, he picked out a piece for the angel's wing, but the match for the head was much harder to find. He wasn't expecting to get anything perfect, just a good match for color and grain. But then he stumbled on a real piece of luck. In a dusty corner behind a repro pine table that was on display, he found a beautiful block of red oak that seemed tailor-made for the job. When he picked it up and turned it over in his hands, he got a real rush of pleasure. He could practically see the angel's face hidden inside it, waiting to be brought out.

He went back to the white clapboard house the next Saturday morning, walking up the front path carrying the canvas bag he'd bought to hold his sculpting tools. He felt good. He felt excited. He told himself it was because he was glad to get back to carving. But it was the girl, too—he was excited about meeting the girl.

She wasn't there this time again. Neither was the kid. Frederick Applebee was in the house alone. As Shannon approached the front door, he saw the old man through the mullioned sidelight.

He was sitting in his armchair, reading the newspaper, smoking a pipe. Shannon thought he looked just like the kind of professorial dad who was in the black-and-white movie about the angel.

Shannon and the old man set up a workplace in the backyard. It was a narrow strip of ground closed in by a diamond-link fence. Before the disaster, there must've been other houses on either side of this house and other backyards alongside this one, but there was only ruination now: empty lots, some strewn with garbage, some overgrown with weeds; lopsided houses, battered and shifted by the floods; blackened shells of houses that had been burned. In the near distance, there were other streets lined with old cars. There were surviving structures and the frames of new buildings just rising from the mud. Farther away, the city's damaged skyline rose black against the blue sky.

At the end of the yard, there was a good flat portion of ground. Shannon and Frederick Applebee put a bench there to hold the altarpiece and a three-legged stool for Shannon to sit on. They carried the altarpiece out together and set it on the bench. Shannon had brought a canvas tarp. He laid this on the ground and arranged his tools and his wood on top of it. He'd used a band saw at work to shape the new wing piece to his measurements. He put the piece to one side on the tarp.

Shannon went to work. He smoothed a surface for the wing attachment. He drilled a hole for the dowel. It was a pleasant, involving business. He could focus on it but still enjoy the sweet, energizing spring air. Applebee wandered into the house for a while and Shannon lost himself in fitting the wing to the broken angel. Then Applebee wandered back out again to watch. He smoked his pipe as Shannon smoothed the new piece onto the old. Now and then, he made what Shannon thought of as "old man conversation."

"Look at this," he said, peering out over the weeds toward the skyline. Biting on his pipe stem. Shaking his head. "It's a shame. It's like we've gone back to the jungle out here. I had to buy a gun. I did. A forty-five. I keep it in the closet in my bedroom. Half the time I'm terrified my grandson'll find it and blow his head off. But what else can I do? We have packs of predators roaming the street at night. Attacking anyone that moves. Breaking in and attacking women right at home in their own beds. Setting cars on fire, houses on fire. The media don't even report half of what goes on. How can they? They're too busy glamorizing slut actresses and gangster music stars. It wouldn't be good for business if they told people what really happens in a neighborhood when morality breaks down. We've got girls here getting pregnant at thirteen without husbands. The fathers taking no care of them or the children. And the sons become predators and it starts again. So help me, all it takes for the world to crumble to nothing is for women to lose their virtue and men their honor."

Shannon gave a sort of smile to himself. It was the usual old man complaint: the world's not what it used to be. It's all going to hell. Back in the day, everything was better. Blah blah blah. As if there was ever much honor or virtue in the world. Holding the angel's new wing piece on his lap now and sanding the edges, Shannon tried to humor him out of it. "I thought you said you weren't a preacher."

But Applebee didn't get the joke. He just went on. "A high school math teacher. Retired now. You can't teach children if they have no discipline. They won't let you discipline them yourself and they get no discipline at home. So it just gets worse. My daughter found that out—yes, she did, for all her idealism."

It was his first mention of his daughter and it turned Shannon's attention. He wanted to find out more. "Your daughter—is she a teacher, too?"

"Teaches the little ones. At least there's still some hope with them. But she finally gave up even on that. In the neighborhood, the thugs come younger and younger. Even the little ones can't be controlled anymore. Now she teaches on the west side, in a private school. That way, Michael can go there free of charge."

Shannon nodded. He liked the image of her teaching little children. It struck him as very womanly. It touched him somehow.

"Oh," said Applebee then, "a preacher." He suddenly got Shannon's joke. He gave a good-natured chuckle. "No, no, no. I guess I *was* going at it though, wasn't I? But no."

"A teacher not a preacher," said Shannon with a laugh.

"Exactly. This house did used to be a rectory, though."

"Oh yeah?" Shannon wasn't exactly sure what a rectory was.

Applebee must've picked up on that. "It was a preacher's house. The church used to stand right there." He pointed with his pipe stem to a field full of garbage. "It burned down years ago. That altarpiece—it was the only thing that was saved."

"Well, I guess the house must've had an effect on you," Shannon kidded him. "Cause for a teacher, you preach it pretty good."

Frederick Applebee laughed. "I'm just a cranky old man, that's all. But cranky old men know a thing or two. That's what makes them so damn cranky. Fact is, I'm no churchgoer and never have been but . . ."

Shannon had risen from his stool and was attaching the wing again. He took a pencil from his pocket and began to sketch an outline of feathers on the wood so he could carve them to join properly with the broken stump. He didn't notice that Applebee had gone into a fugue state and fallen silent.

Then Applebee said quietly, "You ever study calculus?"

"Oh, sure," murmured Shannon, sketching away. "Calculus? That's all I ever do."

"Yes," said the old man, almost to himself. "I understand. No one does anymore. But there's a lot of mystery to it. Infinite limits . . . a lot of mystery." He shook his head slowly. "Sorry. These things—they run around in my brain and I've got no one to tell them to."

"That's all right. I don't mind. It's interesting."

There was no answer. Shannon came out of his focus on the wing long enough to glance at Applebee. Applebee was holding his pipe to his mouth and tapping the stem against his lower lip. He was looking thoughtfully over the arches and jumbles and lopsided spires of the debris lying in the high weeds. Shannon figured he was thinking about the old days. He smiled again. He liked Applebee. He was a good old guy.

Coming back to himself, Applebee noticed Shannon watching him. And he noticed the wing Shannon was working on and how well it fit to the stump on the broken angel and how perfectly and gracefully Shannon had drawn the feathers. "Look at that," he said, perking up, delighted. "Why, that's wonderful. Where'd you learn to do that?"

"I just can," Shannon said with a shrug. "I've always been able to."

At that moment, the little boy—Michael—came bursting out of the house into the backyard. All his earlier solemnity was gone. He was running full speed, squealing with laughter.

"Ho!" cried Frederick Applebee as the boy darted behind him and clutched at his legs, hiding. "What's this?"

Michael's mother cracked open the screen door behind him, peeking around the edge of it with bright, mischievous eyes.

"Where'd he get to?" she said. "I know he's here somewhere."

The little boy giggled behind his grandfather's legs as the woman came out of the house and crept steadily toward him like a stalking cat.

"I know he's here somewhere," she said again.

The boy, unable to tolerate the suspense, broke from behind Applebee's legs and ran for it. The mother went after him and caught him and swept him up in her arms, laughing and tickling him.

Shannon felt a hitch in his chest at this first close sight of her, the sight of her bright eyes and smile and the sound of her laughter. She was wearing loose jeans and a baggy sweatshirt, but Shannon could see her figure moving under them as she wrestled with her son. She was definitely the woman he'd seen weeping in the window, but so different from that woman, so lively and hilarious, that he half doubted the two were the same.

"Henry Conor, this is my daughter, Teresa Grey," Frederick Applebee said.

She came over to them, clutching the giggling, struggling boy in her arms so that his feet kicked and dangled off the ground. She was as pretty up close as she'd been through the window, prettier because she was smiling now. She had big, warm brown eyes, high cheekbones, and a chin like the point of a valentine. She had her father's squashed nose, but smaller, more graceful, like an Irish pug. Her hair sprang out all over the place in corkscrew curls, which Shannon found endearing.

"Hi, Henry," she said. She held the boy in one arm, letting him slide his way to the ground. She offered her free hand and Shannon shook it.

"Look at this," said Applebee, indicating the angel on the reredos. "He's doing a great job so far."

"Oh, I'm glad!" she said. She had a warm voice, on the deep side. "My father loves this old thing. He was crushed when it got broken. Oh, you *are* doing a good job, aren't you?"

"Just the wing," said Shannon modestly. "The head'll be the hard part."

The boy squirmed free of Teresa's hold and dashed for the house. Laughing uncontrollably, he shouted, "I'm getting away!"

"Excuse me," Teresa said to Shannon with a laugh.

Shannon felt another hitch inside him as he watched her go chasing after the child, shouting play threats at him.

He went back to work. He began to carve the delicate wing feathers with an X-Acto knife. The old man wandered into the house and back out again later, standing and watching, chatting about the thoughts he had had on his mind for too long. At lunchtime, the woman brought him a sandwich and a Coke. Now and then, the boy peeked solemnly at him through a rear window. Shannon made faces at the kid and pretended to shoot at him. The boy ducked and came back, fighting down a smile. He was too shy, though, to come out into the yard.

At one point, the old man came out and gave Shannon a key, a small Medeco with a green spot stuck to the bow. "You can get in the back door with this, in through the security gate and the kitchen. In case you want to fetch the altarpiece when no one's around."

Shannon was touched. He had broken into a lot of houses in his life, and he was touched that the old man trusted him with the key.

It was a good day all around. Shannon liked the work and he enjoyed the family and the spring weather was fine. As he carved the delicate feathers, his mind went back to how, not long ago, not very long ago at all, he'd been a hunted man, hiding in a cemetery tomb, of all places, with life in prison or death hanging over him. The thought made him lift his face gratefully to the sun and breathe in deeply.

A breeze reached him and a tendril of decay drifted beneath his nostrils: the stench of the fallen city.

SHANNON FELL IN LOVE with her—with Teresa. It was something entirely new.

Every weekend, he went to the white clapboard house on H Street to work on the altarpiece. He worked long days, the whole day, so that the work progressed quickly. By the end of only the second Sunday, he had the angel's feathery wing piece nearly done.

While he worked, Frederick Applebee and Teresa and the boy Michael would come out in the yard to be with him, each in their turn. Applebee, for instance, would wander out of the house now and then to check his progress. He would stand around and maunder in that old man way of his about the old days and the state of the world, about mathematics and how civilization was crumbling to dust and so on. Then, later, little Michael would come out and stand with his thumbs in his pockets, swiveling his upper body back and forth. He would ask questions—how do you do this and why do you do that? One afternoon, Shannon gave him tools and some wood to play with. The boy gouged some of the wood and glued some pieces together and called it a helicopter and showed it proudly to his mother.

Teresa visited with him, too. She brought him iced tea and sandwiches. She sat nearby and drank a glass of iced tea herself, keeping him company while he worked. She admired his skill at shaping the wing feathers to match the ones on the original angel. She asked him about his life, where he came from, what he had done. He tried to be careful in answering her questions, but he had to say something. He told her stories he'd derived from the black-and-white movies he'd watched in the white room. He said he'd grown up in Utah among the stark rock outcroppings and level desert plains. He told her he'd lived in a small town with his father, who was a banker, and with his housewife mom. He felt bad about lying to her like that, but what else could he do? *What the hell?* he said to himself. It made a strange kind of sense in a way, didn't it? He was telling her about the life he *should have* had because she was the kind of girl he might have known if he had had that life.

That's the way she seemed to him. She seemed part of that life he'd seen in the black-and-white movies, that life he remembered but had never lived. She was the girl he remembered but had never known. She was warm-hearted and generous, cheerful and funny, so completely different from the anguished woman who'd been weeping in the window that he almost forgot ever having seen her like that. She had a natural, unaffected way of praising his work while making jokes about herself. She would tell him how beautiful and graceful his carved feathers were, for instance, and then go into some anecdote about how clumsy she was with her hands. She would make faces and do silly voices as she told the story, slipping from her precise and mellow diction into street rhythms for humor and emphasis, or even sticking her tongue out to one side and crossing her eyes at a punch line to startle him into laughter. She never tried to seem sexy or alluring or mysterious with him. She was just comical and regular, the same way she was with her son. Shannon watched her with her son sometimes. He watched her teasing the boy out of his heavy solemnity with goofy jokes and faces. He watched her wrestle with the boy, giggling in the dirt, or play some madcap version of football with him that was as good as wrestling. She was always full of that kind of energy and cheer.

"I try to make sure he gets to do guy stuff," she told Shannon as she sat beside his workplace on the remnants of a cinderblock wall. A field strewn with garbage spread out behind her. She drank from her mug of tea and kept an eye on the boy where he played with plastic soldiers in the sparse grass at the other end of the yard. "Daddy throws a ball with him sometimes, but he doesn't have the energy he used to have and . . . he was never much into sports anyway. I try to make sure Michael gets to do some rough-housing and . . . you know. That sort of thing. Luckily, he's still little. I don't know what I'm gonna do when he has to learn to swing a bat and stand up for himself in a fight and all that."

Shannon looked up from his work long enough to glance over at the boy—and at the woman watching the boy. A vague under-standing dawned in him. Without really putting it into words, he started to see why they all came out to the backyard to watch him work, why they all talked to him like this and asked him questions and told him their thoughts. It was because of her husband, be-cause her husband had been killed in the war, and now there was an empty place in the family where he had been. Shannon didn't fill that place, he simply stood in it, like those actors who stand in for a star before the cameras start to roll. He could've been anyone—any man, at least—and they would have talked to him because he was in that place, because the boy missed his father and the old man missed the company of his son-in-law and the woman missed her husband. It was as if they were talking to that other man by talking to Shannon.

As this occurred to him in that vague way, Shannon felt a sort of hollow sadness without really knowing why. Without really know-ing why, he said: "The little man must miss his father, huh."

"I guess so," Teresa murmured in a faraway voice—watching the boy and speaking as if she wasn't thinking about what she said. For a moment then, just a moment, Shannon saw her again as he'd seen her first. The same wild suffering shimmered beneath the surface of her distant expression, barely there, then gone. She faced him and smiled. "How boring am I, right? I know how much a man likes to hear a mother talk about her kids." She tilted her head over, shut her eyes, and snored loudly to make him laugh.

Shannon ignored the jokiness this time. "What happened to him? Your husband."

"Oh . . . please. Don't get me started. Talk about depressing. Just what you need, right? Trying to work with me over here sobbing."

"I don't mind. Sob away. I wondered, that's all."

She gave a big sigh, as if to say, *All right, you win.* "He was a staff sergeant in the infantry in Iraq, in a little city south of Baghdad. Some Iraqi engineers had been brought into his FOB, his base, to do some work, and the base came under rocket fire. Everyone went scrambling for the bunkers, but two of the civilian engineers sort of froze, you know, out in the open. Carter—he was the fastest man. He could outrun lightning. He could've gotten into that bunker, too. But he turned around and ran to the engineers instead. Grabbed each one by an arm and shoved them into the bunker in front of him. Just as they got there, another rocket came in and Carter got hit by shrapnel. He was just outside the bunker entrance. The Iraqis didn't get a scratch, but Carter . . ."

She took a leather billfold from the front pocket of her jeans. She opened it and handed it to him. Shannon looked down at a snapshot of her husband, Carter. He was a round-faced man with a grin full of youth and friendliness—nothing like the grim, determined heroes he had seen in the black-and-white war movies in the white room.

"They gave him the Bronze Star with the valor device," she said proudly, "and the Purple Heart and the Combat Infantryman's Badge . . . and here I go." But there was no sobbing, not at all. Her eyes just grew damp. She touched the corners of them and it was over. "I warned you."

"Sounds like a hell of a brave guy," said Shannon, feeling even more hollow than before. He gave her back the billfold.

"That's what I *really* worry about," she said. She spoke in her light, jokey tone again, but he could hear the tears just underneath. "How am I going to teach him that?"

"To be brave, you mean?"

"Everything. All the things Carter just was. I try to tell Michael what he was but . . . you can't even say the words for it anymore without sounding silly. Have you noticed that? Carter had things like honor, things like valor. He was noble. Those used to be good words, right? But somehow they got . . . stupid-sounding, you know? Kind of—*ugh*—heavy and overbearing and even comical. How does that happen to a word? He can look on the TV"—she was talking about the boy now—"he can look on the TV, he'll see all these men struttin' around, all muscle and gold and guns. Struttin' around like they somethin' fine, like they tough, you know? Talkin' about slappin' they hos. Carter was nothing like that. Carter was a *man*. He treated me like . . ." She didn't finish. She fought back her tears. She shook her head. "Even the word *man*," she said. "How does that happen to a word?"

Shannon, at this point, felt like absolute shit. How could he ever compete with a husband like that? He didn't even admit to himself that he *was* competing with him, but he felt bad anyway. He tried to belittle his rival in his mind. *Yeah, big hero. Killing people for the government. Lets the government sell him some line about God and country or whatever and sucker him off to some war they're probably making money off of somehow. Lets himself get blown up for a couple of ragheads who didn't want him there and probably would've stabbed him in the back soon as look at him. What's so great about that, killing people for the government and getting killed for some poor ragheads in some lousy war?*

It was a nice try, but it didn't work. He knew in his heart it was all garbage, just stuff he was saying to keep from feeling so small because he'd never done anything noble or honorable like that. But he still felt small. He felt like absolute shit.

He began his work on the head of the angel. He used the band saw at his job site again. He shaped that special piece of red oak he'd found at the store so that it would fit the broken place where the old head had been. When he got to the Applebee house, he fastened the block of wood to the broken figure with a dowel. Then he went to work on it with a mallet and gouges, hammering away, chipping the block down to the general shape he wanted.

As he worked on it, his misgivings grew. Or that is: he had had misgivings all along, but hadn't acknowledged them until now. Now they came to the surface. When he first accepted the job from Applebee, he had told himself it would be no problem to reconstruct the angel's face from the photographs he had. But the photographs were small and unclear. It was hard to make out the details. Also, there was the wood, this specific block of wood he'd found. It had its own shape to struggle with, its own angel face buried at its core. He saw this face in his mind's eye, but only vaguely, like the angel in the photograph. Like the angel in the photograph, the details were hard to make out.

During the week, he found himself searching people's faces. The faces of the other carpenters and electricians on the site at work. The faces of people at Betsy's restaurant when he ate dinner there. The faces of passersby when he went running for exercise. He was looking for inspiration for his angel, but he couldn't find it. When the weekend came, he chiseled away at the block of red oak, but he didn't know what he was going to make. He began to dread the moment when he would have to start working on the angel's features.

One early morning, he was jogging through a damaged suburb on the edge of the Northern District, the most crime-ridden district in the city. He was in a runner's reverie, focused on his breath and the flap of his sneakers against the pavement. The bald guy didn't register on his mind until he ducked away around the corner up ahead. Only then, when he was gone, did Shannon wonder: *Was that him? Was that the guy from the green Crown Victoria, the drug-thin guy with his cheap suit and his shaved head who seemed to keep showing up everywhere?* Shannon had forgotten about the guy for a while, but now he wondered: Was he back? Was he spying on him?

Shannon increased his speed, hurrying to get to the corner. When he did, he scanned the scene, searching for the bald guy. Instead, his attention was caught by something else: there was a crowd gathered on the lawn of one of the houses here. There were police cruisers parked in the driveway and at the curb out front, their red flashers revolving in the still-shadowy dawn. Shannon slowed to a walk, breathless and sweating. He approached the edge of the crowd. He looked through to see what was going on.

A man had been shot dead. He was lying sprawled in his lover's lap with a black hole in the center of his T-shirt. He was about Shannon's age, small and slender. He had a narrow, weaselly face and a thin moustache. He wore only the blasted T-shirt and his Jockey underpants.

His lover—the lover who knelt on the lawn and held his corpse—was also a man, an older queen wearing a feminine quilted bathrobe and a plastic shower cap on his head. He was holding his lover on his lap and screaming—screaming raggedly, wildly, stretching out his hand to the crowd around him as if appealing to them, begging them to make things right.

A cop stood over the two lovers, looking down at them. Shannon noticed the cop was smirking—probably because the lovers were queers and the older one was wearing that bathrobe and the girly shower cap. But Shannon felt only pity for the screaming man. He could see how much he loved the dead guy. The robe and the cap didn't amount to much next to that. Even them being fags—what did it matter? Look at the poor bastard. His heart was broken.

Shannon started jogging again. He had completely forgotten the bald guy. His mind was playing over what he had just seen. It made him think back to the time he'd seen Teresa standing in the window, crying like that queen, so terribly, so hard. He knew now, of course, that she had been crying for her husband. He understood that she could joke around with him and be cheerful with her son and go to work and do her job and all that, but there was still that part of her screaming and crying inside, the same as the guy in the shower cap screaming on the lawn.

He stopped on the sidewalk at the corner of a broad boulevard. The traffic light was broken here, as many of the lights in the city still were. It hung from the wire above him, dead and dark. The early traffic went whisking past without ceasing. He waited for a break in it, jogging lazily in place with his feet barely leaving the ground.

Slowly, his jogging motions subsided. He came to a full stop. He stood there, going neither forward nor backward, neither left nor right. His lips were parted and he was breathing hard, staring at nothing. This was the first time it dawned on him: he was in love with Teresa. He thought he had been in love a couple of times in his life, but now that he really was, he realized those other times were phony. This was something else, something new. On the one hand, it was a kind of hilarious feeling, like he ought to be wearing a party hat and pulling on his ears and making faces because—*hooray!*—the whole world was a circus. On the other hand, it was agony, total agony—because he felt like he couldn't be whole—like he would never be whole—without her.

It all came together in his mind then. The queer in the shower cap screaming. Teresa crying in the window. This feeling he had, entirely new. The party hat and the agony, the loving and the tears, there was no getting around it: it was all one thing.

On Saturday, when he returned to the backyard of the Applebee house, when he took up chiseling the block of red oak again, he found that he could see plainly the shape that was hidden in the wood. The face of the angel had come clear to him.

NOW HE SET TO WORK in earnest. He carved the angel's features quickly, half-afraid he would lose the image of the face in his mind, but also knowing somehow that he wouldn't lose it because the image in his mind was also, weirdly enough, the very face that was buried in the wood, imperishably there.

That face haunted him. More and more, day by day. Whose face was it? Where did it come from? How had it happened to be in this particular piece of wood? The questions hammered at him as the features became clearer and clearer in his mind and as he hewed them out of the oak with greater and greater specificity. They kept hammering at him after his work was done for the day. After he went home and got in bed at night, he lay awake with his eyes open and they hammered at him.

He recognized some of those features—or sometimes he thought he did anyway. He thought he saw some of Teresa's expressions in them, some of what her face looked like when he first saw her crying at the window and some of what it looked like now when she wrestled laughing on the ground with her son. He also saw the gentle, distracted, putty-cheeked angel from that black-and-white movie he'd watched in the white room. He also saw the old queen screaming on the lawn with his dead lover. And he saw Teresa's husband, Carter. He hadn't wanted to put Carter in the angel's face, but he sometimes recognized him there all the same. He sometimes recognized the grim heroes from the black-and-white war movies, too.

It was a beautiful face in its way, but strange. Neither man nor woman necessarily, though sometimes he saw more of one or the other in it. Neither kind and gentle as you might expect an angel would be, nor stern and pious as an angel might be on Judgment Day. The only words he could think of to describe its qualities were *sorrow* and *joy*. Which made no sense to him because how could you have both at once? But there it was. It was a face—as he saw it in his mind—as it came to reality under his hands—of simultaneous sorrow and joy, as if it were looking down from heaven and saw all the love and all the death on earth happening together at the same time.

It made no sense to him in one way, but in another way he understood. As he feverishly worked the chisel, then the gouges, then the smaller gouges into the wood, he understood that he was trying to carve out the shape of his feelings for Teresa. He was trying to expel them into an oaken semblance of themselves. He knew he loved her and he knew he couldn't have her and so he was trying to give his joy and his sorrow a face. He hoped then they would be outside him and he would be free of them.

But he wasn't—he wasn't free. The more he succeeded—the closer he came to sculpting the face he wanted—the more that face began to agitate and obsess him. It was as if it was watching him, as if his own emotions were now outside himself and looking back at him, staring at him. It was as if the wooden angel had come to feel about *him* what he felt about Teresa, the same agony and celebration, the same sorrowful and joyful love.

And it made him feel bad. That was strange, too, wasn't it? You would think that, since he loved Teresa—since he loved her more and more as time went on—you would think it would make him feel good to have an angel—even just a wooden angel—looking at him with all the tenderness and warmth he felt for her. But it didn't. It made him feel the way he had felt when Teresa told him how her husband died in the war. It made him feel small and rotten. More and more, day after day.

Finally, there came a night, one terrible, terrible night, when he couldn't sleep, when he kept thinking and thinking about the angel's face. He couldn't stop and, after hours of tossing and turning, he sat up naked on the edge of the bed and buried his own face in his hands hoping he could make the image of the angel's face go away. All he could think was *Stop! Stop! Don't look at me!* Because, really, what a piece of crap he was. What a crap life he had led. He was a crappy little thief, that's what. A crappy little tough-guy punk worth nothing to anyone anywhere because he'd never done anything for anyone ever, and if he'd never been born, the world would be the same or even better than it was.

New mang! he cried out in his mind. New mang! New life like princess in fairy tale, huh? Well, bullshit. Bull-shit. How did some plastic surgery and some phony papers make him any different than what he was before? Any thieving punk piece of garbage could get a cut job and a clean sheet. Happened all the time. What did that make him but a liar and a fraud, a fugitive and a fraud? Talking to old Applebee like his long-lost son. Playing with the kid like his father. Flirting with Teresa as if he were man enough to take her husband's place. And what about all those stories he told about himself, those stories stolen from those cornball black-and-white movies? All fake. Even his name was fake. Henry Conor. Every time Teresa called him that, it shot through his blood like grief. What a fraud.

It was an awful night. A terrible, terrible feeling. He sat there naked on the edge of the bed with his body bent over and his hands digging into his eyes and he felt he would do anything—anything—not to be the man he was.

Identity like stain. Identity like stain.

At last, the sculpture was nearly done.

He was putting the finishing touches on it. He had the new head sitting on the dowel, fixed to the body. He was standing over it, brushing at it with sandpaper before gluing it all together and working the angel's robes to hide the join.

"Oh! It's beautiful, Henry!" He hadn't heard Teresa come out of the house, but there she was, standing behind him. "It's better than the original. Even my father says so. It's incredible."

He glanced over his shoulder at her, then turned and faced her. She was wearing jeans and one of those scoop-necked T-shirts, a lavender one that looked good against her skin. She was standing with her hands folded in front of her. Her eyes were bright. He couldn't answer her because of the way she was looking at the angel and the way it made him feel: too filled up to speak. He wanted to take hold of her and feel her soft shoulders in his hands. He thought if he couldn't take hold of her, he would go up in smoke.

Her bright eyes shifted to him. She began to say something and then stopped and then said, "You have a real gift, Henry."

He looked back at the angel. He touched its cheek with a knuckle. It looked at him. *Henry*, he thought, ashamed. She didn't even know who he was.

"It's just something I can do," he said. "I always could."

They were silent and awkward, facing each other in front of the altarpiece.

"Will we ever see you again when it's done?" she asked him suddenly.

"What? Sure. What do you mean?"

"I mean, you won't just go away, will you? When you're finished with the work. You won't just stop coming here."

He was standing there like a kid now, his heart fluttering inside him as if he were a kid. "I guess not. I don't know. I'll be around."

"It's just . . . it's Michael, you know—it meant so much to him having you here."

"Sure," said Shannon. "He likes to have a guy around. He misses his dad. I know."

"It's not just that. It's you. He thinks you're great. We all . . . my father, too. We all think you're great."

"Yeah, but I'm not," said Shannon with an uncomfortable laugh. He had to say this. With the angel looking at him, he felt compelled. "I'm not great. I'm not even really any good." He laughed again. He wished he could stop telling her these things, but he couldn't.

Teresa shrugged, smiling. "Well . . . who is, right? Any good."

"Yeah. Right. Well, not me, that's for sure. I mean, it makes me feel . . . bad, Teresa, you know? That you might think—that Michael might think—that I was something I wasn't. I mean, I haven't told you some of the bad things I've done. And there's a lot of them, too, believe me."

"Everybody's done bad things, Henry. You don't have to tell me."

My name's not even Henry, he wanted to say, but he didn't, he couldn't. "Yeah, but I mean his dad, Michael's dad, your husband, Carter . . . he was a . . . he was a big man, like you said. He was somebody you could look up to. Fighting in the war and all that. Saving those people and all that. I mean, I am not that guy, no way, Teresa. You ought to know that. Michael ought to know that, too. I am so way not that guy, it's not even funny."

"I know," she said—not unkindly, just straight out. "I know you're not. Carter was a great person, an amazing person. But . . ." She gave him one of her comic mugs, lifting up one eyebrow, screwing up one corner of her mouth. She gestured at the sculpture. "He never could have done that. He never could've made that angel's face."

Well, hearing that—that was almost more than he could handle. He was already full with wanting her and that was just one thing too many. He didn't move toward her or anything like that, but he realized that his expression had changed, that everything that was in his heart was right there for her to see now, right there for anyone to see on his face. Then, the next thing he knew, she was looking at *him* differently, too. All the comical mugging was gone and her lips were parted and the black centers of her brown eyes were so large they almost filled them. He thought, *Holy shit!* because he realized she was looking at him exactly like that woman in the movie about the casino, exactly the way she had looked at the hero in the end when he sent her away even though they loved one another. He knew deep down she wasn't really looking at him. He just happened to be standing there where her husband should have been. She was looking at her husband through him, really. But just then, he didn't care. Her husband was dead, after all. He, Shannon, was the one standing there.

So then he did start to move toward her. He wasn't an idiot: he could see she was his for the taking. Her eyes were practically begging him to take her. To hell with his fear and shame and whatever. He wanted his hands on her. He wanted his lips on her and his body against her and inside her. Really, he wanted to break over her like a wave—as if he were a wave and she were brown sugar and he could break over her and wash her away so that they were one thing together. That was the crazy idea of it that came into his mind.

He started to move toward her—just started. But suddenly Teresa blinked as if she was waking up. She let out a little noise, a little breath. And before Shannon could do anything, she had turned away from him, she was hurrying away from him, back toward the house, back into the house, leaving him there alone with nothing but his goddamned wooden angel.

PART IV

AFTER THE FAIR

LIEUTENANT RAMSEY SAT in the coffee shop, waiting for Gutterson. His oval face with its thin moustache was deadpan in its imperturbable dignity. His thoughts were likewise cool, as cool as his expression. His anguish was no longer operational.

His rage at Augie's betrayal, for instance: it had passed. By force of will, he had transformed it into an icy determination. Much the same was true of his hatred of what had happened to Peter Patterson, his hatred of what he had done and how it had come to be done and the way it hung over him and threatened him with exposure and arrest. Sometimes at night, in his dreams, he relived the event: felt the dying man's pulse through the handle of the knife or saw the corpse staring up at him through the flame-lit, rain-riddled water. But in the daylight—here, now—the incident lived in him only as a kind of chill, motive force. His dead mother could haunt him all she wanted, and he loved her. But for now, at least, he could not afford to pretend that he still lived in her innocent Bible-waving world of moral absolutes. If there was a God, he was not here in this city. Just look around. God was gone and even worse, Augie was gone with him. God and Augie Lancaster had withdrawn their attention and protection from this place and they who were left were left alone to fend for themselves. If Lieutenant Ramsey was going to get clear, not Augie or God or Mama was going to make it happen. It would be he, and he alone.

Ramsey had thought it through. Ironically, it was Augie who had inspired him, who had shown him the way forward. Augie on TV all the time these days, with the crowds of young people singing, swaying, cheering, chanting for him: the hero of the flood and fire, the savior of the city. The news media, too — the reporters were in ecstasy over him, not even reporters anymore but simply heralds of his rise, trailing in his clouds of glory like mandolin-bearing cherubs on a church ceiling. *The New Breed*, they called him. *The Man of the Moment. America's Future.* Or once, from their seemingly inexhaustible inkwell of gibberish: *New Emblem of the Transfigured African-American Narrative.* So swept up were they in that narrative that the truth of the matter seemed only to incense them. If anyone spoke up against Augie — if anyone mentioned what Augie had really done in his life or whom he'd really known in this city of his — if anyone simply pointed to what the city had become under his hands, saying *Look at it, look at it!* — the media rounded on the wild-eyed prophet, fanged, and tore at him, drowning out his dying cries with more, almost hysterical, accolades.

Ramsey, in simple envy and ill will at the success of a man who had hurt him, couldn't bear to watch much of this. He had to turn the TV off or turn the channel or turn away, walk away, whenever Augie was on. Ignoring Augie on television, radio, the Internet, and in newspapers and magazines had become part of his discipline, a necessary measure to keep his temper even, his emotions under control. But news of the man was everywhere. Words filtered into his consciousness, images entered his peripheral vision, as these things always will in a city. And they made him think.

Augie Lancaster was a celebrity now, a national name, almost certainly headed for greater success and high office. And it was amazing to Ramsey, amazing how free Augie was of the things he had done here. It was amazing how little his past adhered to him or weighed him down. It made Ramsey wonder, in simple bitterness and envy and ill will: What was his secret? How had he pulled that off? How did a man — a man steeped in such corruption and failure — how did he wreak the sort of havoc he had wreaked here in this city and then just walk away, untarnished, scot-free? Where was the famous burden of history? Where were the consequences of a man's misdeeds? Where was his responsibility? Did these things have no power over Augie Lancaster? Was he uniquely free of them and if so, why?

Ramsey considered these questions a long time. Finally, the obvious answer came to him. Augie was free because he had touched nothing. He had put his hands on nothing. Not for years anyway. He had worked his will throughout the city, throughout the entire state, by a kind of remote control, and he had done that for so long that he had become, in a sense, almost immaterial, an atmosphere of intent, a direction of desire built into the nature of the municipal machine. Things just worked the way he wanted them to. He hardly had to give the command. He had transformed himself from a human being of guilt and responsibility into an intangible force.

Had Augie ever said to Ramsey, for instance: *Kill Peter Patterson?* Had he ever said anything even vaguely like that, anything at all that couldn't be denied completely in a court of law or a TV interview? Ramsey hardly knew himself anymore whether he had or not. Somehow he had simply known that that was what had to be done.

Or take the case of the Reverend Jesse Skyles. A perfect case, that one. Was it Lieutenant Ramsey himself who had formulated the final plan, as he sometimes believed? Was it he who had come up with the idea as a way to calm Augie down, a way to keep Augie from doing something even more radical or violent? Or was it the other way around? Had Augie planted the notion in Ramsey's head, coaxed it out of him in the midst of one of his anti-Skyles ravings? Even now, even sitting here, thinking back, Ramsey didn't know how or where the whole thing originated.

Much the same was probably true of the girl—the girl they had used to bring Skyles down. She probably didn't even know herself what had happened or what she'd done. She was only fourteen years old, after all, one of Ramsey's prostitute informers, already beaten half-crazy by her pimp and poisoned half to death with crystal. She probably didn't know herself where the truth ended and her lies began. That's what made her such a convincing actress. *Oh, Reverend, save me from my life of sin.* She probably didn't even know herself whether she was begging Skyles for salvation or just diddling around for some extra cash.

And even Skyles—even the reverend had to wonder sometimes, too. At that moment, the critical moment, when the girl deftly slipped the strap of her dress down her shoulder—deftly hiked her hem—and slipped her naked breast against his upraised hand and pressed her shaved and shockingly naked slit against his knee, hadn't he hesitated for just a second before he started back and pulled away? It sure looked like that on the security camera footage—it sure looked like he hesitated a long, long second—a clear, open-and-shut case of Lust in the Heart. That was enough to quiet any questions about the girl and her intentions, especially from reporters whose *priest-fucks-kid* narrative fell out of them like dog slobber at a dinner bell. And that was enough, in turn, to make Skyles half believe he half belonged in prison. Wracked with guilt, he could only blither weakly in his own defense while Augie Lancaster's judge and jury members worked their will—his will—Augie Lancaster's ever-unspoken will.

So there it was. The perfect case in point. The reverend wasn't sure if he was guilty. The girl wasn't sure if she was lying. Ramsey wasn't sure whose idea the whole thing was. No wonder Augie Lancaster floated free of history, like a soap bubble carried away on a rising atmosphere of abstract desire . . .

An image that made one corner of Ramsey's mouth lift slightly beneath his moustache . . .

Just then—in keeping with this theme—into the coffee shop came the animal Gutterson. Tromping thump-footed like a troll guarding a castle gate. Wearing a jacket of white linen that looked like it hadn't been ironed since last spring.

He got his coffee at the counter and sank into his chair across the small round table from the lieutenant. He let out a heavy sigh as he sat and said, "Another day, another dollar." Full of earthy wisdom was the detective.

Ramsey didn't even bother to speak. He simply pushed the blue folder across the table at him.

Gutterson sighed again and cleared his throat. He opened the folder with one hand while he raised his coffee cup to his lips with the other.

It was the same blue folder that had been given to Ramsey by Charlotte Mortimer-Rimsky. It held the same blurry photograph of the man in the car outside the graffito house. But now it also held printouts from Ramsey's long, discreet, difficult, and only partially successful investigation.

Gutterson scanned the printouts, staring dead-eyed and working his lips like some knucklehead reading porn.

"Mysterious," he rumbled after a while.

"I need to know what he knows."

"That could get messy." Unconcerned, Gutterson flipped the blue folder shut. He sipped his coffee, looking over the rim at Ramsey.

It was the crucial moment, but it all seemed more or less inevitable. Gutterson's stupidity was of a wholly moral nature. He was smart enough otherwise. He had survived on this city's police force a long time. He was plenty smart enough to divine his superior's will.

"Well, we can't have a mess," Ramsey said.

"No, we can*not*. No, we can*not*," said Gutterson with some unfathomable combination of bloodlust and world hatred. He swept up the blue folder with one paw. "I keep this?"

Ramsey gestured as if to say *Be my guest*.

Then, when Gutterson was gone, the lieutenant sat alone through a half-price refill, looking out the window at the pleasant view of a Westside shopping mall. He daydreamed vaguely about what he'd do when all this was over. How he'd become the law officer he'd started out to be, the neighborhood model of success, self-control, and integrity, his mother's son. He saw himself rescuing fatherless children from their gangster mentors . . . or something. Whatever. He knew full well that it would never happen. He knew full well that "all this" is never over. "All this" is just the world and you make your choices and you pay your way. He was just soothing his conscience, that's all. That was part of his discipline, too, now: quieting the voice of his upbringing, breaking free of his mother's outmoded philosophical apron strings, willing away his shame.

Because that was the real secret of the whole business, wasn't it? That was the great thing Augie Lancaster knew and that Ramsey, meditating on Augie's success, had now discovered: conscience *was* history. Conscience was the weight of history, the only power it had over you. And it, too—conscience, too—was nothing more than a current of mass opinion that could be turned this way or that by a strong man's will.

The thought brought Ramsey back to himself, back to his own predicament—left behind here as he was on the history-flooded earth as Augie levitated into the television ether where the young folks danced and sang his praises and the reporters-who-were-not-reporters-anymore appended choral hallelujahs to his name. The thought brought Ramsey back to the blue folder. It was all about the blue folder now.

To anyone with eyes to see with, to anyone with a mind accustomed to the way things worked in this good old city, in this good old world, the blue folder was nothing less than an order to kill a man. It had come to Ramsey through Charlotte Mortimer-Rimsky, but it was really an expression of Augie Lancaster's will. And now Ramsey had given the blue folder to Gutterson and the folder had become an expression of Ramsey's will. And if ever the deed itself should come back to haunt him, Ramsey would say, "No, no, that wasn't what I meant. It was just a blue folder. I don't know what he was thinking."

Because Ramsey had watched Augie Lancaster on TV. He had seen him floating free of the city and he had learned his lesson.

He had learned how to give an order to do murder without uttering an incriminating word. He had learned how to turn the current of his conscience against the directions of his upbringing, against the fact of his own actions and the tug of responsibility. He, too, had learned how to float free.

He sat stirring an extra half spoon of sugar into his coffee cup and gazed mildly out the window at the passing scene.

ON SATURDAY, after all those days of spring sunshine, it finally rained. That was the day Shannon finished the angel.

He went to the Applebees' house and carried the sculpture into the house's small garage. He worked on it in there, putting on the finishing touches. When he was done, he and old man Applebee set the altarpiece back on the mantel in the dining room. Teresa and the boy came home from the grocery store and they all four admired it.

Teresa made pork chops and mashed potatoes, and they all had dinner together in the dining room by candlelight. There was an atmosphere of celebration in the house as Applebee and Teresa took turns admiring different aspects of the wooden angel Shannon had made, the angel of Joy and Sorrow. Applebee even raised a glass of wine and toasted it. When dinner was over, he went to it and studied it up close.

"You're an artist, Henry," he said to Shannon.

Shannon laughed that off. He was no artist.

"No, I'm serious. You could make a living at it. I mean, this . . ." He shook his head. "It really is remarkable."

Shannon felt good. He was aware of how good he felt. He didn't have that feeling he sometimes got as if his skin were crawling. He just felt good. This was the life, he thought: sitting here with these people as if he were part of the family and holding his love for Teresa half-secret in his heart and having the angel he'd made sitting on the mantel there. Somewhere inside, he knew it all had to come apart at some point, because he knew he was a fraud. The angel looked at him from its perch as if it knew he was a fraud, too, a crappy little thief with a face job and false papers. But he, Shannon, put that out of his mind for now, because this was what he'd always wanted, wanted without knowing it, this was the life, the new life the identity man had promised him: here it finally was.

"Well, we ought to do something," he said. "Go out and celebrate sometime or something." He spoke out of his general pleasure with things, but the idea in his mind was that he would take Teresa out somewhere sometime and they would be alone together.

But the kid, Michael, piped up, "We could go to the fair. There's a fair. Junie went to it, Junie at school. We could go."

And Teresa looked at Shannon expectantly.

So what the hell, the next day, Sunday, when Teresa and the boy came home from church, Shannon took them to the fair.

It was really just a carny on the edge of the city. The usual rides and booth games trucked over from the last town before being trucked over to the next. The kid thought it was magical, though, and that was fun even for Shannon. Michael's usual solemn demeanor fell away. He kept running off to one thing and then another, shouting, "Can we go on this? Can we do this?" The Ferris wheel, the bouncy castle, the whirligig. "Can we do this? Can we do this?" Shannon bought him cotton candy and taught him how to throw one of the lightweight baseballs at the booths. After spending about a million dollars on balls, the kid actually knocked over one of the targets and won a stuffed frog worth maybe a buck-fifty. That practically rocketed him into the stratosphere: "Look, Mama, I won, I won!" He held the frog in a death grip the rest of the day.

Shannon could tell it made Teresa happy to see the boy so excited. Whenever Shannon turned to her, she lit up and gave him a big smile. It really got to him. The smile was about the kid, sure, and he was glad to see that, but it got to him and it made him wonder if they could send the kid off somewhere for a while so he could kiss her. After the way she'd looked at him in the backyard, he was pretty sure she wanted him to.

It was a bright, warm afternoon. Saturday's rainstorm had left the air feeling fresh and clean. The weather brought the people out and as the day wore into blue evening, the fair grew crowded. Shannon and Teresa and the kid had to push their way through the mob and wait on line for the rides, but the kid didn't seem to mind.

He went on the carousel. He wanted Shannon to come along, but Shannon wanted a chance to be alone with Teresa. Maybe the kid understood that, because he tugged at Shannon for only a few seconds, then went off on the ride by himself.

The carousel was small, with colored light bulbs flashing and a calliope playing fairy-tale music. The kid went around on his painted horse every few seconds, waving to them so that they had to wave back. There was no time to go after the kiss. But Shannon and Teresa were standing next to each other behind a low metal barrier and she had one hand on the top of the barrier, leaving the other free for waving at the kid. After about the fifty-seventh time the kid went by, Shannon figured why not and reached out and put his hand over Teresa's hand where it sat on the barrier. He heard Teresa take a deep breath, and then she wrapped her hand around his. Shannon remembered the first time a girl had let him slide his fingers down her pants, when he was thirteen, the first time he had actually felt the magical damp portal into her flesh. It had set off a pretty substantial explosion in him, an expanding fireball filling him with flame. But this was on another order of magnitude, this was nuclear, and it was just her hand in his. Her hand in his and the carousel bringing the kid around and the cheap carny colored lights and the calliope music, that's all. But he really was crazy about her, he really was. He'd never felt anything like it. He turned to look at her, and she looked at him and smiled again, and that was pretty nuclear, too.

Then a movement caught his eye and his glance shifted, and he saw the man who had been following him all this time.

It was that same guy, the same damned guy with the shaved head and the watchful eyes and the cheap suit. It was a different cheap suit this time, but the exact same motherfucker otherwise, large as life, Shannon was sure of it. In that first moment, when Shannon first shifted his gaze from Teresa's smile and saw the bastard through the crowd, the guy was just standing there, just staring his way.

There could be no doubt about it anymore: the guy was watching him.

He was over by the wheel-of-fortune booth. The big wheel was turning and its colored lights blinking behind him. The flashing colors played on him and the fair lights washed over him so Shannon could see him clearly even in the twilight. The bald-headed goon saw Shannon look at him. Caught off-guard, he started. The next moment, he hurried away, losing himself in the crowd.

Shannon felt sick inside. Who was this guy? A cop? He had to be. What else? Deep down, Shannon had known all along that something like this would happen, that someone would find him. But why did it have to be now, so soon? Why couldn't it be in a few months or a year or a couple of years when he'd had a chance to live out his new life, when he'd had a chance to be with Teresa?

The sickness turned to anger in him. He let go of Teresa's hand and said, "I'll be right back, okay?"

"What's wrong?" she said.

"Nothing. I'll be right back."

He left her and plunged into the crowd, going after this guy, this bastard, meaning to run him to ground.

The next minute everything was racing past him and everything was racing inside him, too. The glittering lights of the turning carousel and the muscular rise and fall of the Ferris wheel and the strangely deadpan faces of parents and their children raced past on both sides of him, and his chaotic angry thoughts raced inside him, disconnected. He didn't know exactly what he was planning to do. But something. He wasn't going to just stand around and let this bastard follow him and torment him from a distance. If the guy was a cop, well, let him show his hand. Or if he wasn't a cop. Maybe he was something else, like a blackmailer or some-thing—or an agent of Benny Torrance, out for revenge. Whatever. Never mind. If he had some proof of who Shannon was, let him bring it out. If he wanted to make a play, let him make it. Christ, couldn't Shannon have ten seconds to hold his girl's hand at the fair like anybody would? Was that too goddamn much to ask from the universe?

He reached the wheel-of-fortune booth, where the guy had been. He was breathless, tense and sweating, the wheel's colored lights flashing in his eyes and the barker calling to place your bets, take your chances. Jostled by some dick-swinging trucker who was swaggering past, Shannon turned unsteadily, scanning the people moving along the line of game booths toward an octo-pus ride—eight seats spinning round and round and up and down on the end of mechanical arms.

He saw—he thought he saw—the back of that bald head in the crowd by the octopus. He went after it, turning his body and us-ing his hands to work his way past the people jammed up in front of him.

He reached the octopus, the seats going up and down above him, the calliope music playing loudly in his ears. But the bald guy was already gone, lost in the crowd . . .

No, wait, there he was. At the carnival's exit. Walking fast into the parking lot, walking toward that car of his, that same pale green Crown Victoria with the scrape on the side. Shannon saw its red taillights blink once as the guy pressed the button on his key to unlock it. No chance to catch up to him now, no chance to stop him.

Shannon stood helplessly, jostled by the crowd. He watched helplessly as the guy pulled the car door open and lowered himself inside.

A moment later, the Ford was pulling away.

When Shannon got back to the carousel, the boy, Michael, was leaning against his mother's jeans and sobbing. He was clutching her leg with one hand and clutching his stuffed frog to his runny nose with the other.

"He thought you left," Teresa told Shannon. She didn't sound angry or anything, but she gave him a look of deep meaning, and Shannon understood that this was some kind of big deal because of the kid's father being dead and all. He felt bad about it. He had to force his thoughts back from his run across the carnival, back from that bastard making his getaway in the Ford. He had to force his attention back to the boy—who really did look pretty pitiful clutching his buck-fifty stuffed frog like that.

Shannon knelt in front of him, put his hand on the kid's shoulder. "Hey, hey, hey," he said. "I'm not going anywhere."

But the minute he said it, he felt something dark open inside him. Because it was a lie, wasn't it? He was a fraud—a fugitive fraud with a murder rap hanging over his head. And with this bald guy after him, this new life of his was sure to fall apart at some point. And then he *would* be going somewhere, maybe forever.

The little boy snuffled against his mother's leg, looking at him through his tears, waiting to be told that everything was okay. That's when it hit Shannon full force: if his new life *did* fall apart—or, all right, *when* it fell apart—it wouldn't just fall apart for him now but for this boy, too, maybe for Teresa, too, if she gave a damn, but for this boy more than anyone.

Kneeling there with his hand on the poor kid's shoulder, Shannon lifted his eyes. He saw Teresa looking down at him, and he understood that she was thinking pretty much the same thing.

By the time he took them home to the old rectory, it was late, dark. Teresa sent the boy inside to his grandfather and stood alone with Shannon at the front door.

"Thank you, Henry. That was a nice day," she said.

He could see clearly enough what she was going to say next, and he was desperate to stop her. So he stepped close and took her face in one hand and kissed her. It was no good. It was all wrong, because of the desperation and because he was just doing it to shut her up. Still, she let him do it, and for a few moments he had the drunken sense of what it might've been like, the feel of her mouth giving way and her hair tangling in his fingers and the sweetness of the thing starting up between them, not just the kiss, but the whole thing.

She must've felt some of it, too, because, at first, her hand lifted as if she wanted to take hold of him. But she didn't. It was all wrong, and she didn't touch him. After a while, her hand sank down again. Shannon broke the kiss off and stepped away.

"Oh . . . Listen, Henry . . ." she began—because he hadn't stopped her from saying what she was going to say, he'd just delayed it.

"I know, I know," he said. "Look . . ."

"No, I just have to be sure, you know? It's different when you have a kid. I can't pretend I'm just some girl again and he isn't there."

"No, no, you're his mother, I understand that."

"I can't have people come and then leave. Guys, I mean. I can't just start up with them and let him care about them and then have them leave. I can't let him go through something like that again."

What about us? He wanted to argue with her. *What about you and me—wanting this, wanting each other? Don't* we *get anything?* But he was embarrassed to sound selfish in front of her. "Look," he said, "about what happened at the carnival . . ." But he floundered, because what could he say that wouldn't be a lie?

She smiled her screwy, comical smile and silenced him by putting her hand on his arm, shaking her head. "Oh, you know, do me a favor, Henry . . . I mean, it's not just Michael. I'm not that steady myself. So do me a favor and don't tell me unless I need to know. It's just—if you're leaving, you know, say so. And if you're not, say so. And if you're not sure, then just say that and I'll wait till you know. I will. I mean it. But I can't just start up and have you leave and let him go through that again. I don't think I can go through it again, either. So do me a favor, okay? Just . . ."

He wanted to say something, to answer her, but he couldn't think of a single thing worth saying, not one thing that wouldn't be a lie and make matters worse in the end. So he just had to stand there and take it, stand there knowing that this was good-bye between them, that he was going to lose her. It was a crushing weight of sadness inside him—he wouldn't have believed how bad it felt. As good as it felt to hold her hand at the carousel, that's how bad this felt now. Man, he could've killed that bald-headed bastard for showing up like that. It had ruined everything. Who the hell was he? Why the hell couldn't he just leave him alone?

"Okay," he said thickly. It was all he could say.

Her hand dropped from his arm. She nodded, still smiling but her eyes damp. He stood there another moment. He wanted to tell her how he felt about her, how crazy he was about her and that he loved her—really loved her—but so what? What good was that to either of them? In a way, that would be the worst thing he could say, the worst of all.

He just turned finally—turned with the crushing weight inside him—and walked back up the path to his car.

HE PARKED THE Civic down the street from his brownstone. He shut the car off and sat in it a while, just sort of weighing the car keys in his hand and staring through the windshield.

Though it was not even ten, the area was eerily quiet. It was like that around here, no street life after dark. There were a lot of reasons for that. The worst of the wreckage was right nearby and the gangs of boys might come around prowling, those flood-punks who would kill you for a dime. None of the local nightspots had survived the disaster, so the neighborhood's young people had to drive far afield to find a bar or a club—and the old people weren't much for going out anyway. Plus it was Sunday, the work week beginning tomorrow. So it was quiet.

Shannon sat and weighed the keys in his hand and stared. He was down, way down. Heartbroken, to put it plainly. He wished none of this had ever happened. He wished he'd never come to this city, never carved the angel, never met Teresa—that most of all. He had always known deep down this new life couldn't be real, couldn't last. The bald guy—the cops—someone—he had always known someone would turn up sooner or later and expose him. But it wouldn't have been so bad if he hadn't met Teresa. He couldn't put it into words exactly, but it was like, when he was with her, he could see the life he was supposed to have lived, the shape of the life he was meant for, like a beautiful city in the far distance, a beautiful crystal city in the mist. To find her and then lose her — to have the mist close over that city again just as he'd seemed about to break through to it — that was a real piece of mean luck, cruel, as if the gods were tantalizing him, entertaining themselves with his emotional torture.

He stared out the windshield. Slowly, his left hand went to his right arm and he massaged the spot where the old scars had been. He had a hint in him of that old feeling, that crawly feeling that told him he had to get out, had to do something, find some action, anything, fast. He thought for a moment maybe he'd go somewhere, drive somewhere, some bar where he could get a girl maybe. But he was too down for that, too down in the dumps. He just wanted to go home. It hurt to think about Teresa, but that was all he wanted to do, just go home and lie on his bed and think about her.

He sighed heavily and got out of the car. He walked heavily down the silent sidewalk, his sneakers padding, the only footsteps in the night. There were sirens in the distance. There were always sirens. And when he glanced up, he could see the pale yellow glow of fire on the dark horizon. Something was always burning somewhere in this city. He reached the brownstone's stoop and heavily climbed.

His apartment was on the third floor, three long flights. The decaying wooden banister. The peeling yellow walls. The faded runners beneath his feet. Then he was on the landing. Then down the hall to the wooden door, the keys in his hand.

He stepped over the threshold into the dark apartment. He reached for the light switch as the door swung shut.

He didn't see the man who hit him, never knew the blow was coming. That made it much worse. Before he had a clue, a fist like concrete drove into his belly. He wasn't tensed for it, so it just drove deep. The breath was forced out of him and he doubled over, dropping his keys, clutching his gut, stumbling once in the dark and falling, his knee cracking on the wooden floor, his shoulder hitting the side of the bed as he went down.

He lay there gasping, still clutching himself. The light came on. He had a second to see the lower half of the man's legs, the black shoes, the green slacks. A second to think wildly, *The bald guy . . . ?* Then the guy swooped down and grabbed the front of his windbreaker. Shannon was a big man, but his attacker hauled him easily off the floor. Shannon saw his face. It was not the bald guy. This guy was much worse, much bigger, meaner. He punched Shannon in the head with his concrete fist. Shannon went down again, in a rattled, painful daze, the light suddenly glaring, lancing into his eyes.

The man towered above him. No, it was not the bald guy. It was another guy, big, really big. A linebacker gone to seed. Acne-scarred face and a crewcut that made it look like his hair was standing on end with pure, electric malevolence. And the look on his face—oh Jesus—Shannon was already hurting, but that look weakened him even more with panic and despair because he could tell: the guy dug this shit. He was going to enjoy it.

So in the same second he saw him, Shannon was desperately looking for a way out. His panic and the vibrating pain in his head made the room nauseatingly bright and clear to him. With aching, pulsing clarity, he saw the wood floors and the gray walls and—oh Jesus—the shades on the windows pulled down so no one could see what was about to happen and the rumpled white side of the mattress above him and the dark shadows beneath the bed and the pale, colorless braid rug the big thug was standing on and the red tool bag lying against the mirror on the closet door.

And, at the same time his panicking mind searched for a means of escape, it searched also for an explanation, trying to understand what was happening, racing wildly through the possibilities . . . The cops . . . Benny Torrance . . . the bald guy . . . who the hell sent this thug . . . ?

Then the big man, smirking, opened a knife, and Shannon's thoughts were cut off like a door had shut on them.

The knife was a no-shit killing tool, a short tanto blade unfolding from a butt-pommeled black hilt built to grip. As the big man opened it with his two hands, his white linen jacket brushed open and Shannon saw there was a 9mm Glock in his belt holster, too. With that and the look on the guy's face Shannon got the whole picture like prophecy: he was about to enter a long tunnel of pain and come out the other end dead.

Crazy-scared, Shannon managed to grunt, "What do you want?" Clutching his gut, his head throbbing.

"We're gonna talk," the man said. "But first, you gotta find out I'm serious."

"You got the wrong guy, man."

"You're not the wrong guy."

And Shannon had no answer because who was he? And who was the thug after? Shannon? Henry Conor? Some other guy he wasn't even supposed to be?

But that was the end of the conversation, anyway. The guy knelt down over him, his eyes shining with mean. Holding the knife in his right hand, he grabbed Shannon's ear with his left and hauled his head off the floor, ready to cut the ear off.

Shannon punched him in the balls as hard as he could, but the guy was so tough that only made him grunt, so Shannon hit him again in the throat this time and that got him. The guy gagged and let Shannon go. He clutched his throat, kneeling there, his eyes rolling. But he still had the knife in his hand.

Shannon quickly rolled away from him toward the middle of the room. He was climbing to his feet, his gut screaming with pain, when he saw the guy go for his gun.

The guy still had the knife in his right hand, so he went for the nine with his left. All the same, he drew it smoothly and fast. But by then, Shannon was standing. He lashed a kick at the guy's hand—got him—and the gun went flying—under the bed, damn it, out of sight, out of reach. So Shannon made a move to go after the guy while he was still kneeling, but the guy slashed at him with the knife, driving him back, and then came off his knee and stood.

People joke about how dumb it is to bring a knife to a gun fight but guess what: close quarters, a knife is deadlier if the guy knows how to use it, and this guy did. He was on Shannon fast, in a split second, keeping the knife point toward his eyes so it was hard to see. Shannon only saved himself by grabbing the desk chair. Lifting it. Jabbing the legs at the guy to keep him at bay. The two men shifted so that Shannon's back was to the closet. There was no sound in the room but their breathing. Then the guy managed to get hold of the chair leg with his free hand. He was strong and started to rip the chair out of Shannon's grip.

Shannon held the chair to build up resistance, then let it go suddenly, giving it an extra shove. The guy grunted and staggered back, stumbled, fell on his ass—but never let go of that knife and was already scrambling to his feet.

Shannon turned and leapt to the tool bag on the floor by the closet: the red Milwaukee bag with the hammers and wrenches in the outside pouches. He bent down and grabbed a framing hammer—a real thunder-club with a thick wooden handle and twenty-eight ounces of steel on the end.

Even as he grabbed it, even as he straightened, he saw the guy's reflection in the closet mirror, the guy rushing at him with murder in his eyes and the knife held low.

Shannon spun, whipping the hammer around as he did. He had the guy in the mirror so he could gauge where he was, and the guy hadn't thought of that and was charging top speed to get at Shannon before he had a chance to turn and spot him.

The hammerhead went full force into the guy's temple with a soft and liquid and awful sound. All at the same time, the guy's charge stopped and his eyes went white and his mouth fell open and he dropped to the floor twitching and shuddering and shitting himself, and then was dead.

Shannon had never killed a man before, but it didn't bother him much, not in the circumstances. What did get to him was the craziness of the situation. The dead guy on the floor and his own phony identity and no conceivable reason for any of it, the whole what-the-fuck of it all.

Panting, he staggered over to the bed and sat down on it hard. He held his head in his hands, staring at the body on the floor, which had stopped twitching now and just lay there stinking of shit and still. The malevolence and sadism were gone from the dead man's face. He just looked slack and stupid, staring at the ceiling with his mouth open like an idiot. Shannon wondered if anyone had heard their struggle . . . but there was so much to think about, he couldn't think about any of it at first. What the hell just happened? What the hell should he do now?

He covered his face with his hands and blew into them, thinking, *Okay, okay.* Trying to gather himself and figure it out. When he looked again, the dead guy was still there, still staring up at the ceiling, and Shannon thought, *Okay* again and decided he had to search the guy, find some ID, find out who he was.

He got off the bed and went to the body. Knelt down by it—cautiously—not that he thought the guy was alive or anything—there was no chance of that—but he had this horror-movie image in his head of the guy leaping up at him anyway, dead or no. Flinching at the stench of shit, he held the guy's jacket open and went into the pocket. He found what he thought was the guy's wallet—but no such luck.

He drew the thing out and when he saw it, he groaned aloud in misery. It was not a wallet. It was a leather ID holder. There was a police badge pinned to it, a detective's badge. Inside was the guy's police ID card: Detective Glenn Gutterson.

Shannon had killed a cop.

IT WAS A LONG time before the full extent of the catastrophe occurred to him. Oh, he knew it was a disaster right away, but it was a long time before he could take it all in. With the adrenaline still pumping through him and the cop just lying there dead on the floor, he couldn't think clearly. But he had to think. He had to figure out what to do.

He knew right away he couldn't risk calling the cops—not just because of who he was and who he wasn't, but because he didn't know what this was all about. It might be about anything and he didn't know which way the danger lay, so he just had to keep to himself. Which meant he was stuck with it, stuck with a dead cop and no one to turn to, and a murder rap waiting for him if he zigged when he should zag. That sent some more adrenaline through him. Because maybe someone had heard them fighting and was already dialing 911. Maybe the sirens were about to start up in the distance or maybe right outside or maybe there'd just be a sudden pounding on the door . . .

And what then? What about Teresa? He wasn't thinking clearly, so it took him a few moments to think about her. He was sitting on the bed again by then. Staring at the body, not even seeing it now. Just staring and rubbing the heel of his hand back and forth over his mouth, never mind that his lips were already raw from it. Thinking: What about Teresa and the boy and Applebee? And what about his job and his new life like fairy tale?

Well, that's over with, he thought.

That's when he began to see the scope of this thing. It was global, wasn't it, a total Hiroshima of his hopes and dreams. The new life, the girl, the angel on the mantelpiece—they were all just ashes now. It was a cluster-fuck so epic he couldn't even feel bad about it. What was the point in feeling bad?

Well, maybe he'd feel bad later. Maybe, it occurred to him, he was in shock now. He sure wasn't thinking clearly. It only now occurred to him with any urgency that he really had to get out of here. The sirens might start, the knock might come any minute. That was the main thing, he thought, sitting there, staring at the dead guy, rubbing his mouth raw with his hand.

His new life was over. He had to go.

The things he saw that night—the awful life of the night in that ruined city—it all seemed strange and dreamlike to him as he passed. Everything seemed at once faraway and yet part of him, faraway and yet connected to him, as if it were an emanated dream, a dream that had projected itself onto the world, a world outside that had somehow originated in the nightmare factories of his mind. The tilted, blackened buildings. The slumped buildings with blackened windows like eyes. A building he came to suddenly around a corner with thick black smoke pouring out of it, and crackling, hoarsely whispering flames licking red out of the belly of the blackness. There was a man in the upstairs window, staring out, not even calling for help, not even caring, just staring out as if he was already dead. There were no firemen. No sirens coming. Just a few scrawny beasts of boys watching it like a movie, laughing and exclaiming and slapping hands. He saw another gang of boys in the mouth of an alley not far from there. They were crouched over something alive, like vampires feeding. He saw legs kicking weakly out of the slow melee, flashes of skin and blood. A man leaning against the alley wall smoked a cigarette and watched. A girl crouched at his feet, fearful and fascinated, bright-eyed, helpless and aroused. Shannon moved on.

He heard machine-gun fire. On an empty street, he saw girls and boys-dressed-as-girls taking gangly thugs in and out of an abandoned brownstone. He heard sirens. On a street with no lights at all, he saw an ambulance loom out of the dusky distance, its flashers whirling red. It rushed past him and in the screaming noise and strobic red glow, he saw the silhouette of a man lying in the gutter, clawing at the pavement. And then the ambulance went past and the man sank back into the darkness.

It all seemed far away and it all seemed to come from inside him, his heart enacted in the shadows, his brooding fantasies brought to life. He walked—he didn't know how long—deep into the night. Carrying his tool bag, only with clothes and toiletries in it instead of tools. And the gun, the big cop's nine. He had almost left the apartment when he remembered it, had the door open and his foot on the threshold, when he had stopped and gone back and fetched it from under the bed.

He didn't take the car. They'd have the car made too fast. He'd drive and drive and then they'd put out one call and have him. He knew he wasn't thinking clearly, but he knew enough to leave the car. His cell phone, too: he'd dumped that in a sewer. So he walked and walked, disconnected from everything, and the city was like his dreams playing out all around him.

In the end, he found himself in a neighborhood of small houses ruined by the flood. He didn't know how late it was. He looked at his watch and he still didn't know, it didn't register. A damp breeze that smelled of sewage reached him. The black of the broad sky seemed as if it was slowly being stained from within with a lighter indigo—so he thought it might be nearly dawn.

In any case, he was exhausted now. He looked around him. There were no lights anywhere. The houses were lopsided wrecks, all empty. Animals moved over fields of debris—not just rats and squirrels, not just the bats jiggering in the indigo sky—but big, loping, red-eyed creatures that might have been dogs or something else nosing through the garbage, and great hunched, brooding birds that might have been vultures, and other bony creeping beasts that might have been children or something else.

Shannon made his way to one house that stood slanted like a man with a shortened leg. He saw it in starlight against the sky. Its broken windows stared. Its door hung open. The door flapped and banged and gasped—the latch catching and letting go—as the damp wind smelling of sewage blew stronger.

Shannon went to it. He stood in the doorway and held the door open. It smelled no worse than the outdoors and he could feel the emptiness of it. Nothing moving anywhere. As his eyes adjusted, he could see the emptiness, too. No furniture. Nothing. The place was stripped bare.

He stepped in and pulled the door shut behind him, pulled it hard until it held. He sat down and made a place for himself on the dark floor. He lay his head on the bag. He pulled his windbreaker tight around him. He wasn't thinking clearly. He was worn out and had to sleep. Then it would be better.

He curled up on his side, shivering and clutching his coat. For a moment, his face crumpled as if he would cry, because he had witnessed his own heart in the night city and everything was ashes.

Identity like stain.

PART V

THE BALD GUY

AT HIS FIRST sight of the dead Gutterson, Lieutenant Ramsey had an uncomfortable premonition of nemesis: a sense some evil fate was working against him. He pushed the idea aside as self-defeating superstition. He looked down at Gutterson and thought: *Just good old-fashioned, all-too-human incompetence, that's all.*

Gutterson lay on his back, staring at the ceiling with his mouth hanging open. His head was dented in and there was a small pool of blood under one ear. There was the smell of shit. Ramsey shook his head and sighed. What an idiot.

"Neighbor heard the fight last night. Didn't think to call it in." This was from the wiry caffeine-waif Strawberry, the detective who'd caught the case. He gestured at a short, saggy man looking mournful and self-important in the corner: the building superintendent. "Neighbor mentioned it to the super this morning. Super came up to check it out, dialed nine one one."

Ramsey nodded down at Gutterson. *Jesus.* Acid ate at his stomach lining as his mind went through the various unraveling possibilities, all the ways this could get back to him, bite him on the ass. Henry Conor on the run now, Peter Patterson dead, Reverend Skyles in prison . . . He was reckoning each logarithm of disaster like *click, click, click.* Inwardly grimacing at the acid.

On the outside, all the while, he wore a look of grim seriousness, a show of controlled moral outrage. It was the same look Strawberry wore on a face that usually fluttered and darted with hummingbird energy. It was the same look the two uniforms had on *their* faces and the same one that was on the face of Strawberry's gym-rat partner, James. Even the CSU babe taking pictures of the closet wore the girl version of that look. Even the ME's guy, when he showed up, wore it. It was the official look you wore when one of the animals killed a police. It was a look that said: *I am grieved like you, angry like you, but I am all business, too, a sword of justice, and we will have our revenge together.* It was all show with Ramsey, of course. Personally, he didn't give a shit, because he knew the truth here and, anyway, he had other problems. But he still had to wear the official look. It was more or less a departmental requirement. It was what you wore to a cop-killing.

"Any idea what he was working on?" he asked, as if he didn't know.

Strawberry shook his head. "Found a folder in his car with some casework, a picture, some names and places. Apartment apparently belongs to Henry Conor. A carpenter. Been working for Handsome Harry Hand over at the development. Hit him with that hammer."

It took all of Ramsey's self-discipline to keep from laughing here. Puns about Gutterson getting nailed, getting hammered, getting shellacked flashing through his mind. But really, seriously: How do you show up to deal death with a nine in your pants and get taken down by a carpenter with a hammer? For the sake of his dignity, Gutterson was just lucky he hadn't been stapled to death.

"Conor must've run for it when he saw what he did," Strawberry went on. "Left his car. It's parked outside. Took Gutterson's gun, though."

"I'm personally in charge," the lieutenant announced portentously. He knew that would make an impression and it did. Strawberry answered him with one grim nod, impressed and gratified, because an animal had killed a police and now the lieutenant himself was personally taking charge. Yeah, boo-ra, whoop-de-doo.

Whatever. Ramsey needed to get out of here before he showed them all what he really thought of this mess.

He gave another look down at Gutterson. Gutterson staring stupidly with his mouth open. Gutterson stupidly dead. What a moron.

Ramsey frowned around the room with murderous virtue—one more official display for the troops while the acid ate away the inside of him.

Finally, when he figured he'd given them enough of the old moral outrage bullshit, he headed for the door.

So it turned out there was a problem with this business of moving your minions through the force of your invisible will: idiot minions. Send Gutterson to get some information and kill a guy, and he winds up some carpenter's do-it-yourself home improvement project. It was a while before Ramsey could stop shaking his head and smiling to himself with wry misery.

Still, the more he thought about it, the more he thought there were angles here, unintended positive consequences. The situation was now set up so that Ramsey could get a lot accomplished simply by doing his job. Conor, for instance, had been pretty well neutralized. He had nowhere to go. He couldn't reach out to the feds or the media. Augie Lancaster had the local feds and the media in his pocket. Buses, trains, planes, rental cars—they were all being covered. And there was no chance he would make it out of town on foot either. The first time he stuck his head up, any cop who spotted him would pop him like a duck at a shooting gallery: up, *pop*, he's gone. So the only real problem now—now that Gutterson had shit the bed like this—was finding out exactly what Conor knew and whether anyone else in town knew it. Not the street creatures. They didn't matter. Who would they talk to? Who would care? But there might be others. There was too much mystery around this carpenter to know for sure.

Ramsey murdered Peter Patterson.

Loose ends—that's what it was all about now. Conor was more or less history, but there might still be loose ends.

"He have friends?" Ramsey asked.

He was talking to Handsome Harry Hand now. Little basketball of a guy with a monkey face. They were in the development's messy site trailer, standing together beside the bulletin board. Guy named Joe Whaley was over behind his desk, tilted back in his chair, hands laced in back of his head, watching. Whaley looked like a man who did a lot of watching: a big man with I've-got-your-number eyes. The way he was studying Ramsey, Ramsey figured him for the kind of guy who would know things. But Harry was the boss. So he talked to Harry.

"Any guys he hung out with regularly?"

"Not really," Harry said. "You know, guys he talked to. But he kept himself to himself. Didn't socialize much or . . ." Hand appealed to Joe Whaley with a look. Joe Whaley was the head man on the site.

Joe Whaley pulled a face and Ramsey said, "What? You know something?"

Whaley shrugged. Reached down behind himself to scratch his back. "I think he had *something* going. I don't know what for sure. Something that kept him busy on the weekends, though."

"Yeah," said Harry. "Moonlighting. I got him that. Guy wanted someone who could carve things. You know, work with wood. Conor could do that. Applebee, the guy's name was. I remember 'cause he sent me a letter. Like a thank-you note on a little frilly card."

"You save it?"

"No, but I remember. Cause he had this handwriting."

"Handwriting like . . ."

"Like a girl. And he sent this little frilly card, like I bought him a birthday present or something. Frederick Applebee."

Once again, Joe Whaley made a face, wagged his head. Ramsey caught it out of the corner of his eye.

"What?"

"I don't know. Nothing. I just think there was something else."

"Something like . . ."

"You know, like a girl. It wasn't just a job, that's what I'm saying. It wasn't just moonlighting. I think there was a girl."

"Which you know because . . . ?"

"I don't know, I think. It's just, when you watch a guy, you can tell, that's all. When there's a girl. You can tell."

Ramsey considered. Joe Whaley looked to him like the sort of person who *would* watch a guy and who *could* tell.

"Thanks," he said. Then he said it again to Harry Hand.

He stepped out of the trailer and squinted into the morning sun. The frames of houses rose against the blue sky. The figures of men up on the beams, dark against the brightness. Hammers rising and falling. Big power tools juddering against their bodies. Whapping and buzzing everywhere. All that federal money pouring into the city, you could count on graft master Handsome Harry to get his share. Even the air smelled fresher here. Ramsey wondered who Harry had paid off to get that.

He held the edge of his hand against his forehead, shielding his eyes from the glare. Watching the work with casual interest, his stomach burning.

A girl, he was thinking. *Yeah, that would be a loose end all right.*

IN THE DAYLIGHT, Shannon sat cross-legged on the empty floor and tried to think the situation through. It wasn't easy. His mind was clearer now, but the situation—that was a mess. Here he was in a new town with a new face, all his records wiped out, even his DNA records changed. But from the very start, some bald guy had been following him everywhere. Then, on the night he finally chased the bald guy away, up showed some cop and tried to cut his ear off. What the hell? How did that make sense? Shannon had known a cop or two who would cut your ear off if it served their purposes. He'd even known a couple of cops who would cut your ear off for a laugh. But it was not the usual coplike thing. He did not imagine your average, honest carpenter citizen would get house calls from cops who wanted to cut his ear off. So someone, in other words, knew who he really was or thought he was someone else they knew. Or something.

That was as far as he could get with unraveling that tangle, but there was another area in question, too: what should he do now? Everything inside him—every instinct—was telling him to run. Run fast, keep running. Well, no shit, Sherlock. There was no happy ending to any scenario that involved him staying here. If the bald guy and the cop already knew who he was, then he had a target on his back. And if they had mistaken him for someone else, he couldn't clear himself without revealing who he really was—which could mean death row. In either case, he'd killed a cop, which, in a town like this, came with a mandatory sentence of death-while-resisting-arrest, hold the judge and jury. So it came down to this: running away meant a lifetime of soulless rooms and guttery darkness, but at least it was a lifetime. Running away was the only option if he didn't want to end up dead. It was a no-brainer.

And yet . . .

All night, sometimes in dreams, sometimes in tortured dream-like thoughts, the words had come back to him: *Identity like stain.* The dreams and thoughts were all about Teresa. Teresa seeing on the television news that he'd killed a cop and disappeared or been gunned down by the angry police. They would call him a murderer, a key suspect in the Hernandez home invasion massacre, an accomplice in the slaughter of an entire family. He dreamed Teresa's face when she heard that. And the little boy's face when *he* heard it. And Applebee's. And the face of the angel on the mantelpiece. *Identity like stain.*

He tossed and turned on the floor of the abandoned house in a city full of gunshots and sirens and silent suffering, and he knew he couldn't live with that. If he ran away now, he would run forever, a murderer in Teresa's eyes, a monster to the boy. And okay, he was a lowlife thief, a scumbag nothing, but he wasn't a murderer. He wasn't a monster. He'd lived a crappy life, okay, but there was this other life inside him, this good life, this life he was supposed to have lived. It was like another road running next to the road he was on. When he met Teresa, it was as if the roads crossed for a minute, a day, a couple of weeks, and he saw for a while how things could've been. If he ran now, he would be running down the same old road and leaving the road of that other life behind. He would be right back where he was before the foreigner changed his face. A hunted murderer in the eyes of the world, in Teresa's eyes, in the boy's eyes. Running forever. *Identity like stain.*

Oh, it was too much for him to figure out. He should just get out, hit the wind, that was the smart thing. But, man, he hated it, hated thinking about it, hated the idea of going back to that life. He couldn't have Teresa. He knew that. He couldn't have that other good life. It was too late for that now. He knew. But at least let him be himself in front of her. Let her see that he wasn't a murderer, that he hadn't done Hernandez, that the dead cop was self-defense. Let him clear his name of the killings at least and put some honest picture of his sad self before her. If she saw him on the TV news as he was, as the low thief he really was, well, she could understand that, couldn't she? She could forgive that. She could explain it to the boy and they would both forgive him. *Henry just went down the wrong road,* she would say. *He would've gone down the good road if he could've found it. He just didn't know the way, that's all.* And they would forgive him. That's all he wanted now. Let her see him as he was, only as bad as he was. Let him stay and show all of them who he was, so he wouldn't be evil in their eyes.

Are you fucking crazy? he asked himself, sitting there. *Are you willing to die to do that?* And the answer came boiling up out of him: *Yes! Let me die in the life I was meant for. Keep your identity. Keep your stain. Let her see me as I am. Let me die in the life I was supposed to live.*

It was strange. These thoughts of his—they were all kinds of disjointed and messed up and emotional. But when he was finished, it was as if he'd gone through the whole thing step by step. It was as if he'd figured it out logically. Because now, he knew exactly what he was going to do.

He untangled his legs and stood up off the floor. He took the gun, the cop's gun, the nine-a, out of his tool bag. He chambered a round and checked the safety. He worked the weapon into the back of his belt and pulled his windbreaker down so that it was covered.

Then he walked out of the empty house into the morning.

In all the gray ruins of the city—with all its houses washed to muddy rubble by the flood and its buildings burned to skeletal cinders—the Government Center in the east end of town was shockingly vivid, colorful, and whole. One structure here had a golden dome that glinted in the sunlight. Another was made of white marble with fluted Roman pilasters, graceful and precise in every detail. Yet another had an impressively long wall of tinted windows reflecting the grassy green park with its red and orange and yellow tulips. In the park, men and women dressed in light spring pastels walked along the asphalt paths to glass doors that flashed back the morning as they opened and closed. The Government Center was a weirdly living thing pulsing on the dead city, like some kind of exotic spider feeding on the gray, colorless shape of the butterfly wrapped in its web.

Shannon sat on a bench at a bus stop across the street. His eyes moved over the crowd in the park. It was a bad setup for him. Lots of cops patrolling the park paths, keeping their wary eyes on the building entranceways and the wrought-iron gate in the spiked fence at the park's perimeter. The cops made Shannon nervous, but he acted casual, his arm draped over the bench back, his legs crossed at the knee. These cops weren't searching for him, he told himself. This was the last place they'd look for him, the last wide-open place they'd think he'd come. *These guys were after terrorists and whatnot,* he thought. They were watching out for the random nutjob who couldn't feed his family and came after the government with a gun, because there was no one else left who had a job or a dime.

So he stayed on the bench while long minutes passed. Other people gathered at the bus stop and buses came, obscuring his view. When the buses hissed and rumbled away, the other people were gone and there he still was. Trying to look casual. Glancing nervously at whatever cop was passing near. But mostly—the whole time—he kept watch on the one tower of gleaming steel across from the park's near corner; he kept watch on the restaurant on the tower's bottom floor: the World Café.

That had been the name on the receipt in the bald guy's car. Shannon had seen it when he'd peeked through the scarred Crown Victoria's window. It was the only clue he had to where the bald guy was—and the bald guy was his only clue to why the cop had come after him to cut off his ear, to why he was in the same old fugitive cock-up again when he was supposed to be *new mang*.

At first, he had thought the clue was kind of tenuous. The World Café might be a chain. There might be a dozen of them in the city. He was all prepared to go tromping from one café to another, describing the bald guy to the waiters, hoping for a hit. But it turned out better than that. There was only one World Café, and when he saw where it was, he had hopes the bald guy would show up here sooner or later. This was not the kind of place you traveled to. It was a place for regulars, for people who worked in the Government Center, probably mostly for people who worked in the steel tower, which had letters above the door: Federal Building.

Shannon staked the place out for an hour and a half, so he had a lot of time to think about those letters. Was the bald guy a fed? What were the feds after him for? Why would the feds send a city cop to cut his ear off and kill him? Who the hell did they think he was? Or if they knew who he was, what the hell did they want from him?

No answers. He couldn't come up with a one. So he waited and worried about it and kept an eye on the cops and kept an eye on the Federal Building and the World Café until finally—sure enough—up showed the bald guy.

He came out of the federal building, walking quickly. Same guy, definitely. Same junkie-thin slime-dog in yet another cheap suit, and with his chromey dome glinting in the noonday sun. He didn't go into the World Café. He headed off along the sidewalk instead, parallel to the park. Within moments, he had nearly lost himself in the flow of pedestrians, his bald head appearing and disappearing in the gathering lunchtime crowd.

Shannon unfolded himself quickly from the bus stop bench. Dodging traffic, he crossed the street and went after the guy. He took an angry satisfaction in it. All this time, the bald guy had been following him, now the tables were turned. And it wasn't like at the fair either. He had a plan now. He was going to get the bald guy alone, catch him off guard, corner him, ask him what the hell — fed or not, get the truth out of him. Just thinking about it, just being on the move, brought his anxiety down from the boil and made him feel better. The bald guy had come to represent the whole situation to him, the way it always came back to the same thing, being hunted, being on the run, *identity like stain*.

He reached the sidewalk that ran beside the park's iron fence, directly across from where the bald guy was. Both sidewalks were crowded and getting more crowded every minute as people poured out of their offices for lunch. It was easy for Shannon to blend with the crowd, hold back, and watch from a safe distance as the bald guy hurried along across the street and ahead of him. Shannon had every reason to feel sure the bald guy didn't know he was there. He did feel sure.

Only it turned out he was wrong.

The bald guy reached the corner about a half block in the lead, with Shannon across the street and behind him, watching him over the heads of the pedestrians. The bald guy stopped and waited for the light to change, so Shannon pulled up in the middle of the block, pretending to admire the golden dome through the fence. When the light did change, the bald guy crossed the street and then turned the corner. Shannon had to cross in the middle of the block to go after him, running to beat the traffic. The bald guy continued on down the side street, disappearing from view. Shannon fought through the moving crowds. He reached the corner while the light was still good. He crossed and followed.

He found himself now on a narrower street. There were office buildings all of dark glass to his right. Beside him to his left, taking up the whole block, there was a large parking structure, three stories of featureless concrete. Here, suddenly, away from the Government Center, there were a lot fewer people on the sidewalk. Between Shannon and the bald guy now, there were only a bum and a businesswoman walking along. But the bald guy still kept moving with his quick, determined stride, and it still seemed to Shannon that he was unaware of being trailed.

Then, without warning, the bald guy glanced back over his shoulder as if he sensed Shannon behind him. Shannon froze, startled. In that frozen instant, the bald guy darted sideways and vanished into the parking structure.

Shannon cursed. What now? Had he seen him? Had he somehow known he was there? All at once, he went from having the drop on the bald guy to not knowing what was what, who had the upper hand. It gave him a hot, flashing sensation of frustration and anger. This was the way things kept going for him. Well, not this time. The bald guy wasn't getting away.

Shannon didn't hesitate. He started running, shoving the bum out of his way, getting an acrid whiff of him as he went past. He ran full tilt down the sunlit sidewalk. Reached the entrance to the lot, an archway in the white wall. He charged through the door into the shadows under a concrete stairwell.

He peered out across a still, dark cavern of parked cars, his eyes flicking to the movements of pedestrians here and there. No bald guy. Then, with a sort of instinct, he glanced up—just in time to see black shoes hurrying up the switch-backing stairs above him. He started up the stairs. Already the bald guy was out of sight, though Shannon still heard his footsteps. He followed the sound to the second-story landing and there heard a heavy door opening above him. He charged up toward the third story, the last story. As he reached the landing, he saw its big metal door swing closed. It shut with an echoing metallic *clack*.

Shannon was about to charge through—he *was* charging through, one hand turning the doorknob, the other pushing at the solid gray metal of the door. But as the door opened, some inner sense, some unspoken logic, told him he was being lured into a trap. He kept pushing the door with his left hand, but his right went behind him, to the gun in his belt under his windbreaker. He was drawing it out even as he pushed into the garage.

And it was a trap, sure enough. The bald guy was hiding in a little alcove off the garage roof. As Shannon came clear of the door, the bald guy came out from behind it and jammed a gun against Shannon's temple.

"Fuck with me," he said.

Gritting his teeth in frustration and rage, Shannon figured, *All right, I will.* He whipped up his own Beretta and aimed it at the bald guy's face.

The stairwell door swung shut.

The two men locked eyes over the guns. Then Shannon snorted. Then the bald guy snorted. If they were going to shoot, they'd have shot by now. It was a stupid situation. But neither wanted to be the first to put his gun down, so they stayed like that, the barrels trained on one another. A standoff.

The bald guy smiled. "You're a hard case, Shannon. Most scumbags would've run. You *should've* run. You're a dumb son of a bitch." He had a hard, dark, smooth voice, a voice like asphalt.

"You know me," Shannon said to him.

"I know you, yeah. I even figured you'd turn up. I watched from the window all morning. Saw you sitting out there on the bus-stop bench. So yeah, I know you."

Shannon steadied his gun. He had a strange feeling, a strange jumble of feelings. There was the anger at this fool and the angry anticipation that he was about to get some answers and the fear about where all this was going. And then, beneath all that, there was something else, an understanding he had suppressed from the very beginning, from the very moment he got the text message from the identity man telling him to meet him in the parking lot outside of Eyes. From that very moment, somewhere down deep inside him, he had known that this whole deal made no sense. The foreigner and the white room and the idea that the Whittaker Foundation or some other mysterious "friend" had arranged for him to get a new face and new records and new life like princess in fairy tale . . . Fairy tale was right. It made no sense. When did stuff like that happen? When did new lives get bestowed on people in mall parking lots? All along, he had known the whole setup was a lie somehow. He had known it and had suppressed the knowledge, because he wanted so desperately for the lie to be true, wanted so much to be free of who he was.

Now, as he pointed the gun in the bald guy's face and the bald guy pointed his gun at him, he felt a bright, trembling sense coming up inside him like evil sunrise, a sense that he was about to get some answers to questions he had not wanted to ask.

"Who are you?" he said. "Why are you after me?"

"*After* you?" said the bald guy with a laugh. "You *are* a dumb son of a bitch. I'm not after you, dog. I'm your guardian fucking angel. If you hadn't chased me away at the fair, you wouldn't be in this mess."

Shannon blinked, trying to understand, feeling he was about to understand but couldn't yet, not yet. "What are you talking about? You sent that cop. He was gonna kill me."

"He *was* gonna kill you. But I didn't send him. I sent you."

Shannon tried to understand this, too, tried to figure it, couldn't, shook his head. "I don't . . . What . . . ? What do you mean? Who are you? Why do you know me?"

The bald guy snorted again. He shook his head, smiling a wry half smile. Then he lowered his gun and slid it into a shoulder holster under his cheap suit jacket.

"Know you," he said. "I *made* you, fool. I'm the *real* identity man."

LIEUTENANT RAMSEY WENT to see the old man first. The meeting did not go well. The very sight of the white shingled house standing whole and alone amid the rubble all around it renewed that oppressive superstitious sense of destiny or karma or something at work—that sense that had been haunting the periphery of his awareness ever since he saw Gutterson dead on the floor, the great, staring, stupid lump of him with his brainless head caved in. That whiff of nemesis then—the whiff of dead Gutterson's shit and also of nemesis—of evil fate working against him—an invisible will opposing his invisible will—had been just that, just a whiff, a faint sensation, but it grew now when he saw the white house standing there as if magically unharmed. And when the old man opened the door to his knock, it grew even stronger.

"Mr. Applebee?"

"Yes?"

Ramsey held up his badge. The old man looked at it and then looked back at him, looked in his eyes and then looked him up and down in slow, silent appraisal. He said nothing, only stepped aside to let him enter. A cop gets used to that sort of thing—being hated on sight and all—still, Ramsey had the sickening sense that it was more than that, that he had been judged on his Inner Man and found wanting. That's what made the superstitious sensation worse.

Worse, and then worse as he stepped inside. The musty Negro respectability here was smothering and accusatory, the sense of nemesis clearer and more present, almost an oppressive stringency in the atmosphere. The old man led the way past moldering upholstered furniture and piles of books about jazz and African culture. There was even an antimacassar on the back of one of the chairs, for Christ's sake. Ramsey's mother had used those. What the hell was this place? 1950?

The old man himself seemed as anachronistic as his surroundings. Ramsey had had schoolteachers like him as a child. Putting on intellectual airs and white professorial dignity. Looking down at him with disapproval, no matter how he tried to please.

Applebee led him into the dining room and positioned himself at the mantelpiece. He was wearing a sweater with patches on the elbows, and he leaned one of the patches on the mantel. Ramsey's eyes flicked up and saw the wooden carving above him, three angels, two in profile with trumpets, the third gazing down at him, his hand upraised, his face unpleasantly alive with a look that seemed to echo and amplify the old man's condemnation. *The angel of his nemesis,* Ramsey thought, before he could sweep the thought under.

"How can I help you, Lieutenant?" Applebee said quietly, and the way he said it made Ramsey feel as if he'd been called into the principal's office.

"I understand a carpenter named Henry Conor was doing some work for you."

"That's right, he was."

"He's not here now, though."

"No. He finished the job. He's done."

"So you don't know where he is?"

"He was only moonlighting here on weekends. I assume he's at his usual work or at home." Despite the neutral tone of his words, there was a sort of irony and intelligence in the old man's eyes that made Ramsey wonder what he had done to offend him.

He tried to chalk it up to the usual neighborhood suspicion of the police, rife even among the law-abiding citizens sometimes. But it seemed more than that. Had Conor said something to him?

Ramsey murdered Peter Patterson.

Ramsey glanced up at the angel on the mantelpiece. There was a sort of irony and intelligence in his eyes, too. Annoyed, Ramsey spoke more bluntly.

"He's not in his apartment," he said. "There's a dead police detective there, but not Conor. That's why we're looking for him."

Applebee took a deep breath and shifted his position. A dead detective—that was more than he had bargained for. Still, as the breath came out of him, that undertone of disapproval was there again.

"I don't know anything about that," he said. "I'm sure Henry wasn't involved in killing your detective."

"Oh, really? What makes you sure of that?"

The old man hesitated and then answered, "You get a sense of people." He said it pointedly, Ramsey thought, accusatorily—the old fart—the angel of his nemesis—or was all this just in his own imagination? "In any case," the old man went on, "he did some work for me and now he's gone. You're welcome to search the place, if you think he's hiding somewhere."

Ramsey paused, irritated, giving the old man the eye. "That shouldn't be necessary," he said. "You're here alone, I take it."

"Yes."

"You live alone?"

"I live with my daughter and grandson. She's at work and he's at school."

There was something then—something on the word *daughter*—a shifting of the eyes away and back, a slight hesitation. Ramsey caught it, understood it in a flash. Handsome Harry's site boss, Joe Whaley, had been right. There *was* a girl. Applebee's daughter. Was that the source of the hostility here? Was she the one the old man was trying to protect? That made some sense of this, at least.

"Is there anything else, Lieutenant?" Applebee said—trying to fill the silence, Ramsey thought, fearing he might have given himself away.

Ramsey considered getting tough with him but thought better of it. He wasn't ready to go so far as to put his hands on the geezer and, without that, he didn't think the old man would crack. More likely, he'd just get on the phone when Ramsey was gone and warn his daughter that the big bad policeman was on his way.

So Ramsey gave him a brief smile instead. "No," he said. "Nothing else. I'm sorry to bother you, but I did have to check." He went into his wallet, offered the old man his card. "If Conor contacts you or you hear anything, please get in touch."

Applebee took the card without a word. Without a glance at it, he stuck it in his sweater pocket.

The irony and disapproval in the old man's eyes and the irony in the eyes of the angel of judgment and his own self-aggravating superstition continued to annoy Ramsey, but he exercised his famous self-control—merely smiled again and nodded. None of it mattered, none of it was to the point. It was best in this situation just to be polite and move on.

The daughter was the one he was really after.

He knew her. The moment he set eyes on her, he understood exactly who Teresa was. *The good girl,* he thought, *the church girl.* It figured, her being Applebee's daughter and all. And it gave him fresh insight into Conor's trajectory.

He was sitting in his Charger now, parked in a no-stopping zone in back of the school where she taught. It was a Westside private school, a big old cathedral-like building of red brick with rounded mission gables. There was a fenced-off asphalt courtyard out in back with some playground equipment and some painted white lines for field games. Ramsey was parked in front of that.

The lunch hour was just passing. At the sound of a bell, the boys poured out into the yard in their neckties and the girls in their plaid skirts, all of them shouting and laughing together, a surflike roar. Ramsey was just about to get out of his car and go inside to find Teresa when he saw her step into one of the rear doorways. She stood there, watching the children at their play.

He knew her face from her license photo in the computer, but he hadn't had a real sense of her until he saw her now. Now he felt a sort of helpless admiration for her and a dark resentment toward her and a dark attraction. *The good girl, the church girl.* His wife had been one of the same. She was the girl who didn't drink or do drugs or smoke or party. The girl who sang in the choir and decorated her notebooks with marker drawings of hearts and flowers. The girl who said "Aw" when she saw pictures of small animals and "Oh no! What're you going to do?" when her friends got themselves knocked up. She was the girl who walked swishing past when the brothers talked jazz at her passing ass, because she wasn't going to come over here, baby, not even if she was so fine, aw really, he'd be so careful, swear. She had her life all laid out in her mind, her plans confided to her diary, and they didn't include no baby-baby-baby, because she wasn't going to have no baby before the clock struck married. She was that girl.

And here was the thing about it. Girls like that—for some reason, they were love magnets for weak and damaged men. It was some kind of save-me-mommy deal. His wife had told him all about it. They wanted her sympathy, her kindness, her "Oh, you poor thing." They wanted her to make them better than they were, but, fucked-uppedly enough, they wanted to drag her down to their level, too. "I used to tell them if they wanted salvation, they could get themselves a Bible," Ramsey's wife had said. "If you want *me,* you gotta walk like a man."

That's what they held out for, these girls. Men. Military men. Cops. Long-haul collegiates going for the big degrees, business, engineering, even medicine or law. That's what his wife had done—she'd held out for him. This one, too—Teresa. Got herself a hero soldier, the records said. Only she got handed the short stick of God, didn't she? Husband killed in Sandland. So she was stuck with the kid-and-no-husband scenario, like it was nigger fate.

The thought drew Ramsey's mind back in bitterness and melancholy to his wife. Who had gotten the short stick, too, in the long run, you might say. But that was a whole 'nother story, and he didn't have time to torture himself with it now.

He got out of the Charger. There was a gate in the schoolyard fence. It was padlocked and an older man, a janitor in dirty greens, was sitting in a chair beside it in lieu of a guard. Ramsey showed the man his shield through the diamond links. The janitor rose creakily and opened the padlock.

As Ramsey walked across the yard toward Teresa, the children chased each other all around him. Their surflike roar broke into individual voices, cascades of laughter and wordless cries. These seemed to feed the melancholy in him somehow, seemed to increase his brooding awareness of the evil fate arrayed against him. So, too, did the sight of Teresa as he came closer and closer to her, as she reminded him more and more of his wife.

She had moved from the doorway to settle a dispute between two boys over a kickball. She was turned half away from him and didn't see him approaching. She was bending forward to talk to the children. His eyes went over the curves of her body, and over her profile. *Why isn't she teaching in the Northern District public schools where they really need her?* he thought—because he wanted to resent her for something other than the fact that she reminded him of his wife, as the laughing children reminded him of his son and daughter.

"Ms. Grey?" he said. He flashed his badge again as she straightened and turned to look at him. As she came around to face him close up—gave him the whole cornball valentine-shaped face with its high cheekbones and warm brown eyes—the jolt of his attraction to her was startlingly sharp. He was painfully aware that he had once been the sort of man she would have held out for, that now he only seemed to be that man—as his wife had finally understood.

"*Mrs.* Grey, yes," she corrected him—which he also resented, without quite knowing why.

Then her eyes went to his badge, and they were startled and filled with worry. She hadn't expected him, hadn't known he was coming. The old man hadn't called her—or maybe he'd tried to and she kept her phone off at work. Conor hadn't contacted her either. Which meant she probably didn't know about Gutterson yet. The news wouldn't have made it onto TV—in fact, there was only one television station and maybe a website or two where anyone still thought a murder in this city *was* news.

He said, "I'm Lieutenant Ramsey," and she turned to him expectantly. He couldn't tell whether she recognized his name or not. Was it possible Conor had never mentioned him to her? Or was she just pretending that he never had? He couldn't tell.

"Mrs. Grey, do you know a man named Henry Conor?"

"Yes, I know Henry. He did some work for my father. Why, is something wrong?"

"What sort of work?" he asked her. "Carpentry?"

"Some . . . carving work, that's right."

The little hesitation gave him everything he needed. She was not thinking about Conor's carpentry. She was thinking about the man himself. She was the girl in question, all right.

"Is that it? Is that your whole relationship to him? He worked for your father?"

"Well, I'm not sure what you mean," she said reluctantly. And then—in case he already knew—she confessed: "We were friendly. In fact, he took me and my son to the fair yesterday."

"To the fair."

She made the classic female defensive gesture, defiantly brushing her hair back with her hand. "What's this about?"

"We're looking to question Mr. Conor about a police detective who was found dead in his apartment this morning. He was killed with one of Conor's hammers."

He said it brutally and got the effect he wanted. She was staggered, her lips parting, her pupils becoming pinpoints. For a moment, he thought she might actually swoon to the asphalt.

So Ramsey thought he had the whole picture now. A lonely widow with a man in the house, a man who would include the boy when they went to the fair. She had been falling in love with Conor, her feelings flowing powerfully, maybe only checked a little by the memory of her husband and by some mental wrangling a girl like her would do out of obligatory protectiveness toward her son. But hesitation or no, mental wrangling or no, she'd been falling for him. And now here was Ramsey telling her there was a dead detective, that Conor was on the run, being hunted by the police. Telling her, in effect, that Conor was just the sort of damaged criminal-type she had been avoiding all her life, just the sort of bad, needy boy she had fended off while waiting to meet the real man she married—the sort of man Ramsey seemed to be. He sensed all this in a second and sensed he had a moment of psychological power over her here, a moment when all her instincts would tell her to turn away from bad boy Conor, to turn toward the nice policeman who reminded her of her dead husband, and tell him everything.

"That's . . . Henry wouldn't do anything like that," she said.

"Really. You know him that well?"

"Well, I . . ."

"You know where he came from? What he was doing here?"

"He was a carpenter, working as a carpenter."

"Did he ever tell you why he came to this city in particular? Doesn't seem like a very nice place to come to. A lot of people are leaving, as I understand it."

"He said he came for the work. He said there's a lot of work here—because of all the rebuilding."

"Did he ever mention a man named Peter Patterson?"

"Peter . . . Uh . . . No. I don't think so."

"What about Jesse Skyles? The Reverend Jesse Skyles."

"I don't think so. I've heard of him. The story in the paper—about him and the girl. Henry and I talked about a lot of things. We may have talked about Skyles. I don't remember."

"You may have, though."

"I'm sorry. I just don't remember."

"But you talked about a lot of things."

"He would carve out in the backyard. I would go out there and talk to him sometimes. To keep him company."

"You and your son or just you?"

"No, and my son. And my father, too, sometimes."

Ramsey thought he had the whole picture. "But you can't remember what you talked about?"

"Not everything. It was just conversation. You know."

"Did he ever mention my name? Ramsey? Did he ever mention me?"

"No. Why are you asking me these things?"

"Mrs. Grey, do you have any idea where Conor is now?"

"No. No, I don't. I thought he would be at work."

"He's not at work. He's gone. A police detective has been murdered in his apartment, and Conor has disappeared. If you know where he is, it would be a good idea to tell me."

"I don't know. I already told you. I don't know. Henry wouldn't do anything like that, I'm sure."

Ramsey felt a strange flutter of doubt. Something was wrong here, very wrong, but he couldn't place it. For one thing, he couldn't tell whether the girl was lying or not. His instincts told him she wasn't, but he thought she had to be. Would Conor have kept all his purposes secret from her? As they became close, as they became intimate even, wouldn't he want to share with her the burden of his mission? It didn't make sense that he would ask questions and jabber freely on the street and suddenly become secretive with the girl he was romancing. Something here, anyway, didn't make sense. Ramsey felt he had a bright, clear picture in his mind of what had passed between this girl and Conor, but he couldn't quite put that picture together with the Conor he thought he'd come to know. It was as if, outside the bright clarity of his understanding, there was deep shadow—shadow that hid a hunkering disaster. Nemesis.

"Ms. Grey—*Mrs.* Grey—I feel you're keeping something from me."

"I'm not. I'm really not. Why would I?"

"Are you certain Conor never said anything to you? About why he came here? Why he came to this city?"

"For the work, that's all. He said he came for the work."

"All that time you talked to him, and your father talked to him, and your son, that's all he told you." He couldn't stop himself. He couldn't let go of it. Something didn't make sense.

"Look . . . Henry didn't murder anyone," she answered. "He wouldn't do that."

"That isn't what I'm asking you."

"I know, but . . ."

"He never mentioned Patterson? Or Skyles? Or me?"

"No. I don't think so. No. I'm almost sure."

"I find that difficult to believe," he said, looking hard into her eyes, his doubt mixed with anger now because she reminded him so much of his wife.

A bell rang in the big old cathedral-like building, a long, loud rattling bell. The laughter and shouting of the children came back to Ramsey as if it had been gone, as if the volume of it had dropped to nothing while he talked to Teresa Grey.

"I—I have to go," she said. "Recess is over. I have to go back to work. You're wrong about Henry."

But he could see she was uncertain as she turned away—uncertain enough, he thought, that she would have told him what she knew. Or was it all a performance? Was she hiding Conor? Protecting him? Was she that good a liar? She could have been. No one lies better than a good girl in love. And Conor *would've* said something to her. He must've. It didn't make sense.

Ramsey stood there another moment, aware of the woman's peculiar valence—the way she touched on his personal sorrows—and yet unable to distinguish it from that lingering suspicion of a shadow zone outside the zone of his understanding, that strange darkness sheltering nemesis and disaster.

He stood there and watched her walk back into the building, her skirt swishing as the children rushed past on either side of her, as they crowded before her through the schoolhouse door.

For the first time, he felt afraid of what he was about to do.

"ALL RIGHT," said Shannon. "Tell me."

They were in the green Crown Victoria now. The bald guy was driving. The bald guy's name was Foster, it turned out. Foster glanced over at Shannon and laughed.

"Where'd you think you came from, dog? Your mama's tummy? You think the stork brought you? You think you were born again through water and the spirit? Or maybe someone told you one time that dirt-bag thieves get brand-new lives for free."

Shannon faced forward, expressionless, looking out the windshield at the miserable boulevard. Stores boarded up. Holloweyed whores. Predators slouched so deep they were shaped like question marks. All this on a bright spring Monday afternoon.

"I guess I wondered . . ." he said glumly.

"Yeah, I'll bet you did. I'll just bet you did. But you're all alike, you bottom feeders, every one of you. You think someone's gonna hand you the moon on a platter. You think someone *should*, like they owe it to you. *Oh, I'm so poor. Oh, I'm so put upon. Where's my money?* Like you earned it somehow by virtue of being a worthless piece of shit. Every time I wanna round up a fresh batch of dumb-ass bail jumpers, all I gotta do is tell them somebody's giving them something for nothing. Free tickets to the Super Bowl. Free house. A new car. Never did shit for nobody nohow, but out of the woodwork they come like it's only their due."

Shannon could've said it wasn't like that for him. He could've said he had been desperate, on the run, wanted for murders he hadn't committed and a break-in that he had. He could've said a lot of things, but he just said: "So this whole new identity thing was—what? Like, a setup?"

"Of course it was a setup! Why should anybody give *you* even the smell of his ass?" Foster shook his head and snorted. "I don't know whether to be amazed or amazed that I am still amazed."

The car turned a corner onto a side street of shattered houses, some no more than dust and lumber piled on dead grass. Shannon stared out at them but hardly saw them, immersed in what the man was telling him, still all murk and confusion. His sluggish effort to work out the truth of the matter was getting him nowhere. This was way beyond his powers.

"So what was it then?" he said. "What was it—some kind of scam to steal money?"

Foster let out a big guffaw. "A scam to steal money? Son, I work for the federal government. We don't need a scam to steal money. We *are* a scam to steal money. Look up 'scam to steal money' in the dictionary, there's a picture of the federal government right there. Scam to steal money! God save me from an uneducated public."

Slowly, Shannon turned to face him. Close up, Foster's aura of seediness was even more apparent, the threadbare shine of his suit and the wasted-junkie thinness of his frame even more painful to look upon. Close up, he had a fidgety, watchful junkie demeanor, too, something frantically alert in the smart, bright eyes.

"That cop," said Shannon. "Gutterson . . ."

"Gutterson!" Foster spat back the name as if the dead detective had been a bill for back taxes.

"He was never after me, was he?"

"Ah!" Foster took one hand off the steering wheel and tapped a finger against the side of his own head. "Now the clock is beginning to tick."

"He was after Henry Conor."

"The mist is parting. Finally."

The fields of rubble and dead grass fell away as the car turned another corner. Here was a long side street of antique office buildings with elaborate cast-iron facades. Between their tiers of pillars, arched windows, some broken, some just dark, exuded emptiness like a vapor, an atmosphere of abandonment coiling above the entire block. Vaguely, Shannon recognized where they were, realized they were not that far from his own brownstone.

"Who is he then?" said Shannon. "Who's Henry Conor?"

"Henry Conor is you," Foster answered, turning the wheel. The Crown Victoria slid to the curb, into the shadow of a building bleak with ruin. "Least, he's you—or he's no one."

Shannon waited for more. Foster shut the car down with swift, jerky movements, scoping the area all the while, his head turning back and forth, his sharp eyes darting here and there. He pulled the car keys out of the ignition and fiddled with them nervously.

"I made Henry Conor up," he said with a quick, mirthless smile. "I invented him, dog. And then I got you to take his place."

Into the louring building. Up four flights of dark stairs. Graffiti on the gray, abandoned walls and chips and scars in the paint where the plaster showed through like an exposed nerve. Down the gutted hallway to a carved wooden door where Foster knocked out a quick code, then used a key.

Shannon followed him across the threshold. Inside: a loft stripped bare. Chairs and card tables and a cot under the exposed heating pipes and fluorescent bulbs. There were three laptops, two playing various squares of video footage, one showing a series of oscillators. Shannon saw images of his apartment, Gutterson's outline traced in chalk on the floor.

Two men were here, both in shirtsleeves, both wearing guns, one weaselly, playing Patience at a table, one slick and handsome, lying on the cot, reading a magazine about pretty girls in their underwear.

Foster shut the door.

"You were watching me," Shannon said to him. It made him feel sick to see it.

"Listening, too," said Foster flatly.

"Don't worry," muttered the slick guy on the cot, turning a page. "We covered our eyes when you jerked off."

"I didn't cover *my* eyes," muttered the weasel dealing cards. "I dug it."

"We were watching out for you, boy," Foster said. "You were our guy in place. You were Henry Conor. We knew they'd come for you."

"You invented this guy . . ."

"A follower of Reverend Jesse Skyles, a friend of Peter Patterson, a man who knew what Patterson knew, a man on a mission."

Shannon looked at the videos of his empty apartment, the hallway outside the door, the street outside the brownstone. The whole place must've been rigged with cameras and microphones.

"Why me?" he asked.

"You showed up for it, darling. You answered the call and came to the mall. Guess you wanted it more than the others we tried. Or maybe you were just the first one stupid enough to check his cell phone. I don't know."

"No," said Shannon. "No, I mean . . ." He stared at the videos, fascinated, thinking about all that time he was being watched. "No, I mean, why me instead of one of you? If you needed a man in place, why didn't you use an agent, one of your own?"

"We're breached, baby face. Augie Lancaster's got more men in my agency than I have. That's why we're flying a little bit off the radar here. Way off the radar, the truth be told. What you're looking at right now is every agent I have that I can trust, minus a higher-up who's funneling the money."

The two men waved without looking up from what they were doing. Shannon stared at them dully.

"Anyway, I didn't need an agent. I didn't *want* an agent." Foster moved to one of the big arched windows. He stood to one side and looked out and down, checking the street below. "All I wanted was a body, an identity. A treasure at the end of the treasure hunt. Someone the trail led to, if you see what I mean."

Shannon did not see what he meant. "The trail . . ."

"The clues. We left clues for them to find. Computer traces. E-mails. Graffiti in empty houses. Remarks made to informants on the street. A photograph of a man sitting in a car. Signs that Peter Patterson hadn't been alone, that he shared his information with someone—and that now that someone had come to town, a man on a mission, looking for justice."

Shannon shook his head. More murk, more confusion.

Foster, glancing over at him from the window, laughed. Gestured at him for the benefit of his colleagues. "Look at this fool. Doesn't even know who Lancaster is." Then, explaining it to Shannon: "Lancaster runs this town. Runs this state. Could run this country if no one stops him. And his network goes so deep, we've never been able to get near him without getting derailed or blown or reassigned. Then—by the grace of God—literally by the grace of God—along came Peter Patterson. Low-level city bookkeeper, nobody even knew he was there. But he was well enough placed to see where the money was going, federal money, state money, programs, going where it always goes, into the pockets of the people who control it, in this case Lancaster and his gang. For years he lived with it—this Patterson, I mean. Sure, he lived in a bottle to kill his conscience, but it seemed to be working for him. Then, one day, he heard the Reverend Skyles preaching in some asshole of a church somewhere and he got the word and came to Mr. Jesus. Climbed out of the bottle. Found his conscience. Began to make overtures to us. Feeling us out. Working up his courage, you know. We were reeling him in slow by slow. We almost had him. But we're so damned breeched. They got to him first."

Finally—and it really did feel like clouds parting in his head—the light began to shine for Shannon. He began to understand. His lips parted as he gazed at Foster. "They killed him. Your informant—Patterson. Lancaster killed him."

"Had him killed. Just as dead as ever he could be. Right in the middle of the storm and the riots, too, so whatever evidence there was was lost in the rain and confusion. There was no way to make the case. Oh, we knew who did it, all right. Only one man Lancaster could trust with a job like that. But we'd never have broken him. In fact, with our agency so corrupted, we could barely move without giving ourselves away. So we had nothing. Again. And in a single leap, Augie was free—free and going national to boot. A hero because his city was so corrupt it collapsed in a rainstorm. That's the government for you: it fails upward. It has three new remedies to fix everything it just destroyed."

Foster had moved away from the window now, moved back toward Shannon, talking. Shannon, a much bigger man, stared down at the frenetic, seedy little figure.

"So you made them think there was someone else, another guy with the same information Patterson had. A guy you just made up."

"Henry Conor. Another Skyles disciple. A private detective from down the road. A man on a mission. We needed someone we could trust, someone no one knew, someone who couldn't give himself away, because even he didn't know he was the guy . . ."

Everything happened at once then. Shannon understood—and erupted, furious. He grabbed Foster, both hands on the front of his jacket. The weasel jumped up, his chair falling backward, a handful of spades and clubs and hearts and diamonds flying, red and black everywhere, as he drew his gun. Likewise the slickster on the cot: riffling pages of cleavages, bras, and panties went airborne as he leapt up and charged into the melee.

"You knew they'd come to kill me!" Shannon managed to say before the weasel stuck the gun barrel in his eye and the slickster wrapped an arm around his throat and pulled him off, with Foster shoving him away for good measure. "That's all I was there for—just to die! You missed the first murder, so you wanted to make sure you witnessed the second!"

Foster had fallen backward, angrily smoothing his threadbare jacket, his chintzy tie. The other agents held Shannon fast, one with his chokehold, the other with his gun. Foster gestured them away.

"All right," he said.

They let Shannon go, sneering as they backed off. The slickster fetched his magazine. The weasel holstered his gun. He righted his chair and began to gather the playing cards.

Shannon and Foster stood glaring at one another.

"We didn't *want* them to kill you," Foster said.

"You just didn't give a shit if they did."

"Why should we? You're a lowlife. You don't mean anything to us. You don't mean anything to anyone, Shannon. If you died, so what? Who cares? But we figured they wouldn't kill you right away. We figured they'd do exactly what they did do: try to find out what you had, where the info was, who else had it, who else knew. Maybe if you hadn't chased me off at the fair that night, I'd've been nearby when they made their move, could've gotten there to help you. As it was, we had to watch from here—and by the time I reached you, it was over."

Shannon gave a bitter laugh. "Bad break for you, me killing *him,* huh?"

"That it was. That it surely was. If he'd killed you, we'd've had him. Busted him, turned him, traded our way up the ladder right to Augie himself. We'd have had them all. As things stand, with Gutterson dead instead, the whole operation's blown, a great big waste of time and taxpayer money. When they murder you now—and they will—it'll just be SOP for a cop-killer—shot trying to escape—we get nothing out of it. So congratulations, Shannon. We fucked you? You fucked us right back."

For another moment, Shannon glowered at the little man. Then, disgusted with him, disgusted with himself and with all of it, he turned away, shaking his head at the dusty floor. He had one more burst of anger in him: "Didn't occur to you bastards that if you gave me a new life, I might live it, huh? I mean, when you contacted me, I had nothing, I had nothing to lose, but now . . ."

Foster shrugged. "Poor baby. Like I said, Shannon, you don't mean a thing to us, not a thing. Just a scumbag thief living off other people's money. Sort of like the government, come to think of it, only they're not looking at three strikes and hard time. But then, what can I tell you? Life's unfair."

Still studying the dust, Shannon hooked his thumbs in his belt. He nodded. He couldn't argue with the man there. Life was unfair all right, and hard time was what he was looking at for sure.

The other agents had now settled back into their places. The slickster was on his cot again, paging from one cleavage to another. The weasel had finished gathering his playing cards, had settled back into his chair, had racked up the deck with a few quick bangs of it against the tabletop, and was dealing himself a new hand.

"What now?" Shannon said. "You gonna turn me in? Send me to prison?"

Foster waved him off. "Nah. I don't want to have to explain this mess to anyone. Better for all of us you just disappear. Do your thing, man. Into the wind with you, there's a good lad. Unlikely you'll get out of town alive anyway. And if you do, well, after today, Henry Conor's gone. Your license, your papers—they'll all vanish from the computers. They'll all be about as useful to you as a teenager's drinking ID. We'll be setting your fingerprint and DNA records straight, too, so the first time you're busted, you'll go down for good. The arc of the moral universe is long, boy, but it bends toward you getting screwed."

Something occurred to Shannon now. He turned his face from the floor, raised an eyebrow at Foster. "You keep calling me a thief."

"You are a thief."

"But not a killer. You don't pin the Hernandez killings on me?"

"Ha! Listen, you add together the IQ of everyone who works for the United States government, you'd get enough intelligence to make one retard with his hat on sideways—but we're not *that* stupid. Benny Torrance looking for payback ain't even *my* idea of a good lead. We never would've used you if we thought you were a mad dog."

"But on the TV they keep saying it, telling people I'm a suspect. I've heard them."

"They'll keep saying it, too. We're not the police. You're a suspect till they bring you in and beat the truth out of you."

"So meanwhile, that's it. I just walk out of here."

"Like I said. Unless . . ."

"Yeah? What?"

"Well, this is gonna unravel fast. Our target is smart—a cop— Ramsey, his name is—he's smart and he'll unravel this jig-time once he starts looking for you, digging into your life. He'll go everywhere you've gone, talk to everyone you've met, and sooner or later, he'll figure out there's nothing there and it'll dawn on him he's been played. On the other hand, if we act fast, if we let him find you—let *him* find *you*—maybe he'll come after you. He's out of allies, so he might well do it himself. Then we'd have him."

"You mean come after me like Gutterson did?"

"Right. Find out what you know, work you over, maybe give himself away."

"Or he might just pop a cap in me."

"Or that. Probably that."

"And if he doesn't—and if you get him—what's in it for me?"

"Uh . . . shit."

"Nothing?"

"Not a thing."

"You still gonna make Conor disappear, put my records back, and all that?"

"Got to. Like I said, we're flying way off the radar here. After today, you're Shannon again, whatever happens."

"You won't even offer me—you know . . ."

"Immunity? Son, I'm gonna be lucky if I don't end up in jail my own damn self. There's some small chance, if everything goes just right, we might be able to work something out for you higher up the line. But no guarantees, and as things stand, I wouldn't pin your hopes on it. A bullet to the head's a lot more likely."

"So if I help you, either I get killed or I get busted for life."

"Pretty much."

"I guess I'm missing something. I want to do that because . . . why?"

Foster's whole hairless head seemed to quirk upward as he broke into a self-mocking grin. "Civic duty? Stop the bad guys? Save your mother country from political disaster?"

Thumbs hooked in his belt, head hung, Shannon stood looking at the man a moment.

"Have a nice day," he said then — and walked out.

He made his way back to the abandoned house, his hideaway. He tossed his gun in his tool bag and zipped the bag up and grabbed the handles and lifted it, ready to go, ready to leave town, hit the wind. But he didn't go. He set the bag down again and stood there, staring at it.

He didn't know what it was, what stopped him, but he couldn't move from the spot, even though the tension and urgency of his danger twisted his gut inside him. Then, after a few moments of standing there, staring, he did know. It was Teresa. He couldn't leave because of her.

Slowly, he sat down on the floor. His gut went on twisting, the tension terrible. He knew he had to go, had to run, had to get out of this city any way he could or the police would kill him. So he loved Teresa — so what? It wasn't as if she was going to run away with him. Hell, if she did, it would only ruin her life. And he didn't have to worry anymore that she would think he was a killer after he was gone either. Now that he knew the truth, he could write her a letter and explain it all. Why should he stay because of her?

But the answer was already in his mind, beneath the tension, beneath his conscious thoughts. Foster's words were there:

Our target is smart — a cop — Ramsey, his name is — he's smart and he'll unravel this jig-time once he starts looking for you, digging into your life.

He'll go everywhere you've gone, talk to everyone you've met, and sooner or later, he'll figure out there's nothing there and it'll dawn on him he's been played.

Ramsey. He was the one who had murdered this Peter Patterson. He was the one who had sent Gutterson to his apartment, the one who was looking for him now and who would go to his worksite and would find out about the Applebees, and who would go to the house on H Street and look for him there.

Shannon lay down, his bag under his head. He stared up at the ceiling. He didn't think Ramsey would hurt the Applebees—why would he? He didn't think so, and yet his sense of their danger was even more urgent to him than his own.

He lay there a long time, thinking about it. The sunlight shifted to slanted afternoon beams in which motes of dust were dancing. He stared up through the yellow beams, through the dancing dust, his mind drifting, his stomach in knots.

What could he do anyway? What could he do about Ramsey? How could he protect them—Teresa, Michael, the old man? It wasn't as if he was really Henry Conor, an honest guy free to play the hero without fear. All that—his new life—had just been a lie, not even a lie, an illusion, a federal setup, a lawdog scam, gone not even like mist in the morning, more like a dream of mist in the morning, because it had never been real to begin with. So? What? Was he just trying to keep that fantasy alive? Was he just looking for an excuse to see her again? Wouldn't Ramsey be waiting for that? Wouldn't he be waiting for him to turn up at the house on H Street? Maybe he'd kill Shannon there, and then the Applebees would be witnesses and he'd have to kill them, too. Wouldn't he just be bringing more trouble to Teresa's door if he stayed, if he tried to protect her?

He lay there with the sun above him slanting and the light of the sunbeams growing mellow. He thought and thought about it. He had to go. If he didn't get out, they'd kill him. There was nothing he could do if he stayed. But to just run like that, to just leave her behind with this Ramsey bastard coming after her . . .

His mind drifted. He saw himself in the future. Maybe on the run, maybe in prison. It was bound to be one or the other. He thought he would be able to bear the fact that he would never see Teresa again. Hell, he knew he could bear it. He would be sad, but so what? He would not have the life he wanted, the good life he thought he had been meant to have, but so what? A broken heart wouldn't kill you. The sadness would get better over time. He would forget that other life. He was a hard guy—he had always been a hard guy. He could deal with all that if he had to, all that and a side of fries if he had to.

What he couldn't bear, what he couldn't bear even to consider —even just now, even just lying there on the floor—was the idea that some harm might come to Teresa because of him, the idea he might be in his cell one day or hiding in some backwoods town one day, and news would reach him. A murder in the city . . .

Teresa's face came to him. The boy's face. The angel's face. Their eyes.

He lay there. He thought about it. He thought about . . . well, he thought about a lot of things. He thought about sticking his Beretta in his mouth and blowing his brains out—anything just to end this tension and indecision and helplessness. He thought about walking out in the open and letting some trigger-crazy cop do the job for him. And he daydreamed about going to see Teresa one last time, not to try anything with her, he told himself, not to convince her to come with him or even to touch her, so help him, he wouldn't even touch her—but just to warn her, to explain himself, justify himself to her, face to face, and see the forgiveness in her eyes and warn her to get out, to run, to save herself and her family . . .

All through the day, tortured in his heart, he lay there in the dust on the floor of the ruined house, his head on his bag, his hands behind his head, staring up through the motes in the slanting afternoon sunlight, watching scenarios and disasters play out in his mind, trying to figure out what to do, and waiting for nightfall.

LIEUTENANT BRICK RAMSEY waited, too, suffered tortures that long day, too, tortures of indecision and of what he disdained to name as fear. But he *was* afraid—there was no other word for it. It had been building in him since that morning.

It had started when he'd seen Gutterson lying dead on Henry Conor's floor. There had been that wisp of superstitious dread, that suspicion of nemesis working against him. Then there'd been the old man in the white house—Applebee—leaning on the mantelpiece under the wooden carving of the angel, the old man looking at him and the angel looking at him as if they knew what he'd done and who he was inside.

Finally, there'd been the daughter—Teresa—and his sense that something was going on here that he didn't understand. That sense—and the old man's look—and the wisp of dread he'd felt when he saw Gutterson—they'd all combined until he felt like a kind of darkness was closing in on him, strangling him. That's when he began to suspect what he would have to do. That's when he began to become afraid.

He went back to the Castle—that was what they called Police Headquarters. He went up to his office on the tenth floor and sat alone. Swiveling back and forth in his high-backed chair. Gazing out the long window without really seeing the expanse of the fire- and flood-blasted city laid out below him.

He tried to think things through, but there's no point in following his logic. There wasn't much logic, in fact. It was all just that strangling sense of things closing in. The superstitious dread. The look in Applebee's eyes, the angel's eyes. Teresa.

They knew. That, at last, was the only sense he could make of it all. That explained the old man's hostility, and the girl's ignorance, which had to have been feigned. They knew what Conor knew. They knew who Ramsey was and what he'd done. They were part of this — this *thing* he was feeling, this evil fate that he felt in the air around him, this will opposed to his will. That's what he was battling here. That's what was lurking in the shadows beyond his understanding, that spirit of nemesis like a stern, relentless phantom, her hand upraised as she waved the Book of Judgment at him, hammering it against the darkness as she hunted him down.

Sitting there, swiveling back and forth, staring blindly out the window, Ramsey realized there was no way out of this for him anymore. He was going to have to see it all the way to the end.

Across town at that hour, the fifteen-year-old gangster who called himself Super-Pred was committing an act of violence so grotesque that even the thugs who attended him found themselves nauseated and quailing. The gnarly-assed junky called Speedball had been scamming on the Pred, no question, and had shorted a detective on his payoff, pocketing the skimmed cash to feed his own habit. Which was not only dishonest but unforgivably stupid, because the cop was a cop and sure to complain. Everyone knew S-P was going to deal out some shit to the junky, and everyone also knew that when the Pred got going, he sometimes lost himself in the work. There was always, therefore, a 50 percent chance that Speedball might not survive the discipline — which was probably why the poor zombie pissed himself when he saw Super-Pred had come to deal with him personally. Still, no one was prepared for the elaborate bloodfest that followed. It was something you'd expect to get more from some Afghan warlord than a city g. When Super-Pred finally hitched up his pants and strutted out the warehouse door, the boyos he left behind could only whistle and curse and steal frightened glances at each other as they mopped up what was left of Speedball's body and the pools of their own vomit besides.

As for the fifteen-year-old lad himself, he was still impossibly wired with triumph and self-horror when he returned to the garage he used for an HQ. Much, indeed, like a warlord of old, he summoned women to him, two of the child-whores he ran, and worked off his excess energy in unspeakably cruel sexual acts that left one of the children bleeding and sniveling and the other mocking her and lording it over her because she felt that was her safest bet.

So there, finally, Super-Pred sat, enthroned in an old leather chair, bloated with satisfaction, his mind a sort of red silence, with even the voice of his self-horror barely a dim cry, no more than what you might hear from a starving baby in an abandoned building as you were driving away. He was drinking a beer, watching a movie on the laptop set on a mechanic's workbench, laughing while two of his minions slouched on the sofa, drinking beers and laughing with him as the gangster on the monitor buzz-sawed a rival in two.

The garage's side door opened then and a shaft of afternoon light fell through it. The gangsters were still laughing as they turned to see who dared disturb them.

Ramsey's silhouette cut its shape out of the light.

Aware of all the ramifications, Ramsey felt slightly nauseated as he stood over the boy reclining in his chair. Super-Pred—making a show of being unafraid of a fresh beatdown from the lieutenant —gave him a lazy salute with his beer bottle and said, "What's up, daddy."

Ramsey gestured with his head and the two other thugs were dismissed.

Then, when he and the Pred were alone, Ramsey said, "There's a white shingled house on H Street . . ."

PART VI

THE RUINED TOWER

NIGHT FELL. Far away, beneath a chandelier flashing rainbows over a fine ballroom in the nation's capital, Augie Lancaster was bestowing the high, ringing ideals of his oratory on the upturned faces of worshipful celebrities. But here, in the alleys of the city he'd created and left behind, there were a thousand little crucifixions. Girls who still had secret dreams of romantic dances were on their knees in the dust taking a mouthful of dick for a handful of dollars. Boys in the animal rage of manhood-without-nobility were strutting the little distance between their hard-ons and the grave. Gunfire was everywhere. A teenager was gurneyed into an ER with a slug in his chest. He'd leave in a wheelchair: dead-eyed, drooling. Wailing drifted through every half-opened window. A little girl slapped her baby because it wouldn't stop crying long enough for her to hit her methamphetamine pipe in peace. *Tsk, tsk, tsk,* said the old men shaking their heads. Old, dried-up, moralizing men locked behind the barred doors of their houses to keep them from souring the juicy life of the street; chewed-up old men spat into the gutter of the juicy street life. And the women? So mean. Thirty-year-old grandmothers: nasty, bullying.

Why you so mean, woman?

'Cause you so weak!

In the churches, meanwhile, they preached other men's sins, so who could fail to say *amen?*

• • •

Then there was the white shingled house on H Street. Strange it should still stand there, surrounded by all that ruin and debris. All those empty lots. Those piles of rubbish rising gothic against the starless sky. Unfair, it almost seemed, to the gangsters staring at it balefully from the dark. Why should it go untouched by the disaster when whole other neighborhoods—their neighborhoods—were gone? The yellow glow of the lights in the windows touched some inborn notion of home they didn't even know how to imagine, and so instead of yearning for it they felt a sort of gibbering justification in their intentions, an instinct to destroy what obscurely moved them and threatened to reveal them to themselves in the light of their best desires. What they had come to do was only right, they felt somehow: the rape and the murder and the flames. It was only as it should be, their privilege and their calling.

They glanced fitfully at their leader, wondering why he hesitated to give the word.

Inside the house, there was squealing and comical chatter, a comical music of *zwits* and *boings*. The boy, Michael, was lying on his stomach in the living room, looking up from his crayon drawing at an old cartoon on the TV. Teresa checked on him from the archway and then returned to her father in the front room. He was sitting in his reading chair, fiddling with an unlit pipe. She sat across from him on the sofa, leaning forward, her elbows on her knees.

"He'll turn up," the old man told her without much conviction.

She shook her head. "I don't think so. I think he's gone for good."

"He'll come to say goodbye. If he can, he will. You'll see."

She frowned. "I'd just like to hear Henry's side of it, that's all." She didn't like to admit her feelings for Conor, even to herself, but she knew them now and she knew her father knew them and it made her feel exposed and embarrassed. "It's just—that policeman, that detective . . ."

"Oh, he was . . ." The old man waved the stem of the pipe in the air before him. "I wouldn't believe a word he said. In this city? The police are worst of all, worse than the criminals. I took one look at him—I knew he was after Henry for his own reasons. Believe me."

"I don't know. He seemed . . . like he might've been a good person."

"I think that's what he's good at: seeming like that. Probably was one once. Which makes him even worse. I'm telling you, I took one look in his eyes and . . ."

Applebee stopped short. He cocked his head, listening. There were only the *boing*s of the cartoon music and a comical chattering.

"What? What's the matter?" said Teresa.

"Did you hear something? In the kitchen? In back?"

"I don't think so . . ."

With his eyebrows lowering, the old man pushed himself out of his chair. Teresa instinctively stood up, too. They hesitated a moment, looking toward the back of the house, listening for a noise.

Then, with violent suddenness, the gangsters burst in through the front door.

There were three shotgun blasts, thunderously loud as they blew off the door's security cage. Even as Teresa recoiled in shock—that quickly—they kicked the door in and charged through.

The old man had a second to lean toward the stairs, toward the gun he kept in his bedroom. Then one of the bangers whipped the butt of the shotgun into his face. The old man staggered back, his knees buckling as he hit the wall and tumbled down to the floor.

Teresa screamed for her son: "Michael!" She turned toward the archway. Two bangers grabbed her by the waist and legs and lifted her into the air as she twisted and struggled. Another thug stalked past her into the living room. He came out laughing with the writhing child helpless in his arms.

"Mommy!" screamed the boy.

Super-Pred gave an avuncular laugh. "You a fierce little man, ain't you?" he said. He glanced through the archway, charmed for a moment by the cartoon rabbit and the cartoon hunter on the TV screen.

"Leave him alone!" Teresa shouted.

Rage flashed in the gangster's eyes, and he spun and grabbed her as she struggled in the grip of his two thugs. He pincered her cheeks with one hand and leaned his nose almost against hers.

"You don't talk to *me*, bitch! You just a bitch!"

Teresa tried to twist her head free, tried to talk to him. "Please! You can have anything you want. Just leave him alone!"

The Pred laughed again. Grabbed her face again. Grabbed her breast hard so that she cried out in pain.

"Mommy!" screamed the little boy.

"Bitch, I can have anything I want anyway!" Super-Pred said. He glanced at his companions. "Spread that shit around."

He meant the gasoline in the cans they'd brought with them. The thug who'd whipped the old man leaned the shotgun against the armchair and grabbed a red can. Another thug grabbed another can, and they began splashing the room with gasoline, splashing gasoline over the old man where he lay gasping and coughing in his own blood.

"He look like he burn good," said a banger, laughing.

The little boy struggled and shouted. The thug holding him was surprised and angered by the child's strength. He cursed and lost his temper and hurled the boy face first into the wall. Teresa let out an anguished scream. The boy fell dazed to the floor. The thug kicked him.

"There!" he said.

And the other thugs spread gasoline on the boy, too. The boy coughed and curled up, gripping his stomach.

"Hold off a second," said Super-Pred.

He was in that zone of his now, that mental zone of unpredictable fury. He grabbed the front of Teresa's blouse with two hands and tore it open. That set the fire going inside him.

"Bring her in here," he said.

Gripping her arms and legs, they hauled and dragged and hustled Teresa through the door into the dining room. Grunting and crying out, she kicked and tried to tear free and tried to bite their hands, but she was helpless.

"Put her on the table," Super-Pred said, following them through the door.

They forced her, struggling, onto the table, while the Pred, with a great show of lordly calm, wandered around the room, studying it with mock appreciation.

He noticed the reredos on the mantel.

"Shut that bitch up," he said casually over his shoulder as he approached the wooden sculpture.

One of the bangers punched Teresa and the other groped and clutched between her legs. They tore at her clothes.

Super-Pred looked up at the three angels, confronted the central angel staring down at him from the mantelpiece. He liked it. It gave him a feeling, a feeling that he and the angel were actually communing in some way. He could see the depth of love and sorrow carved into the angel's expression. It made him laugh because he felt this was a joke that he alone in his uniqueness understood. Someone else might *ooh* and *ah* at such a face, but he was special and got the joke of it. With the sound of the bangers taunting Teresa behind him, the sound of their punches and her anguished gasps, the Pred reached up for the reredos almost with a sense of fellow feeling and affection. Inevitably, he lifted it from the mantelpiece and hurled it to the floor. The wing splintered with a cracking sound. The head snapped off and rolled free.

The force of the action bent the teenager forward slightly, just on the threshold of the kitchen doorway.

Shannon curled around that doorway and put the Beretta nine against the side of Super-Pred's head.

He had let himself in through the kitchen door. He had used the key old Applebee had given him, the small Medeco key with the green dot on the bow. He had come to the house without knowing what he would do, just wanting to make sure Teresa was safe, just following his instinct to watch over and protect her. He had lingered outside a long time, uncertain. Then he had seen the gangsters arrive and had slipped in the back way using the key.

Now, he stood with the gun pressed to the gangster's head. Super-Pred glanced at him, gauging his chances.

Shannon smiled. "You think I won't kill you?" he said. "Look in my eyes. I'll kill you. I *want* to kill you. Tell them to let the girl go."

Super-Pred looked into Shannon's eyes and even his usual pretense of courage deserted him; he knew he had never been so near the precipice of oblivion.

"Let her go," he said—but his voice was hoarse, barely more than a whisper, and his boys were busy working the girl over. He had to shout it at them a second time: "Let her go!"

Then the bangers noticed the new situation. They stumbled back away from Teresa, clumsily reaching for the pistols in their belts.

By then, Shannon had the fifteen-year-old gangster king by the collar, was holding him in front of himself, holding the nine up under the punk's chin.

"Better tell them how it is, son," he said.

"No guns. Put the guns down," said Super-Pred quickly.

"Drop 'em," said Shannon.

Teresa had rolled off the table. She had fallen to her knees on the floor. She braced herself on the floor with one hand and clutched at herself with the other, clutched at the shreds of her clothing, trying to cover her nakedness. Blood and snot and tears were dripping from her. She was crying with a wild rage.

Shannon paid no attention to her. He was already filled with her and looking for a chance—hoping for an excuse—to kill every one of these little shits, every single one.

Super-Pred knew it and a note of hysteria entered his voice as he shouted, "Put the pieces down, motherfuckers!"

One thug dropped his gun, but the other hesitated and Shannon killed him. He shot him quick in the chest and by the time the kid went down dead, he had the pistol under Super-Pred's chin again. It felt good to kill the kid, and Shannon hoped some of the others would try something. Even if they riddled him with bullets, he would kill them all. Even if they shot him dead, he would come back from hell and kill them.

"Move through the door," Shannon said.

The banger who was still living had his hands in the air. His whole body was quaking. His eyes were wide because his friend was suddenly dead and he saw what Shannon was now, he saw what Super-Pred saw. He didn't need the gangster king to repeat Shannon's order. He nearly leapt to the dining room door.

"Tell them to drop 'em!" Super-Pred shouted after him, his voice cracking.

The other three bangers in there had heard the gunshot, but it didn't occur to them it wasn't one of theirs. They figured Pred had shot the bitch, that's all. One of them was even moving to the door to get an eyeful of the bloodshed. But just then, his pal came through, babbling, "Put the guns down, man, put all the pieces down!"

The gangsters saw Super-Pred hustled into the room, Shannon holding him and holding the nine-a to his chin.

"Put the pieces down!" Super-Pred was shouting, and the other thug kept babbling, "Put 'em down, man, he's serious!"

Two of the gangsters dropped their guns. The third one gave it a second's thought, but dropped his, too, before Shannon got the chance to kill him.

Shannon shot a quick glance over at the old man on the floor. The old man was crawling to the boy. Now the old man cradled the boy in his arms, blood dripping from his mouth onto the back of the boy's head. The whole place stank of gasoline. Antic cartoon music filtered in from the back room pathetically. Shannon wanted to kill every g he saw.

The gangsters could see the murder in his eyes, and one of them said stupidly, "Man, we didn't mean nothing."

Shannon shot him in the leg just for that. The punk went down howling.

"Shut up! All of you, shut up!" said Super-Pred, his voice cracking.

"Get out," Shannon ordered quietly. He saw they would do whatever he said now. He was half sorry about that, sorry to have no excuse to kill them. He shoved the gun up under Pred's chin hard. "Get out, I said. Drive away. Look back and I blow this fucker's head off. Then I come after the rest of you. Get out and drive away."

The bangers crowded to the door so fast, Shannon had to shout after them. "Take this one! Take this one with you!"

They came back for the one he'd shot in the leg. The wounded punk was blubbering like a child in pain as they draped his arms over their shoulders and hustled him to the door.

When they were gone, when it was just Shannon holding Super-Pred at gunpoint, he looked down at the old man. "Applebee," he said. "Can you stand up?"

The old man nodded painfully, holding the boy. "Yeah."

"The boy okay?"

"You're okay, aren't you, son?"

"I think so," said the boy.

"Go upstairs and get some clothes for your daughter," said Shannon.

"I'll get them." It was Teresa in the doorway. Clutching the shreds of her clothes to her, her bloodied face still, her cheeks tear-stained, her eyes luminous with fury.

Shannon nodded at her. She went unsteadily to the stairs.

"Mommy!" the boy called after her.

"I'll be right there, sweetie," she mumbled. "Stay with Grandpa."

She went up the stairs quickly.

Shannon heard the bangers' cars start up outside. He heard them roar off into the night. He moved away from the old man and the boy. He yanked the punk gangster to the door and kicked it shut. Now it was quieter inside and they could all hear the cartoon music filtering in from the back room.

"You know what I'm thinking," Shannon said in Super-Pred's ear.

"Come on, daddy," said the boy.

"I'm thinking of killing you. It'd be good."

The punk trembled in his grip. "Come on, man."

"Come on?"

"Yeah, daddy. What the hell, you know?"

"Yeah, well . . . maybe this wasn't your idea."

"It wasn't. I swear."

"I know it wasn't. Fact, I know whose idea it was."

"So you know. So don't kill me, man. What the hell, right? It's like I had no choice."

Shannon shoved the gun in his chin even harder. He spoke in his ear through gritted teeth. "You had a choice."

"Don't . . . don't . . ."

"I want to hear you say it. I want to hear you say the name. If it's the right name, I might let you live. If you lie to me, you'll be dead a second later."

Super-Pred couldn't think that fast. He tried to weigh the dangers. He stalled for time. "She your girl, is that it?"

"Shut up. Mention her again, I'll blow your balls off. Tell me the name."

"Ramsey," said Super-Pred. He could hear his own death in every word Shannon spoke. He could feel his feet hanging over the pit of death. "The cop. The lieutenant. The Brick they call him. He big. It's like he say it, you gotta do it, man. You gotta."

"He told you to come here, do this."

"Yeah, man, swear."

"He say why?"

"Just said do 'em, daddy, didn't give no reason."

The stair creaked and Shannon glanced over to see Teresa coming down. She had pulled on a pair of jeans and a gray army sweatshirt. Her cheek was swollen and bloody. Shannon wanted to hold Super-Pred up in front of her so she could watch while he pulled the trigger.

Teresa went to her father and her son. The old man had gotten hold of a chair arm. He had pulled himself to his feet. Now he was bent over, helping the boy up, too. "Come on, son, come on." The boy rose slowly, clutching his stomach.

Teresa reached them. She put her arms around the boy and murmured to him.

Shannon turned his attention back to Super-Pred, breathing hard. "If I let you live," he said, "can you get a message to Ramsey?"

"Yeah, daddy, yeah. Sure, I can get a message to him easy. Tell him anything you want."

"Tell him we can deal. Him and me. You understand? Tell him I have what he wants and we can deal for it. I get my payoff, I leave town, he'll never see me again."

"Yeah. Yeah. I can tell him that, sure," said Super-Pred.

Shannon glanced over at Teresa. She was standing with the boy clutched against her. Her father leaned on her shoulder for support, wiping blood from his face with his hand.

Shannon gestured with his head toward the dining room. "Take them into the kitchen and wait for me," he told her.

Teresa shepherded the boy to the door. The old man went with them, his hand on her shoulder.

Shannon waited until they left the room. Then he said to Super-Pred, "You tell him what I said. Tell Ramsey I'll be in touch and we can deal."

"Okay, okay, I'll . . ."

Before Super-Pred could finish, Shannon drew back his arm and stabbed the butt of the pistol into the punk's temple. The kid collapsed in his grip, unconscious. Shannon let his collar go and dropped him to the floor.

That was that. Shannon stood, looking around the place, breathing hard. The smell of gasoline was nauseating. The comical cartoon music tinkled and banged in the next room—pathetic. The punk lay still at his feet for only a second. Then he began to stir and groan. Shannon sneered down at him. The image of Teresa struggling on the dining room table flashed in his mind. He had stopped himself from thinking about it before, but now it came to him. He forced himself to stop thinking again. He needed Super-Pred alive to deliver his message.

He stepped through the door into the dining room. The other thug lay dead on the floor in there. He lay on his back beside the dining table, his arms splayed, his mouth open, his eyes staring. That made Shannon feel a little better. He was glad he'd gotten to kill one of them at least.

He crossed the room quickly. He went to where the angel altarpiece lay smashed near the kitchen door. Without breaking stride, he stepped over the wreckage and went through to join Teresa and her family.

He brought them around to the front of the house, leading the way, holding the gun out before him with one hand and keeping the other on Teresa's arm. He led them to her car, a gray Ford, in the driveway. He stood guard as the three of them got inside. He opened the door—and just as he was about to lower himself behind the wheel, he heard a ragged scream from inside the house. It was a scream of unholy rage and frustration. It barely sounded human—barely even sounded animal to Shannon, but more like something subnatural, like some sound effect from a horror movie. As Shannon paused to listen, it came again, and then there came a string of terrible and Tourettic curses howled at full volume. There was a crash, another crash, the sound of glass shattering. Shannon saw Super-Pred stumble past the window as the gangster hurled a chair across the room in his fury. A light must have broken, because the front room flashed and went dark. Then, a moment later, there was another sound—a deep and airy utterance under the boy's raving—and a new, weirdly lightless light raced up over the walls, swift, giddy, and explosive, as if it were the living expression of the gangster's malice. He had torched the gasoline and set the house on fire.

Shannon got in the car and started the engine. As he backed out of the driveway, the blaze seemed to leap up around the white shingled house on both sides like two enormous red hands rising from the earth to grab hold of the place and drag it down.

At the same time, Super-Pred staggered out into the night, a small black figure against the great, red, rising flames. He had a gun in his hand and was firing wildly at the darkness as he went on screaming curses.

Shannon saw all this in the rearview mirror for another second or two. Then he guided the car around the corner, and there was nothing of it visible behind him but the orange glow against the blue-black sky, and that was quickly fading.

It was only one more of over fifty fires burning just then across the night city.

SHANNON DROVE ON through the dark streets. The old man sat beside him. Teresa sat in back, cradling her son in her arms.

"You all right?" Shannon asked the old man.

"Yeah. Yeah, I'm all right. Where're we going?"

"How about you back there?"

"We're okay," said Teresa.

"Where're we going?" Applebee said again.

"I know a place," said Shannon. "Just hold on."

Then he drove in silence. He darted glances here and there, watching the street for danger. He caught the eyes of gangsters who looked up to check him out as he passed. He caught the eyes of whores and hustlers looking to deal. The scenes back in the house kept flashing in his mind. The bangers holding Teresa on the table. He was furious and ashamed, and he wished he had killed them all. It wasn't his fault this happened, he told himself. It was this guy Ramsey's fault—and Foster's fault, too, the seedy federal bastard who'd set him up. But it didn't matter what he told himself. He felt as if it was his fault anyway. He felt he had come to Teresa and her family and brought this down on them. It didn't matter how it happened. He felt as if it was all because of him.

"Where are we going, Mommy?" said the boy faintly in the back seat.

"Shh," she said. "Henry is taking us someplace safe."

"I want them to see a doctor," Applebee told Shannon.

Shannon nodded. He drove in silence.

He came onto a street of brooding darkness, old office buildings rising on either side. Most of their big, arched windows were dark, but here and there a light shone through thin curtains. Here and there, firelight flickered, too, as squatters on some abandoned floor huddled around a flame.

Shannon pulled the car to the curb and switched off the engine. Applebee glanced at him.

"I gotta go see someone," Shannon told him. "You all better come with me."

"Where are we, Mommy?" said the boy.

"Shh. I don't know."

Shannon got out and came around the rear of the car, scanning the street's shadows. The old man climbed out more slowly. Shannon opened the door for Teresa and held it as she slid out with the boy in her arms. When she set the child down on his own and straightened up, she faced Shannon and looked at him. It was not a hard look—or a soft look either. It was neither angry nor kind. She was just searching his face for an explanation.

He wanted to explain. He wanted to tell her it wasn't his fault. He wanted to tell her he was sorry because he felt like it was his fault even if it wasn't. There was no time to tell her everything he wanted to.

"My name is John Shannon," he said finally.

Teresa nodded, as if that were enough for now.

The lock on the building's front door was long broken. Inside, there were no lights working. It was nearly pitch black. Shannon had to feel his way to the stairs and whisper at the others to come to him. The little boy kept asking questions: "Where are we going, Mommy?" Teresa kept answering, "Shh. I don't know."

They climbed the stairs slowly in the dark, clinging to the rutted banister. It was eerily silent. When they reached the fourth-floor landing, they went down the hall, brushing their fingertips against the rough, pitted wall to feel their way. Shannon could see a dim light gleaming under the door at the end.

He reached the door. He remembered the coded knock and rapped it out with his knuckles. There was an instant response from the other side. A chair shifting. Quick, soft footsteps approaching. A whisper from within: "Who is it?"

"Shannon."

He heard the locks turn. Foster opened the door. He looked at Shannon. He looked at Teresa and her family.

He laughed and stood back to let them in.

At the far end of the stakeout loft, there was a small enclosure formed by plywood dividers. There was a card table in the enclosure and a couple of folding metal chairs. Shannon sat on one of the chairs and waited there alone, leaning forward, his hands clasped together between his knees. He could hear the voices on the other side of the dividers: Foster and one of his men—only the slick agent was in the loft tonight—talking to Teresa and to Applebee and the boy. After a while, he heard footsteps. He sat straight as Foster stepped into the opening between the dividers and came into the little room with him.

The small, narrow man was in shirtsleeves, his tie loosened. His gun was in a shoulder holster. He was fidgeting, shifting his neck in his collar.

"We're going to take them to a doctor," he said. "We have a car coming to pick them up. They'll be safe."

Shannon nodded. "Thanks. I wasn't sure you'd still be here."

"We were going to close up shop first thing tomorrow."

"Well, happy days then. You're back in business."

Foster gave a series of quick, nervous expressions and gestures: smiles, shrugs, winces. Then he settled into the chair across from Shannon. After that, for once, he seemed to stop moving. He became unusually focused, his features unusually still.

"Okay," he said. "Let's hear it."

"I sent Ramsey a message," Shannon said. "I told him I'd deal."

Foster's eyes shifted once, away and back, as he took this in. Then he was still and attentive again. "Okay. You figure he'll get the message?"

"He'll get it."

"And then?"

"Then . . . I figure—you brief me on what it is I'm supposed to know. I go in wired, meet with the guy, deal with him, maybe draw him out. When you hear what you need to hear, you move in and bust him."

There was another moment of stillness between the two of them, Foster's eyes on Shannon, Shannon's on Foster, both men silent. Murmuring voices came from the other side of the dividers, the other end of the loft. Then Foster's face went bright with a grin. He shook his head. He laughed.

"What?" said Shannon.

"No, no, dog, nothing. It's a great plan. Great, really. Except if you go in wired, he'll find it in half a second."

Shannon thought about it. "Not wired then. We set it up somewhere you can mike."

"He won't come into anything like that. He won't come just anywhere."

"He'll come. He'll have to."

"No. He's not stupid. He'll have to feel safe."

Shannon thought some more but couldn't come up with anything.

Foster helped him out. "We have some tools available. If they work, we'll be able to listen in."

"There you go. Do that then. Use your tools."

"What we won't be able to do is stay close. If he's smart—and he is smart—we'll be too far away to get to you."

"Why do you have to get to me?"

"Stop him killing you. We won't be able to get to you in time to stop him killing you."

"If he kills me, then you've got him. Isn't that what you said?"

232

Foster shook his head. "That was before. Now you're a cop-killer."

"He still can't just kill me. Not if you're listening in."

"Maybe."

"All right then. It's a plan."

"He *will* kill you, Shannon. You know that, right? He may talk to you, he may not. He may just open fire."

"Then you've got him. That's what you wanted."

"I'd say *probably*. I'd say he'll *probably* just open fire."

"Well, then you've got him," Shannon said again.

"And if you do live . . . in the unlikely event . . . man, I'm telling you—I can't promise you anything. Not thing one. I'm not in that position."

"Doesn't sound like it's going to be an issue, does it?"

Foster laughed again. "No, it doesn't. No, it definitely does not." He lapsed into another silence—silence and stillness—studying Shannon.

"Is there a problem?" Shannon said.

"Maybe. I don't know. I'm not reading this. It makes me uncomfortable."

"I guess we all have to take our chances, don't we?"

"Maybe. I mean, give me a clue—what am I dealing with here? Is it silver bells, Christmas time in the city? You suddenly discover your inner good Samaritan . . . ? Oh wait . . . The girl."

Shannon said nothing.

"You're kidding me," Foster said. "This is about the girl?"

"And the boy and the old man, too."

"Well, well, well."

"Whatever."

"What do you want exactly?"

"I want them out of here. They're not safe in this city. The cops are after them, the bangers are after them. The cops and the bangers are the same people here—what the hell? I want them safe. I want them out. New city, new job, new names if they need them."

233

"New life, like princess in fairy tale, huh."

Shannon's lip curled. The skeevy federal bastard had been listening to that, too. "That's right. Why not? They'll never be safe here now."

"No, they won't. You're right about that. They're dead if they stay."

"So what's the problem? Can't you do it? They're clean. They got no records. Nothing you got to clear or pull strings for. You got programs that handle stuff like this, don't you?"

"Oh yeah. We can do it. For them? It'd be easy."

"So there it is. That's the deal."

"You go in, Ramsey kills you, we get Ramsey, the girl and her people are safe. That's the deal?"

"Well—who knows? Maybe he won't kill me."

"Oh, he'll kill you, Shannon. I don't mind making the deal, but that's what it is. He'll kill you."

"All right. But you'll make the deal?"

"I might. Is that everything?"

Shannon hesitated, pressing his lips together. He didn't like to tell this skeevy bastard any more than he had to. "Tell her how you set me up. When it's all done, tell her how I didn't know. When I came into her house, I didn't know anyone was after me. I wouldn't have brought them into it, if I'd known."

"That's right. It was my doing. I'll tell her that."

"And about Gutterson, how that happened. And how I never did Hernandez. I was never anywhere near that."

"Your last will and testament, huh?"

"Whatever. Don't be an asshole. Just tell her."

The federal agent sat still, watching him, thinking it over. "I don't think I've ever seen this before."

"The world is full of things you don't see."

"Is it? I wouldn't know." He stood up quickly. "All right."

Shannon stood up. "We're good to go?"

Foster nodded. He stretched his neck, moving his shoulders up and down in an undulating rhythm. The tics and nervous shiftings had begun again. "We're good. We'll have to move fast before Ramsey figures it out."

"That's your department. Do what you do."

Foster moved away, moved to the edge of the plywood divider. He paused there. He glanced back at Shannon.

"What now?" Shannon said. "For Christ's sake, Foster."

"All right. All right. But it's kind of out of character for you, this, isn't it?"

"I guess it's not, since I'm doing it."

"I guess that's right." But he studied Shannon another moment or two.

"We all have to take our chances, Foster," Shannon told him.

"I guess that's right," Foster said again. He walked out.

Shannon stayed where he was, alone in the little enclosure. He paced back and forth behind the plywood walls. He didn't want to go out in the loft and see Teresa. He didn't want to see Applebee or the boy, either. He just wanted them to go so he could do what he was going to do and get it over with. It would be easier without seeing them.

But the boy came running the length of the loft. Shannon heard his footsteps, and then the kid came into the enclosure.

"Hey," said Shannon, looking down at him.

"The car is here to take us to the doctor."

"That's good. The doctor'll fix you up."

"I don't even hurt anymore."

"Well, you're a tough guy."

Teresa came looking for her son. She took him by the shoulders. "Come on, Michael, we have to go."

The boy stood looking up at Shannon. "You beat the gangsters," he said.

"That's right."

"There were a lot of them, too."

"They won't hurt you anymore. You'll be safe now."

"Come on, sweetheart," said Teresa.

235

"Isn't Henry coming to the doctor?"

"We have to go," she told him. "The car is waiting."

"I'll see you, kid," Shannon said.

"Go wait with Grandpa," Teresa said.

She sent the boy back into the loft. She stepped into the enclosure with Shannon. She stepped close to him. Her face was swollen and lopsided, but it didn't bother him. He looked in her eyes and he was crazy in love with her. He wanted to explain that he hadn't known he was dangerous to her or he would never have come to her house in the first place.

"Listen . . ." he said.

She put her hand on his face and drew him toward her and kissed him. It was a good kiss. When she drew back, he couldn't find any words.

"We'll talk later," she said softly.

"Sure," he said.

"We'll figure it all out. Nothing's impossible."

He was crazy in love with her; he couldn't believe how much. "I'll be seeing you, Teresa," he said.

"See you."

She walked out of the enclosure. He listened to her footsteps, moving back across the loft. He listened to the voices. He heard the door closing. Then the loft was quiet.

He was glad they were gone. They just made it harder. Now he could do what he was going to do. Now he could get it over with.

IT WAS A LONG NIGHT—a long, long night. The waiting was bad. *The waiting is always the worst part,* Shannon thought. He lay on the cot where the slick agent had read the girly magazine. He lay with his eyes open, staring up at the pipes zig-zagging through the shadows on the loft ceiling. He thought that this was what it must feel like to be on death row. The weird combination of suspense—as if you didn't know what was going to happen—and the sickness of inevitability. Shannon figured you felt the suspense because even though you *did* know what would happen, you couldn't help hoping you'd be saved from it somehow. Where there's life, there's hope—that's what makes the whole business so terrifying.

Funny, he thought, he had done all this to escape from death row and yet here he was. But then what did you expect in the long run? In the long run, it was all death row. There was only one way out of the world.

Foster and the slick agent stayed with him through the night. Mostly, they sat silently in the metal folding chairs. Once or twice Foster went into the enclosure. Shannon could hear him in there, murmuring into his cell phone, but couldn't make out what he said. After a while, Foster left the loft altogether. A few hours later, he came back and the slick agent left. Shannon figured they were going somewhere to get some sleep.

Shannon himself slept now and then. He would doze off and then wake with a start, realizing the morning was now that much closer. He figured it was just as well to sleep since the waiting was awful, but still, the end was that much closer, and the suspense and the sickness of inevitability grew worse.

Finally—suddenly—he saw blue dawn at the loft windows and figured he'd dozed off again. There was something lingering in his mind as if it had come to him while he was asleep. It was a story someone had told him a long time ago, when he was a little boy. He must've been very little, because he couldn't remember who had told him the story. He only had the sense that it had been a woman and he'd been sitting cross-legged on the floor looking up at her and she had been very kind. It was strange the things that came back to you and the things that didn't.

As for the story itself, it was about a boy who went to a magical country in his dreams. Shannon couldn't remember the details of it, only that the boy had met a magical fairy and she had given him a golden ring. Then, at the end of the story, the boy woke up in his bed and realized it had all been a dream—but when he looked down in his hand, there was the ring. It was still there. As a little boy, Shannon had been very impressed by the story and had found the ending wonderful.

He lay there on the cot for a moment, gazing out the window at the lightening sky, sick with the waiting and inevitability. He hadn't thought about that story in a long time, but he sort of understood why it had come back to him now. It was *his* story in some sense. What had happened to the boy had also happened to him. He had had a dream, too—a dream that he could have a new life with a new name and a new face in a new city—and now he was awake and it had only been a dream, but he had met Teresa there, and the way he felt about her was like the gold ring in the story.

Who was it who had told him that story, he wondered. It seemed to him he should remember someone who had been kind to him when he was a boy . . .

The loft door opened and Foster came in. Shannon had not realized he was gone. He was carrying a bag with him from a local diner. Shannon could smell coffee.

"Let's get ready," Foster said.

Shannon swung his legs over the side of the cot and sat up, rubbing the sleep from his eyes.

He was glad the waiting was over.

Now it was full day. Shannon was sitting in one of the metal chairs in the main part of the loft. He had his elbow propped on the card table to steady his arm. He was holding the handset of an old-fashioned landline phone to his ear, the kind with a coiling wire. His grip on the handset felt weak. His palm was sweaty.

He looked at Foster. Foster sat next to him, leaning toward him. He had an earpiece in his ear, wired to the phone so he could listen in. He fiddled with the earpiece and with the wire and tapped at a nearby computer keyboard. The phone was hooked to the computer, which was running some kind of program that Foster said would foil a trace, fooling the electronic switching system into thinking the call had come from somewhere else.

Shannon waited for Foster to finish with the keyboard and give him the go-ahead. He was growing more and more nervous by the second. The other two agents stood over them, pretending to be nonchalant, but watching the whole thing intently.

Now finally, Foster drew a breath and nodded at him. Shannon pressed the buttons on the phone. He waited. The phone started ringing. Shannon listened. He licked his lips to wet them. His heart was beating hard. The phone rang again. Foster tapped at his keyboard. Shannon switched the handset to his other hand. He wiped his wet palm on the leg of his jeans.

The phone began to ring again—then it broke off. Shannon's breath caught. Foster stared at him. The weasely agent and the slick agent stood straighter. There was silence on the other end of the line. Then a voice:

"Yes?"

Foster nodded. It was Ramsey. It was a moment before Shannon could speak.

"Hello?" Ramsey said.

"You know who this is?" said Shannon.

"Yeah," Ramsey said. "I know."

"You want to meet me, I'll be at Betsy's Café at noon."

"No. That's no good for me."

"You're not in charge of this," said Shannon gruffly.

"We've both got to feel safe."

There was a pause. Shannon didn't know what to answer.

"You know Anatomy?" Ramsey said. "It's public, crowded. We can sit in plain sight and talk it out. Everyone goes home happy."

Shannon glanced at Foster. Foster shrugged and nodded.

"Yeah," said Shannon. "That's all right. Noon."

"I'll be there."

The phone line went dead.

Shannon hung up. He let out a long breath. "All right. What's Anatomy?"

"Restaurant downtown. Ground floor of One CC—One City Center. It just reopened about a week ago. They'll be booked solid—that's why he picked it. The place has strong connections with the city machine—obviously, or it wouldn't have that location. We won't be able to get a man in there without Ramsey knowing. You'll be on your own."

"But if it's crowded like he said, he can't just kill me."

"Oh, he'll kill you, Shannon."

"But not just right there with everyone looking."

"Maybe. Or maybe he'll just shout, 'Everyone get down, there's a cop-killer' and open fire. I don't know."

Shannon wiped his hand on his jeans again. "I don't think he'll do that."

Foster took out his earpiece and tossed it down on the table. "That must be nice for you," he said. "But believe me, he'll find a way."

THE BUSINESS DISTRICT had been hit hard on the night of the disaster. Water had damaged luxurious lobbies and atria. Rioters had smashed massive storefront windows. Mobs had marauded through skyscrapers, ransacking offices at random. There had been fires everywhere.

No one knew exactly what had destroyed the upper floors of One City Center. Its distinctive spire had somehow been torn free of its moorings and had speared down forty-five stories through the flaming night before piercing the floodwaters, hurling great waves in every direction, and pulverizing itself on the pavement underneath. What was left of the building's top windows had been shattered. Its offices had been gutted by flames. From a distance, the building now seemed a looming charred-black tower rising to a jagged, mangled confusion of light and shadow. It darkened the whole skyline with an aura of malevolence and ruination.

Below, at the building's base on Center Street, there were still rows of boarded windows. There were lobbies and offices still filled with debris. But there were lights on, too, a checkerboard of lighted panes. Revolving doors were turning, people going in and out. The banks and financial and legal businesses had opened again wherever they could. So had the restaurants that served them. Pedestrians crowded the sidewalks and cars passed hesitantly under the sporadic traffic lights, edging around the barriers protecting the broken place in the street where the tower had crashed.

Foster and his agents had found an office directly across from the restaurant Anatomy. The office was abandoned, all the furniture removed, the walls torn up, the insulation underneath exposed. The paneling was gone from the ceiling, too. Wires hung down and light fixtures dangled. The floors were covered with dust.

Shannon and Foster stood together at a filthy window, looking out. They were on the second floor. They could see the front of the restaurant below, but they couldn't see inside through the tinted window. The slickster and the weasel were there behind them, each sitting on a metal chair. A laptop computer was set up on a third chair.

Shannon kept his hands in the pockets of his jeans. They were unsteady and he didn't want Foster to see them shake. It was annoying. In his mind he was pretty calm now that the waiting was over. In his mind he was thinking: *What the hell, right? Everybody dies.* But his body was afraid and unsteady.

"Need another look?" Foster said. He held his cell phone out in front of Shannon. There was a photograph on the phone's screen: Lieutenant Brick Ramsey. He was a solidly built man with a serious, oval-shaped face and a thin moustache. He seemed to have a sort of stillness and dignity about him. He looked like an upright guy, the kind of upright guy every tough neighborhood needs. The priest, the cop, the coach—the kind of father figure they need in these neighborhoods where there are no fathers, where it's all women without virtue and men without honor, like Applebee had said. If this had been one of those old black-and-white movies he had watched back in the white room, a guy who looked like Ramsey would've been the hero of the picture, except for his being black and all. *But the real world was different from the black-and-white movies*, Shannon thought. *The real world was always right on the brink of falling completely the fuck apart.*

"I've got it," Shannon said. "I'll recognize him."

Foster put the phone back in his pocket.

"And you'll be able to hear me, right?" said Shannon. He just said it to say something because he was nervous. He didn't really want to know how the whole thing was going to work.

"Maybe," said Foster. "We may be able to hear you. We sent a text message to Ramsey's cell phone. When he picked it up, it downloaded a Trojan horse—malware—software—that turned his phone into a listening device."

"Really? You can do that?"

"Maybe. I guess we'll find out."

"Hell, if you can do that, why didn't you just do it before? Why do you need me?"

"Because every warrant we've ever gotten in this city, the target's been alerted within forty-eight hours."

"Great. So what's different now?"

"We got the warrant twenty minutes ago. We may have some time before he finds out."

"But what if . . . ?" Shannon started to say.

"If the Trojan horse doesn't work? Or he turns off his phone or he somehow spots the download or the warrant's already been blown or any of another million ways we can be fucked? Then we'll be fucked. That's just the kind of fly-by-night operation it is, dog."

Shannon's hands clenched in his pockets. "My tax dollars at work," he muttered.

"If we knew what we were doing, we wouldn't be working for the government, believe me. We'd make our own damn money."

Shannon glanced at a clock that stood above the boarded storefront of a bank. It was nearly noon.

Foster said, "All right. Let's go."

It was during the next few moments that Ramsey had his revelation. Until then, there had just been his burgeoning, amorphous dread and superstition, an increasing sense of persecution by unseen forces too powerful to resist and an increasingly desperate idea that none of it mattered anymore anyway. Ever since his meeting with Super-Pred, he had felt like that. He had felt vague and distant, indifferent, dead. When the phone call from the gangster reached him, when he heard that Teresa and her family had escaped, that this plan, too, even this one, had been foiled by the forces arrayed against him, he accepted the news with a sort of spit of laughter, as if to say, *What else could you expect in this unfair world?* He no longer seemed to care whether or not he saved himself. He didn't even feel as if he *was* himself any longer. He was just the sullen vessel of his own resistance to the inevitable end. But the end was inevitable all the same.

So he sat in the booth, waiting. Anatomy was an upscale Italian restaurant. It had soft lighting and yellow walls. There were square tables under white tablecloths throughout the open room. There were booths with brown leather seats against one wall. Hanging on that wall between the sconces here and there were large plaster sculptures of body parts. That's what gave the restaurant its name. There were enormous arms and hands hanging up there, huge legs and feet and an oversized torso. And there was one table under a gigantic woman's breast and another under a gigantic pair of buttocks. That's where Ramsey was sitting—in the booth under the giant ass.

There were people at almost every other table, and the empty tables had signs on them marking them reserved. The crowd was mostly men in suits, but there were some women, too. Everyone was talking and the room was filled with voices and laughter.

Where Ramsey sat—under the plaster buttocks—he had a clear look at the front of the place. The bottom half of the long window was blacked out and there were venetian blinds on the top half. The blinds were partially open, so he could see the people passing on the street. The door was clear glass. He would be able to see anyone approaching.

He sipped from a glass of water, set the glass down, and checked his watch. It was nearly twelve. When he lifted his eyes, he looked out through the front door. He spotted Henry Conor crossing the street.

Ramsey hadn't realized until then that he despised Conor and was afraid of him. Maybe he'd denied it to himself because he didn't like to think he was afraid of any man. But now he felt the full force of it. This nemesis that he sensed was dogging him—this evil fate he'd got himself all worked up about in his mind—what was it, in the end, but Conor really? Conor inspired by the Reverend Skyles as Patterson had been inspired by Skyles. Conor coming after him to avenge Patterson like he was Skyles's vengeance or the vengeance of God. Conor killing Gutterson. Getting the drop on Super-Pred and his g's. Conor and Patterson and Skyles and God and his mother—it had all gotten wrapped up together in Ramsey's mind until it felt like the work of some persecuting power. But now that he saw the man in the flesh he realized: it was just this man, this one man. All he had to do was get rid of this one man and his problems would be over and he'd be free.

Yet, even as he thought that, once again, he felt that instinctive doubt, that awareness of shadow and uncertainty beyond the edges of his understanding. Something still didn't quite add up. Something was wrong.

And then, as so often happens in the moment of crisis, circumstances brought the revelation he needed.

Because, just as Conor reached this side of the street, just as he was approaching the door, his hand lifting to push it open, a waiter came up beside Ramsey. The waiter was a husky crewcut blockhead who looked a lot like a police detective in a white waiter's outfit. He handed Ramsey a pink square of paper from a message pad. Ramsey glanced at the paper. The words on it were scribbled in pencil:

They got a warrant to Trojan horse your phone.

Ramsey looked up sharply. Silently, he mouthed the word: *Who?*

The blockheaded waiter-who-was-really-a-cop mouthed a word back at him: *Feds.*

• • •

Shannon pushed through the restaurant door. The voices and the laughter rose around him as the door swung shut. He saw Ramsey sitting in the booth along the wall. The lieutenant was wearing a fine gray suit and a fine burgundy tie. He was holding a pink message slip in his hand, talking to the waiter standing next to him. Then the waiter moved away and Ramsey looked over and saw Shannon coming toward him and Shannon saw the look in his eyes and it was a look like murder. For a second, fear rose uncoiling like a cobra in his stomach, and he actually thought the scenario might play out the way Foster described it: Ramsey just pulling his gun, just shooting him down right there with everyone watching. But no, that didn't make sense. He took a breath and managed to force himself to keep walking forward.

Ramsey stood up as Shannon reached the booth. The waiter stood close to Shannon so that both men blocked him from the restaurant's view. The waiter was a cop, too, it turned out. He searched Shannon quickly, his hands going over his sides, his stomach, down to his ankles. Shannon let it happen, glancing up idly at the enormous plaster buttocks hanging on the wall. What the hell was that about?

Then the waiter was finished searching him. He nodded at Ramsey and moved away. Ramsey sat back down. Shannon slid into the booth across the table from him. He wagged his thumb at the ass over his head.

"I hope that's not a working model."

Ramsey gave a barely visible hint of a smile. "Could be." He crumpled the pink message slip and put it into his jacket pocket. He came out with his cell phone. He placed the phone in front of him, a small black machine on the white tablecloth. "In your case, it could just be."

The lieutenant's calm, still, dignified eyes held his eyes steadily. It made Shannon even more nervous. And that cell phone on the table, the phone that was supposed to act as a listening device . . . Shannon glanced away, looked around the room at the men and women talking and laughing over their plates of pasta. At least the restaurant was full of witnesses in case anything bad happened.

"You have something to say to me?" Ramsey asked.

When Shannon looked at him again, Ramsey was toying with the cell phone on the table in front of him, turning it this way and that as if he was getting ready to spin it around. Had the warrant been blown? Did he know the phone was bugged? Did he know this was a federal operation? Shannon couldn't face the possibility. He decided the lieutenant was just playing with the phone, that's all.

Shannon leaned toward him, leaned toward the phone.

"I was there the night you took down Patterson," he said. That was how Foster had told him to open it, go for the shock value. "I was Patterson's backup. I saw the whole thing."

Ramsey turned the cell phone on the tablecloth this way and that. He gazed at Shannon mildly. "Take down Patterson? What do you mean?"

"You know what I mean. I was there. I saw it happen."

"Saw what? I don't know what you're talking about."

"You know damn well. He gave me copies of his records, too."

"You're not making sense." Ramsey turned the cell phone in his hand, gazing at Shannon.

"I'm not here to bust you, Ramsey. That was Patterson's thing. I don't care. I'm just after money, that's all."

"I'm sure you are," said Ramsey calmly, turning the phone in his hand. "But this is all a mystery to me."

Shannon felt cold sweat break out on his temples and under his shirt. This was bad. It was wrong. He could feel it. He could feel disaster coming at him, a train on a track. He leaned toward Ramsey, his face damp, his arms on the table. He was vaguely aware that the restaurant noise of voices and laughter had grown dimmer around him.

"Look," he said in a harsh whisper. "You brought me here. I thought you wanted to deal. You don't want to deal, don't waste my time."

"You're the one who's wasting time," said Ramsey coolly, smiling slightly. "I thought you had information for me about a murder case. Now you sound as if you're trying to blackmail me. But over what? It doesn't make sense."

It was such a smooth performance that Shannon stared at him. And as he stared, he noticed for the first time that the sounds of voices and laughter all around him had died away completely. The restaurant was quiet. There was a clink of silverware against a plate, then nothing.

Feeling the sweat roll down his chest, Shannon turned. The people sitting at the tables—the men in suits, the women here and there—had all stopped talking, stopped eating. They were all just sitting there at their tables. They were all turned toward him, every single one of them. Just sitting at their tables and staring at Shannon.

Shannon sensed a movement behind him. He looked over his shoulder in time to see a waiter—or a man dressed as a waiter —close the venetian blinds that covered the top half of the front window. Now the whole window was covered. Shannon turned farther at another movement and saw another waiter directly in back of him locking the front door, moving to stand in front of the door so that no one could see past him.

Now there was no noise in the restaurant at all. The place was silent and he understood: they were *all* cops. Everyone in the restaurant. They were all Ramsey's people. It was all a setup, all of it.

Shannon slowly turned back to Ramsey, his eyes passing over all those people—all those cops—at the tables staring at him. When he faced front again, Ramsey gazed at him just as mildly as before. A line of sweat ran down Shannon's temple.

Without looking down, Ramsey opened his cell phone. He pressed the power button. The cell phone gave out a tone and went dark.

"Now let's really talk," Ramsey said.

• • •

In the abandoned second-floor office across the way, the weaselly federal agent leaned forward in his chair, his face close to the laptop. He was listening to the voices of Ramsey and Shannon coming through the speaker.

"Man," he said. "Thing's working great. They're really coming over five by five."

Foster was still standing at the window, still looking down at the front of the restaurant below. "Well, well," he said. "Will wonders never cease?"

Then the voices coming from the computer crackled once and died.

"Wait a minute," said the weasel. "I think we lost them."

"I guess that answers that question," Foster murmured.

He narrowed his eyes, peering down at the restaurant. His hand was lifted near his face, his thumb rubbing his fingers as if he were feeling a piece of cloth—a nervous gesture. He noticed a movement now at the dark windows. It took him a moment to figure out what it was, then he realized: the venetian blinds had closed. His heart sank.

"Shit," he said. "They've got him."

Shannon felt the silence all around him, the eyes all around him. He felt his own breath go in and out and looked in Ramsey's eyes, which were calm and sad and unmovable. He hoped that Foster was on the run, coming like the cavalry to save him, but at the same time, he knew this was just hope, the everlasting reflex of hope: no one was coming, no one could. Ramsey's mild gaze—no wonder they called him Brick, his mild gaze was like a brick wall, like the dead end of yet another blind alley in a luckless life full of blind alleys, full of brick walls. And all those people—all those cops—sitting at all those tables, in all those booths under the plaster body parts, staring at him without mercy and without a sound . . . No one could save him here.

"It's funny, you know." Ramsey frowned down at the cell phone on the table. He considered it, turning it this way and that. "I was actually beginning to get superstitious about you. No, really. All this time, I sensed there was something wrong, something working against me. I thought . . . I'm not sure what I thought. But there's a reasonable explanation for everything, isn't there?"

Shannon breathed in and out, and the sweat trickled down his face. He knew it showed his fear, but he couldn't stop it.

"Who are you?" Ramsey asked him quietly. "Who sent you here?"

Shannon licked his lips and started, "I told you, I—"

"The smartest thing"—Ramsey interrupted him without raising his voice—"the smartest thing you could do for yourself now would be to tell the truth quickly. Because otherwise, we'll take it out of you slowly, bit by bit."

Shannon wiped his face with one hand. There was no point trying to hide the sweat; there it was for everyone to see. He took a long, deliberate look around the room—at the giant plaster nose, the torso, the cold, plaster, comfortless breast, and all those expressionless faces underneath the body parts that might as well have been plaster, too.

"Pretty good," he said, nodding. "Pretty good, Ramsey."

"I'm going to ask you one more time," Brick Ramsey said. "I need to know who you are and who sent you. I need to know how far along this has gotten. You're going to tell me eventually, so why don't you just tell me now."

Shannon opened his mouth. His tongue felt as if it were coated with some sort of sour dust. He felt all those merciless eyes on him and all those cold, plaster body parts and Ramsey's merciless eyes. And no one was coming to help him.

"Go to hell," he said. He looked around the room and swallowed the sour dust and raised his voice. "You can all go to hell."

Ramsey barely lifted his chin in answer and the blockheaded waiter-who-was-a-cop stepped up behind Shannon swiftly and stuck the hard, hurtful barrel of a Beretta into the hollow behind his ear.

• • •

The slick agent now rose thoughtfully from his chair. He moved to stand beside Foster. Foster remained where he was, standing at the window, staring out the window at Anatomy across the street, rubbing his fingers with his thumb, rubbing them.

"Should we go in?" the slick agent asked him.

Foster hesitated, gazing down at the restaurant, thinking through the possibilities. Finally, he shook his head. "If they see us coming, they'll kill him on the spot. It'd be over before we got there. Just another dead cop-killer, they'd say." Rubbing his fingers. Thinking. "No. Ramsey is going to want to know who he is, who sent him. If our guy holds out, they'll take him somewhere, somewhere they can work on him, make him talk."

"Why would he hold out?" said the slick agent. "He's just a punk. Why would he?"

Foster's face was blank, his lips parted. He went on rubbing his fingers with his thumb, in a reverie, thinking. "The girl," he said, in a distant voice. "If he gives us up, they'll get to us before we can get her into the system. If he talks, they'll get the girl."

The slick agent considered that, looking from Foster to the window. He grimaced. "He's a punk. He'll just tell them everything."

But Foster shook his head. "He won't. They're going to have to move him somewhere. To work on him."

Now the weasely agent got out of his chair as well. He moved to stand next to Foster and the slick agent, and they all three stood at the window, looking out.

"They're going to have to bring him out—get him into a car," said Foster. "We'll have a chance then, a shot at stopping them. They've got to bring him out and when they do, we'll see them and make our move."

But he was wrong. They took Shannon out of the restaurant through the service exit in the kitchen. It led to a hall off the ground floor of One City Center. It was an empty concrete hall that led to a service elevator.

Ramsey led the way. Shannon followed him. He had no choice.

The blockheaded cop dressed as a waiter was right behind him with the Beretta nine trained on his back. The blockhead kept the gun close to his side so there was no chance to grab it. Shannon knew the blockhead would kill him if he tried.

Ramsey used a Homak key to summon the elevator. The door opened at once. He stood back and let Shannon walk in. Then the blockhead walked in with the nine. Then Ramsey walked in.

Ramsey worked the Homak key in the elevator panel and the door closed. The elevator started up.

Then Ramsey turned and drove his fist deep into Shannon's midsection, right above the groin.

Shannon felt the air rush out of him and doubled over, sick. He was already falling to the floor when Ramsey hit him again, a lead-knuckled blow to the side of the head that dazed Shannon and made his knees give way.

Shannon lay gasping at Ramsey's feet. The moment before Ramsey kicked him, Shannon knew it was coming, but there was nothing he could do about it. Ramsey kicked him in the midsection hard and then kicked him again, aiming for his balls. Shannon spit puke and tried to cover himself. Ramsey grabbed Shannon's windbreaker and lifted him off the floor and punched him, dropping him back down again.

Shannon lay curled on the floor, groaning. He hurt and he was sick, but he didn't think there was anything irrevocable yet, anything broken inside. At the same time, he didn't see any hope of escaping, not with the blockhead holding the gun on him. They would just keep beating him until they were finished, and then they'd shoot him and he didn't see any way out of it. It made him sicker still with fear.

The elevator stopped with a heavy jolt. The door came open. Ramsey grabbed Shannon roughly, lifting him.

"Get up," he said.

Shannon had to take hold of Ramsey as he tried to get his feet under him. He couldn't think straight because of the blows to the head and because his whole body was weak with pain and sickness. He managed to stand up with Ramsey holding him. He stumbled out of the elevator. They were in another concrete hall. Ramsey grabbed him by the collar and hurled him face first into the wall. Shannon felt his nose break, which sent a unique and terrible pain through his head. Hot blood poured down over his face. His legs went rubbery and he started to collapse, but Ramsey grabbed him, held him up, and frog-marched him down the hall.

Shannon saw a door coming at him, but by now he barely knew what was happening. The door opened in the center of a nauseating whirl. A gritty wind bearing the first dead heat of summer washed over Shannon's face. The next thing he knew he was outside, out in the middle of the sky, in the middle of the hot wind. Ramsey dropped him roughly to the floor.

Shannon lay there bleeding, trying to lift his head, trying to look around and get a glimpse of things through his haze of pain and concussion. He saw the naked sky through iron beams, walls in shreds like torn fabric, charred like burned paper. The dark towers of the skyline were visible through the gaps. Great, billowing clouds raced behind the towers on the hot, gritty wind.

Shannon understood where he was. He was on one of the top floors, one of the ruined floors, of One City Center. It was like being in a room that had exploded. The walls were smashed clear through, the beams visible, the windows shattered, the remnants burned. All that was left was the charred wreckage of the place on an open platform in the sky.

He knew what they were going to do to him, too. They were going to throw him off the building. He would fall so far, hit the pavement so hard, his body would be crushed to cinders, and no one would be able to tell what had happened to him. They would get their medical people to say it was an accident or suicide. That would be that.

The fear of dying in that particular fashion made him even weaker, even sicker, but there was nothing he could do, he was too beaten and dazed now to fight back. He tried to think of something that would make it easier for him. He thought of Teresa. He thought he still had the way he felt about her. It was like the gold ring in the boy's hand after his dream in the story—he still had it. He thought she would be safe now. If he could just keep his mouth shut till they killed him, she would be safe, and Michael and the old man—they would be safe, too. So he could die feeling how he felt about her and knowing he had kept his mouth shut and kept her safe and that was something. Otherwise, yeah, it had been a crap life all around. Maybe there was a better life when this one was over. Maybe God would forgive him for some of the bad things he'd done because, in the end, he had helped Teresa, then he would have a better life. But even if there was no God and no better life, Teresa would be safe. Maybe she would even think about him sometimes. So there was that, too. And basically Ramsey could go fuck himself.

The gritty wind blew over him with a roar. The shredded walls shook and fluttered loudly. Shannon lay on the floor and fought against his sickness and the fear of falling.

The weaselly federal agent and Foster and the slick agent stood together at the window and stared down at the restaurant. Foster rubbed his fingers with his thumb, his face blank.

"What do you think?" said the weaselly agent finally. "They're in there a long time."

Foster wasn't sure what he thought. He stood there silently.

Then he saw a flash at the window. The venetian blinds had opened.

"He's gone," Foster said. "Damn it. They took him out. Let's go."

Ramsey worked Shannon over on the floor of the shattered room at the top of the ruined tower. He kicked him in the gut and in the spine. He stomped on his hand, breaking his fingers with a snapping sound. He lifted him up by the jacket and punched him. The blockheaded cop in the white waiter's outfit looked on absently, holding the gun vaguely in Shannon's direction. The hot wind blew through the torn walls and the walls shuddered with a loud noise.

At first, the blows hurt Shannon, each one a fresh pain. He tried to cover himself and when he couldn't cover himself, he tried to crawl away. When he couldn't crawl away, he just lay there on the floor and went through it. After a while, it was all pain, a sort of throbbing, indivisible suffering mixed with the mess of blood and vomit on him and the sad understanding that they would kill him when they were through. He tried to think about Teresa, but after a while he couldn't think about anything except how bad it was. He just wanted it to stop, even if they did kill him.

"Now," said Ramsey, breathless with the work. He knelt down next to Shannon's head. He knelt on one knee and draped his arm over the other. He looked at Shannon mildly. Shannon flinched at his every move, afraid of more blows. "You're going to tell me who you are and how much you really know and who runs you," Ramsey said.

Cowering, his hands over his head, Shannon tried to answer him, but it just came out a sobbing groan.

Ramsey reached down. He pulled Shannon's hands away from his face and slapped him in the nose lightly with his knuckles. With his nose broken and his cuts raw all over, the blow sent a fresh explosion of hurt through Shannon's head.

"I didn't understand you, boy. Speak up," said Ramsey.

Shannon swallowed blood and tried again, louder. "You killed Patterson."

"Is that right? Who told you to say that?"

"I saw."

"You're lying. I want to know who runs you."

Shannon wearily mumbled his answer.

"What did you say?"

"Said . . . go . . . to hell. And fuck yourself on the way down."

Ramsey laughed at that. He glanced at the blockhead standing guard. "He's a tough guy."

"He is," said the blockhead reflexively. He wasn't really listening and didn't really care.

Ramsey looked down at Shannon's blood-soaked face. Shannon's eyes blinked whitely at him out of the blood. "Are you a fed? Or are the feds just running you?"

"Killed . . . Patterson . . ."

"You're going to tell me everything, Conor," he said. "Really. Why make it so hard?"

Shannon gave a weak laugh. "Already hard."

"It's going to get a lot harder, son, believe me."

Shannon tried to curse him out but could only cough up blood.

"You don't want to die, do you?" said Ramsey.

Shannon coughed some more. "Not afraid," he said.

Which wasn't strictly true. He was full of fear, but he knew he could get through it. It had been a crap life and now Teresa would be safe. Fuck Ramsey.

Ramsey rabbit-punched him in the testicles. Shannon doubled over, gagging and sobbing.

"I want to know who sent you," Ramsey said quietly.

Shannon could not feel the hot wind on him anymore, but he could hear the walls rocking and shuddering. He could see patches of blue and clouds flying past towers as his head lolled over. He prayed to God to let it end already, to let him die, even if there was no better life.

Foster sent his two agents into the restaurant and good luck to them, but he went another way. He pushed through the revolving doors into the lobby of One City Center. He strode to the reception desk, flashing his federal ID. There was a male security guard there and a female receptionist.

"How many ways are there out of the restaurant?" Foster barked at them.

"There's a door into the lobby and one into the service hall," the receptionist said. She was a short, busty woman with an air of competence.

"There a way out of the service hall?"

"A back door to the Dumpsters and the elevator. You need a key for the elevator." The woman slapped a Homak key down on the black marble reception desk.

"This way," said the security guard. "I'll show you."

Foster followed him across the lobby. He already had an idea about where they'd taken Shannon.

Ramsey didn't have to slug or kick Shannon anymore. He could just probe his torn and broken places. Shannon screamed and sobbed at the pain. After a while, Ramsey knelt over him and studied him, expressionless. He was startled at how much he hated this man, how much he wanted to break him and kill him. The sadistic feelings disgusted him, as if they were some squirmy thing he wanted to hold at a distance from himself. Every time the man screamed, Ramsey felt some satisfaction in it and that disgusted him, too. He wanted to end this—and he would have ended it if it weren't for his pride, his fierce desire to break the man's resistance, to have that victory over him before he threw him off the building.

"Damn it, I'm going to find out the answers anyway, whether you tell me or not," he said quietly. "Tell me what you know and who else knows and who sent you, and we can be done."

Shannon tried to say *fuck you* but couldn't get the words out.

Ramsey grabbed Shannon's broken fingers and made Shannon scream again.

"You said you saw me," Ramsey said.

"Saw you kill Patterson," Shannon managed to answer.

"You're lying. You've got nothing. That's why they sent you, isn't it?"

"I saw you."

Ramsey made him scream again, squeezing his fingers.

"You're lying, aren't you? They sent you because they've got nothing."

"You killed Patterson," Shannon managed to mumble.

Ramsey's anger rose in a red tide. He could feel that he was about to lose control of this. Maybe he already *had* lost control and just didn't know it yet. He was furious and disgusted and he knew he had to finish it, but he couldn't finish it. So maybe he had lost control. *What difference did any of it make?* he reasoned with himself. He could trace the warrant, find out which feds had slipped out of the net. They would make the proper phone calls, take care of them, get rid of them. Whoever ran this operation would end up checking parking meters on the moon . . .

Still . . . still . . . this man here. He couldn't quite rid himself of the feeling that this man *was*, in fact, the nemesis that had pursued him all this time, that was still pursuing him. He wanted vengeance on him for forcing him to go to Super-Pred, forcing him to degrade the very meaning of his biography—his rise out of the ghetto, his service to his country, his service on the force—by begging favors from that fifteen-year-old nightmare version of himself, by letting that nightmare version of himself become his agent in the world. This man had done that to him, forced him to it. He would not be beaten by him now. He would not be defied.

He stood up over the trembling Shannon. He drew his Beretta. He pointed it down at Shannon's knee.

"Look at me, boy," he said.

Shannon looked up at him, blinking through the blood.

"You're making this uglier than it has to be," Ramsey said.

Shannon blinked up at him, open-mouthed. Even in the haze of pain, he realized what Ramsey was going to do. "Aw, don't," he begged.

"Are you going to talk to me or not?"

"Please . . ."

"Are you or not?"

Shannon sobbed in expectation of the agony. "Fuck you," he said. "Fuck you."

"God damn you!" Ramsey said.

His finger was tightening on the trigger when Foster charged through the door.

It was all like a slow-motion dream to Shannon. He was staring up at Ramsey and he saw the gun and he understood what was about to happen and he couldn't do anything but pray and pray for God to let him die and then there was a bang and he thought he'd been shot but he wasn't and he saw movement and there was Foster in some vague, unfocused distance charging across the background of blue sky and tower tops, shouting words Shannon couldn't hear through the wind noise, holding his gun out before him in his two hands.

Then Ramsey was turning, his gun still pointed down at Shannon, and the blockheaded cop in the white waiter's uniform was whipping around toward Foster and lifting his gun. Shannon heard the first shot, not loud, a distant snap almost drowned by the hoarse roar of the wind and the walls rocking and shuddering. He saw the smoke and fire explode from the barrel of Foster's nine. Then the blockheaded cop was flying backward and crumpling to the floor next to Shannon's feet.

Then there was another shot, a blast echoing through the wind. Shannon didn't know where it'd come from. But then he saw the blood and flesh explode on Foster's shoulder and the agent's face contorted with pain and his body twisted and his gun flew from his hand as he went falling toward the sky.

Shannon blinked upward through swollen eyes and saw that it was Ramsey who'd fired, his gun trained on the spot where Foster had been, smoke curling from the barrel of it.

Foster now lay at the edge of the floor, inches from a break in the charred wall, an open space into emptiness, a forty-story fall. The agent was wounded, writhing like a hurt animal, trying to crawl away from the edge to recover the gun that had fallen out of his reach.

All in that vague, unfocused slow-motion—all beneath the

hoarse, shuddering roar of the hot, gritty wind—Shannon saw Ramsey glance down at him from far above to make sure that he wasn't moving, that he was helpless there. And then Ramsey walked away, walked across the room to finish Foster off.

And a thought came to Shannon that was almost like a voice in his ear—that clear—the first clear thought he'd had since Ramsey had started working him over: *The gun! The blockheaded cop's gun!*

Shannon looked up at Ramsey's back as Ramsey walked into the unfocused distance to kill Foster where he lay, and then he, Shannon, looked over at where the blockheaded cop lay on his back on the floor at his feet. And, sure enough, there was the weapon, the nine the cop had been holding—there it was on the floor not far away, so that Shannon realized that if he could only move, if he only had the strength to move, he might get the gun. He might get the gun.

Shannon understood that this was what he had to do, an unlooked-for chance he had to take. He did not feel he had the strength to move or that his body could stand the pain of moving, but he knew he had to. He did not think or pray. He was all prayer and all pain—unbelievable sickness and pain—as he began to curl his body toward the gun, moving his flesh as if it were a mountain of stone under which he was buried, moving it around by what seemed like inches at a time, over a time that seemed like hours. He still saw Ramsey in his peripheral vision, the gray back of him moving away toward Foster. And then Ramsey was gone, and Shannon thought there must be no more time left and that it didn't matter anyway because the pain was just too much, he could not move another inch, but he kept moving—another inch and another—because he understood this was what he had to do, an unlooked-for chance.

It was his left hand that was broken. He reached for the gun with his right, flinching with the agony of the movement but trying not to cry out. Suddenly he felt the wind again and the grit of the wind stinging his wounds. He reached the gun. He closed his fingers around it and began to lift it, his hand trembling weakly and the weight of his flesh and the weight of his pain crushing him down so that every inch of movement required more strength than he believed he had.

He squinted across the room at Ramsey and his vision cleared so that he saw the lieutenant standing over Foster now, lifting his gun to put a final bullet in him. Shannon could not bring his own weapon to bear fast enough. He could not stop Ramsey in time.

So he shouted out "Ramsey!" through the wind.

And he saw Ramsey, startled, spinning around, turning the gun quickly from Foster to point it straight at him.

When Ramsey heard the shout and turned and saw the blood-soaked figure bringing the gun to bear on him, he knew what was going to happen next, it seemed inevitable. All in a moment, he felt overwhelming desperation, rage, and terrible shame. A wild, silent cry of regret, a silent cry of yearning for his mother's comfort, tore from his guts and filled him. All in a moment, he saw: it was his doing, all his doing, and he was sorry for it.

Maybe that's why he hesitated just a fraction of a fraction of a second before he began to pull the trigger.

But it was too late by then. Shannon shot him.

It was a wild shot. The bullet hit only the fleshy edge of Ramsey's thigh. It didn't even knock the gun out of his hand. But the jolt and the searing pain made him stagger back a step and he tripped over Foster lying there and he staggered back another step and fell off the edge of the floor into nothingness and went down and down and down, screaming in helpless terror and sorrow for what felt like forever.

Shannon saw Ramsey fall back into the sky and vanish in a finger snap as by some terrible magic, and he understood that it was over. The weight of the gun and the pain overwhelmed him then. He collapsed onto the floor in a spreading puddle of his own blood.

He closed his eyes. He felt himself sinking away into darkness—death or unconsciousness, he didn't know which. Either way, he was glad—glad and grateful for it. It was over. He had done everything he had to do.

He let himself go and was gone.

EPILOGUE

IT WAS STRANGE to be back in the white room. For the first day or two, he was in a painkiller fog, and it was very strange. He hung suspended in the fog as if in midair, and the fog drifted by him, sometimes black and sometimes gray and sometimes full of present shadows or past faces he remembered. He saw the white room through the breaks in the fog for shapeless moments at a time, and he wasn't sure whether it was really there or he was dreaming. And when he thought it *was* there, that he *was* back in the white room again, he wondered if the rest of it had been a dream—the ruined city and the wooden angel and Teresa—everything a dream while he had been here in the white room all along.

Slowly, day by day, the fog thinned. He wafted down from the air and intermittently felt the bed beneath him. The sound of a door opening or footsteps on the floor would alert him and he would fight against the weighted haze, trying to sit up and see more clearly. He caught glimpses of men with guns. Different men at different times. One would stand over him with his thumbs in his belt and look down at him with a deadpan face. Another would sit in a chair against the wall and page through a magazine. Yet another would just sit in the chair and stare. Lawmen of some sort, standing guard.

There were other men, too, sometimes—and sometimes women: doctors or nurses in scrubs with stethoscopes around their necks.

They fussed at him and shifted him on the bed and stuck needles into him. Sometimes they gave him water through a straw and he drank gratefully. When they spoke to him, they spoke as if he were an infant or a dog—as if he couldn't really understand or answer them. When he did answer, they always seemed surprised and a little resentful. Then he would be gone again and when he woke up it was all so hard to remember.

One day, he opened his eyes, and there was Foster. Same old narrow, bald, seedy agent in yet another cheap suit. Shannon squinted through sleep and saw him fidgeting in a chair at his bedside. He was wearing a blue sling on his right arm and Shannon remembered that Ramsey had shot him.

Foster rubbed his neck with his good hand. He shifted his neck in his collar. He looked up at a woman working a machine by the bed.

"All right?" he said. "I need him clear."

If she answered, Shannon didn't hear her. He saw her walk away. With lazy nausea, he moved his head so he could look at Foster.

"Teresa," Shannon said. He had a feeling it was not the first time he had said it.

"Yeah, yeah, she's all right," said Foster. "I told you. They're fine, they're in the system. New city, new life. No one even knows they were involved. They'll be okay."

Shannon closed his eyes and let out a breath. It was a great relief to him. He shifted uncomfortably. He was beginning to become aware of a new, unwelcome clarity. The drugs were wearing off, the tendrils of painless fog losing their grip on him, falling away. He could feel cool reality drifting over his skin like air drifting over a rotting tooth. He understood for the first time—or for the first time he could remember anyway—that his body was broken and wrong and the drugs were keeping him from the full feeling of it. He opened his eyes.

"How bad?" he mumbled. "How bad am I?"

Foster gave a jerky shrug. "You got a beating, dog. Ribs broken.

Nose, fingers. Lost your spleen. Muscles torn up all over. You'll live, though."

Shannon nodded.

"But we better talk fast," the agent went on. "I need you clear. I need you to understand what I tell you. But once the drugs wear off, you'll be a traveler in the unhappy lands, my friend. So let's get it over with, so we can put you back under."

Shannon managed another nod. "What . . . ?"

"Focus, boy. You understanding me?"

"Yeah, yeah. I hear you."

"All right. Here it is. The situation out there in the world is currently pretty bleak, not to say dire, for both you and me. We're getting hit good and hard. The media have put their heart and soul into the Augie Lancaster dream of life, and the idea that he's the most corrupt, power-hungry organism in the galaxy isn't sitting well."

Shannon had to fight hard to understand this. His head was clearing, but as it cleared, he felt the pain closing on him like a fresh skin of knitted nerve endings, closing on him until it passed through, and he couldn't tell whether it was outside him or rising from within . . . It was distracting. "Yeah? Okay?"

"Well, you know how the media thing goes," said Foster. "The way they tell it, it's all *our* fault. It was an illegal operation, blah, blah, blah. We're just trying to bring down a great reformer and defend the status quo, doncha know. We're racists taking vengeance on Augie for exposing the white man's incompetence during the flood. Whatever. People will do and say just about anything to keep from admitting they're wrong. They're wrong about Augie, but they don't care. They'll die to keep from admitting it."

"Right, right, right," said Shannon. He was starting to breathe harder, to flinch with the spark and play of his pain. "So what's the point?"

"The point is: I'll probably be fired. Possibly I'll do some prison time. Which means you've got no friends anywhere."

"Well . . . I never knew you were my friend anyway, so no loss."

"It's a sad fact, dog, but I'm all you've got. Without me, they'll be in here trying to charge you with shit you never even heard of. You don't get yourself a good lawyer, you'll die in prison, maybe get the lethal I."

"Well . . ." Shannon took a sharp breath as the pain shot through him. It was a tough situation, but he couldn't think about it now. "It is what it is," he said.

"Yeah," said Foster. "It surely is." He stood up out of his chair and moved the chair in front of him and moved to stand behind it. He looked here and there around the room. "The way it's going to go is this. A lot of serious-looking men and women wearing expensive suits the taxpayers were forced to pay for at gunpoint are going to come through here in the next few days and weeks and ask you questions in stern, serious tones of voices the taxpayers were also forced to pay for. They will be full of shit, every single one of them, and they will be attempting to convict you of anything they can in the hopes they can support Augie Lancaster so that the media will make them look virtuous and they can continue to live off the ever-dwindling fat of the land. That is called your government, son, and when it is finished with you, it will put you in one of its prisons or kill you dead. Now you've been warned."

Shannon gave a small groan. Man, he hurt. He hurt all over. He forced himself to focus through it. "Okay. Okay. What do you figure I should do?"

Foster frowned. "Tell the truth. They're not used to it. It fucks with their heads. That's what I'd do. But it's your call. I just thought you ought to know what's coming."

"Okay. Okay, thanks. Don't worry about—" The pain cut a jagged path through him like lightning. He tensed and fought down a cry.

"Hey, Doc," Foster called.

The woman came back into the room. Foster nodded at the machine beside Shannon's bed. The doctor went to it and pushed the buttons.

Foster continued to stand there behind the chair, looking down at him. Holding the chair back with his two hands, drumming his fingers on it. "They gave Ramsey a hero's funeral yesterday," he said. "Bagpipes and everything."

Shannon felt the tendrils of the drug growing back over him like vines. The pain began to ease, his body relaxing. "Did they? What a comedy."

"That's what I'm talking about. That's what I'm trying to say. They'll tag you for that, if they can. Killing him. Killing a hero cop. I can only do what I can do."

Shannon gave a small laugh. "I don't expect any breaks. I know how it is." The tendrils spread into fog. His breathing grew deeper.

"Did you hear him at the end?" he heard Foster ask from a dreamy distance. "Ramsey. Did you hear him scream as he went down?"

Shannon shook his head slowly, his eyes fluttering shut. He had not heard. He only had seen Ramsey disappear into the sky like magic. He saw it now again.

"I heard him," said Foster. "Man, I'm still hearing him. At night? It's like he's still around somewhere, still screaming."

Shannon smiled dreamily, letting himself sink away. "I wouldn't worry about it, Foster."

"Yeah, I guess," he heard Foster say. "But when you work for the federal government, it's not such a big leap to believe in hell."

The men and women came in their expensive suits as Foster had said they would. By then, the pain had become bearable. The fog of drugs had thinned to a mere mist. Shannon lay on his bed and gazed quietly at the men and women as they asked him questions and pointed their fingers at him and sometimes leaned over to shout in his face. He told them everything that had happened. He did not hide anything. This only seemed to make them angrier. They accused him of lying. They accused him of murdering Ramsey. At one point, one man, an old guy with big eyebrows bouncing up and down, told him that he was going to go to death row and be executed if he didn't change his story right this minute. Shannon gazed at him from the bed. It was odd, but he was not afraid. He was not afraid of any of these people or of anything they might do to him. At first, he thought maybe it was the drugs dulling his feelings. But it was not the drugs. The drugs were very mild now. He just wasn't afraid, that's all. He just told the truth and lay on the bed and gazed at the government people as they came and went.

One day, Sharpstein came. Sharpstein was a large, flabby man with a large, flabby face. He wore glasses with black frames. He said he was Shannon's lawyer. Shannon never knew who sent him.

Shannon was out of bed by now. He was dressed in jeans and a black sweater when Sharpstein walked in with his brown briefcase. He was sitting on the couch in the main room, the room where he had watched all the old movies on the DVD player the last time he was here. But the DVD player was gone, so he was just sitting there.

Sharpstein set his briefcase on the table. "Don't they give you a TV in here?"

"No. I could use a TV. One of the doctors brought me some comic books, but I read them all."

"No computer? No Internet?"

"No."

Sharpstein's big, flabby face seemed to expand. "Jesus. That's gotta be a violation of something or other. What do you do all day?"

Shannon shrugged. "Work out. Try to get my body back. I still sleep a lot." He also spent hours daydreaming about Teresa, making up scenarios in his mind about the life they would never spend together, what it would have been like. But he didn't tell Sharpstein that. Who the hell was Sharpstein anyway?

"Man!" said Sharpstein. "Stuck in here all day with nothing to do? It'd make my skin crawl. Doesn't it make your skin crawl?"

Shannon's lips parted in surprise. He stared at Sharpstein for a long time. "No," he said, wondering. "It doesn't make my skin crawl. You're right, it should, shouldn't it? It always used to. But no—no, it doesn't." It was like not being afraid of prison or death row. It was another odd thing he noticed.

"So no one's telling you anything either? You have no idea what's going on out there?"

"No," said Shannon. "What's going on?"

Sharpstein laughed. He had a high-pitched laugh that made his jowls quiver. He seemed full of glee at the absurdity of people. He told Shannon that a big struggle was taking place. It was all political and hard to understand. As far as Shannon could make out, the people who talked on the radio were battling the people who appeared on TV. It had started with Foster. He had been suspended from his job and had gone on the radio to talk about it. The people on television had not let him come on, but the people on radio let him and he told his story. Then, a detective told *his* story on the radio. It was the detective Foster had shot on the rooftop, the one who dropped the gun that Shannon used. Somehow, he had changed sides and decided to talk on the radio, too. The people on television didn't like this. They brought people on to attack the detective and to prove he was a bad man and a liar. And he *was* a bad man and a liar, and they *did* prove it. But the thing was, when they proved it, they accidentally also proved that Ramsey was a bad man and that he was corrupt, and then the people on the radio began talking about that as well. After that, the public started to get interested, so the politicians also started fighting. The way Sharpstein told it, the politicians who wanted to look virtuous on television were squaring off against the politicians who wanted to sound virtuous on radio and they were arguing back and forth.

Shannon didn't get any of this. "What's it got to do with me?" he asked.

"Well, it saved your life for one thing," Sharpstein said. "The TV pols wanted you moved to prison so you could be killed by a fellow inmate before you gave any public testimony."

"Really? They said that?"

"No! Of course not! They don't just say things like that. What're you, crazy? They don't even know you exist yet. They just know there are witnesses being kept in seclusion, namely you. And they want you put in prison where you can be killed. They call that transparency."

"Me getting killed is transparency?"

"Or the public's right to know. Something. Anyway, luckily for you, the radio pols managed to embarrass the TV pols enough so they backed off on that and let you stay here for now where you're relatively safe . . . Listen, this is ridiculous. We gotta get you a television in here. And a computer so you can find out what's happening."

"Ah . . ." Shannon made a face. He didn't care about any of this. He didn't care what they did to him. "Forget it," he said. "Just . . . Could you get me one of those movie players? And some of those really old movies? You know, the ones before they had color in them."

Sharpstein took a big yellow pad out of his briefcase and put it on the table. He wrote on the pad. "You want to watch black-and-white movies."

"Yeah," said Shannon. "I like those. They're good."

So Shannon went back to watching old movies and working out in the white room, just like before. And now, when the people in expensive suits came to question him, Sharpstein was there and Sharpstein answered most of the questions for him. Shannon appreciated that. He started to like Sharpstein. Sharpstein was entertaining. Sharpstein laughed at the people in the expensive suits—and when he laughed the suit-people looked worried, as if maybe their flies were unzipped and they hadn't noticed it.

"I love this!" Sharpstein said once to a crow-faced woman in a tan pants suit. "My client is telling the truth and you're trying to plea bargain him into lying. It's beautiful!"

"No one wants anyone to lie," said the crow-faced woman grimly. But she had that is-my-fly-unzipped look in her eyes. It was very entertaining.

• • •

Then there was a startling moment.

Shannon was alone, except for the lawman who, he knew, was sitting in a chair outside the door of the white room. Shannon was watching an old black-and-white movie on the TV Sharpstein had gotten him. The movie was about a British pilot during World War II. The pilot was shot down by the Nazis, and he went diving down to earth in his plane to crash and die. But his plane went into the fog and in the fog Death couldn't find him, so even though the plane crashed, the pilot *didn't* die. It was a fantasy movie.

So, anyway, the pilot went off to a hospital and he met this girl and he fell in love with her. But then, Death finally caught up with him and wanted to take him away. But the pilot said, well, hold on a second, that's not right, you made a mistake and now I'm in love and it's not fair to kill me because it's all your fault I'm in this situation to begin with.

Shannon was doing sit-ups during the movie, but when it got to this part, he stopped and just sat up and watched. Because wasn't this exactly what had happened to him? Through no fault of his own, he had been given a life he wasn't supposed to have and he had fallen in love, and then they had come to take him away and it wasn't fair.

In the movie then, the pilot had to go up to heaven for a big trial that was judged by all the good people who had died, like Abraham Lincoln and so on. They argued back and forth over whether the pilot should die or be allowed to live and have his love. Shannon thought this was like what was happening now, outside in the world, between the TV people and the radio people. They were arguing back and forth and in the end they would decide what happened to him.

In the end of the movie, the judges decided that if the pilot could prove the girl really loved him, he could live again. So the pilot went back to earth and he collected a tear the girl had cried because she thought he was going to die, and he brought the tear back to heaven as proof of her love. Shannon gaped at the TV screen, because he saw it was just like the face of the angel, wasn't it? The girl's tear in the movie was just like the face he had carved when he had fallen in love with Teresa. He couldn't put it into words exactly why it was the same, but he knew it was the same. And suddenly he understood why he wasn't afraid of prison anymore or even of death row. He understood why his skin didn't crawl when he was just sitting around like this. He couldn't put any of it into words, but he understood that somehow he had won some kind of big victory, that even though good things had never happened to him and he had never had a chance in life and even though they were going to put him in prison or even send him to death row, he had somehow won anyway, like some kind of sports hero in the impossible last minutes of a game, and now his skin did not crawl and he was not afraid and whatever happened, he would be all right and his life was good. His life was good.

The final credits of the movie rolled and Shannon put his face in his hands. He was filled with a gigantic feeling of sweetness that he couldn't describe even to himself. He had no words for any of it, and he just sat there with his face in his hands.

It ended suddenly. Things were just going along, and then it was over.

Sharpstein came. He said, "We're done." Then two large men came into the white room. They pulled Shannon's arms behind his back and put handcuffs on him.

"What's happening?" Shannon said to Sharpstein.

"Augie Lancaster's been indicted. Foster's guys on the inside worked the pyramid. They've got testimony all the way up. Lancaster's done. Foster's been reinstated. It's over. The good guys won."

The two big men were pulling Shannon roughly toward the door. Sharpstein followed him to the threshold.

"Where are they taking me?" Shannon said.

"They don't need you anymore," Sharpstein told him. But that was all he could get out before the door shut in his face, and the two men hustled the handcuffed Shannon down the hall.

• • •

274

It was a blazingly bright morning. The air was warm and lazy, but there was a bracing hint of autumn, too, and Shannon smelled grass. The two large men hurried him over a scraggly field to a dark limousine parked on a dirt road. Shannon lifted his eyes, yearning to see the world. He had a glimpse of a vast plain running to a broad open sky. Then one of the large men opened the back door of the limousine and the other lowered Shannon inside.

It all happened very fast. Before Shannon fully understood what was going on, one of the large men reached behind him and unlocked the handcuffs. Then the man pulled out of the limousine and shut the door.

The limousine seemed very dark after the bright day. Dazed, Shannon tried to see the driver, but he was an obscure figure behind a divider of tinted glass. The car started moving.

"We meet again, eh?" said a voice from beside him.

Shannon turned and, son of a bitch, there was the identity man, the foreign guy who had given him his new face. Shannon gave a startled laugh. The disreputable old buzzard cut an elfin figure sitting there in his tweed jacket with his spotty hands and his slicked-back red-silver hair and his unkempt eyebrows. And that gleam of disdainful foreign humor in his eyes.

"Hey!" Shannon said. "What are you doing here?"

"You are not happy to see me?" said the foreigner. *Cheppy*, he said. You are not *cheppy* to see me, with the *ch* being the sound you make when you're about to spit.

"That depends," said Shannon. He didn't know what to think about any of this. "Last time I saw you, you stuck a needle in my neck and cut my face up."

That made the foreigner chuckle. "I remember. Good times, yes?"

"You gonna do that again?"

"Only if it amuses you. For my part, it is not necessary."

"Yeah, then I'll pass, thanks."

Shannon felt the car begin to speed up. He turned to look out the window. They were on a freeway now, racing past long fields of sparse grass. It was the first moment since Sharpstein had barged in on him that he had had a chance to think. Now, he began to put things together. What Sharpstein had said: "They don't need you anymore." The fact they had taken the cuffs off him. The identity man. There was a slow dawn of hope and amazement inside him.

He turned back to the foreigner quickly.

"We're not going to prison? No prison?"

The foreigner had turned to look out his window, too. He answered without turning back, casually, as if the whole business meant nothing to him. "No prison, Shannon. You are to go free."

Shannon was surprised at how powerfully this hit him. He had not been afraid of going to prison. He was resigned to it. He had not even been afraid to die, if it came to that. But when he heard it would be this way instead . . . When he heard: *You are to go free* . . . Well, there was a great surge of pleasure and celebration inside him, champagne corks and fireworks all around.

"No kidding," he said. Then the interior party sort of rose up and overwhelmed him. He put his hand over his eyes. "No kidding. Free."

The foreigner glanced at him and shrugged. "Look at you. Great powers are going back and forth in world, winning and losing. You are nothing in it. Just cork on sea."

Shannon took a breath to settle himself. "I don't care about them. The great powers. I just want my life, that's all."

"So. You have life. Lots of life, all the life you want. No one cares damn about you. They are just as happy for you to go away."

Shannon nodded. "Sure. Foster. I'm just trouble for him, aren't I? That whole stupid operation. Now he's a hero and I'm just an embarrassment to him."

The foreigner gave another of his disreputable chuckles. "There is no one who wants anything from you except you disappear."

"Right," said Shannon. "Right." Thinking of Foster, he felt a wave of gratitude toward the seedy little agent. Or something. He did not know what he felt. There was too much to take in.

After that, they drove for a long time in silence. Shannon looked out the window, thinking about things, a lot of things, letting his mind range over it all. He kept coming back to Teresa. He kept wondering if there was any way . . . Probably not, but he couldn't help hoping. That was the thing: he just couldn't help it. He thought about being with her all the time. He didn't seem to be able to let her go.

At one point, after a long silence, the foreigner broke into his thoughts. "I hear you make statue," he said.

Shannon came out of his reverie. "What's that? Oh. Yeah. Yeah."

"I am curious. You can do this?"

"I can carve wood, yeah."

"You learn this somewhere?"

Shannon shook his head. "Not really. I can just do it. I always could."

"Yes?"

"Yeah. Sure."

"You read book or . . ."

"No, I just . . . I just find a piece of wood, that's all. And I see something in it. It's kind of, like, it's partly in the wood and partly in my head. And I carve, I guess, until the thing in the wood and the thing in my head come together into one thing. It's cool. I like it."

The foreigner studied him thoughtfully.

"What," said Shannon.

"You are interesting case."

"Oh yeah?"

"Different."

"Really? Different how?"

"I did not expect."

"Well," said Shannon. "There you go. You never can tell, right?" The foreigner shook his head, his eyes humorous.

"What?" said Shannon. "What's so funny with you all the time?"

"You Americans," said the foreigner. "You are so stupid you

277

don't even know what you know." He turned away to study the passing landscape.

Shannon shrugged. Maybe he was stupid. Maybe he was American. Let the foreigner laugh. It was all right with him.

They drove on a long time and passed over mountains into meadows. Towns went by with mountains in the distance against the sky. Then there was a cluster of towns, more and more traffic on the freeway around them. They were coming to the outskirts of a city.

The foreigner cleared his throat. He took a manila envelope from the pouch on the door beside him. "Here," he said. He handed the envelope to Shannon.

"What's this?"

"You wanted life. It is life. Papers, records, license, and so on. Some money to start with." He reached down to the floor. There was a small, soft overnight bag there that Shannon hadn't noticed. The foreigner set it on the seat between them. "Change of clothes," he said.

"But no new face this time, huh."

"You do not need. No one is looking for you. No one wants to find you. They hope you are gone for good."

Shannon took the envelope. "So who am I this time?"

"Your name, you mean."

"Yeah. What's my name?"

The foreigner's eyes gleamed with wit and contempt. "You are John Shannon. But not *that* John Shannon. You are new John Shannon. No crimes, no record with police, no—what you call?—strikes against you."

Shannon weighed the envelope in his hand. He made a face of appreciation. "Not bad. How'd you manage that?"

"I am very good identity man."

"I guess so. Whole new life again, huh. Just like that."

"Not even scars on arm."

One corner of Shannon's mouth lifted. "Right. Just . . . identity like stain."

The foreigner hesitated. He seemed more thoughtful than usual. "You are interesting case," he said finally.

"Oh yeah? No identity like stain?"

The foreigner tapped the envelope with a thick finger. "We will say it is like block of wood with shape inside and shape inside your head."

Shannon laughed. "Fair enough." He unzipped the overnight bag and wedged the envelope inside and zipped it up again.

Soon after, the car pulled to a stop.

"Here we are," said the foreigner.

For a moment, Shannon just sat there. He didn't know what to do.

"Well?" said the foreigner. He gestured toward the door.

"I just get out?" said Shannon.

"Unless you want to live in car."

A dozen questions went through Shannon's mind. Where would he go? Where would he work? Where would he start? But he didn't say anything. He would figure out the answers himself. They were no one's business but his. He would find his way.

"Well . . ." he said. He offered the identity man his hand. He didn't know what else to do. The foreigner smiled contemptuously and shook it. Shannon took the handle of the overnight bag and got out of the car.

He found himself standing on a road that passed through a small field. Wheat was growing high on either side of him. Up ahead, he saw a little house, and beyond that he saw another house and then houses spreading away into the distance until there was a city glinting silver in the afternoon sun.

He shut the door of the limousine. He set the bag down on the road at his feet. He stood beside it. He looked back over his shoulder at the fields and then off toward the silver city. He figured he would start walking toward the city and see what was what.

While he stood thinking about it, the limousine backed up on the road and maneuvered through a Y turn and turned around. It came to a stop beside him. The identity man lowered his window and looked out, considering him.

"You are interesting case," he said again.

Shannon smiled.

The next moment, he saw a movement out of the corner of his eye. He turned to it—it had come from the nearest house. It was a small green house with a gray roof. It was right at the edge of the field of wheat. The door of the house was opening. As Shannon stood watching it, Teresa stepped out onto the front step.

Shannon drew a slow breath. He had known it was going to happen as if he had seen it in a dream, and yet when it did happen, it was too big, his heart could barely hold it. He had never had a good break in his life and now it seemed like there was one good break after another and, even if they weren't much in the way of the whole world and all the powers working in it, they were a lot for him and he was moved and grateful.

Teresa held the door open and looked out of the house, this way and that. She was looking for him, Shannon realized. She was waiting for him. Then she saw him, and her face brightened with a smile. She lifted her hand to wave. His heart could barely hold it.

"Shannon," said the identity man.

Shannon forced himself to turn away from Teresa and look at him. Looking out the window of the car, the foreigner glanced back to where Teresa was standing in the doorway and then glanced back at Shannon with the gleam of old humor in his eyes.

"Carve good, yes?" he said.

Then he laughed and the window went up and the limousine rolled away.

Shannon didn't watch it go. Teresa was waving eagerly to him from where she stood in the doorway at the end of the field of grain.

He picked up his bag and started walking toward her up the long road.